Sean started writing at university as a way of escaping his engineering degree, before becoming a trade journalist working out of a brick shed. He writes full time, and published four novels under his real name, before changing style, content, publisher and identity to something much more fun. He's a single dad and lives on the south coast with his little boy. He has never owned a cat, and each year more and more of them go missing in his neighbourhood.

Praise for Sean Cregan:

'Sean Cregan is that real deal you've been looking for – a thriller writer that actually thrills' Ray Banks

'[An] edgy, frenetic thriller . . . Cregan's evocation of *The Levels* is filmic, the location intensely realized, as much a character as the protagonists themselves . . . [Cregan's] taut prose propels us through to the explosive ending of this gothic-punk thriller' *Crimeculture*

'A convincing, engaging and constantly surprising industrial thriller, it marks the arrival of a huge new talent' Steve Mosby

'Breathlessly classy pulp' *Telegraph*

By Sean Cregan and available from Headline

The Levels
The Razor Gate

THE
RAZOR GATE

SEAN CREGAN

headline

First published in 2011 by
HEADLINE PUBLISHING GROUP

First published in paperback in 2011 by
HEADLINE PUBLISHING GROUP

1

Cataloguing in Publication Data is available from the British Library

ISBN 978 0 7553 5809 0

Typeset in Aldine401BT by Avon DataSet Ltd,
Bidford-on-Avon, Warwickshire

Printed in the UK by CPI Mackays, Chatham, ME5 8TD

Headline's policy is to use papers that are natural, renewable and
recyclable products and made from wood grown in sustainable forests.
The logging and manufacturing processes are expected to conform
to the environmental regulations of the country of origin.

HEADLINE PUBLISHING GROUP
An Hachette UK Company
338 Euston Road
London NW1 3BH

www.headline.co.uk
www.hachette.co.uk

For A and J

ONE

The man was tall and gaunt, his face hidden in the shadows of his hood and the steam of hard-blown winter breath. He had less than two minutes to live.

Maya, mind wandering and head bowed against the cold, didn't see the man step from the deeper darkness of the narrow alleyway until she blundered into him. The smell of fresh sweat, alcohol faint in the background, white eyes glittering at her. She mumbled an apology and stepped back, letting him cross the sidewalk in front of her, watching him weave along the kerbside as if he was trying to find a cab. And good luck with that, she thought. Traffic was backed up all along Green Street, Newport City's evening rush in full swing. Crowds of people streamed along on foot, bathed in the glow of storefront fluorescents, while the blue light of LCDs advertising perfume, underwear, jewellery, shimmered cold and artificial from the slush and ice.

'I'm sorry, Maya,' Kevin McMahon at the *Newport Post* had told her earlier that afternoon. 'The board would never sanction my putting you on staff. After the Saganowski case they won't let the paper touch you. There'd be too much bad press if we did, and the perceived risk of something similar happening would be too high. You know how it goes.'

'Sure,' she'd said. The *Post* had been her last chance of finding real news work short of cheap supermarket tabloids, and she still had too much self-respect to spend the rest of her career writing about Hitler being alive and well and working in Burger King.

'If it was up to me . . .'

'Thanks, Kev. I appreciate that. Worth a go, you know?'

'Yeah.' He'd sounded guilty. 'Look, if you come up with something special we can run and it's a solid story, I can take it off you freelance. Get you back in the game. Maybe we could turn it into a semi-regular gig if it works out.'

She'd thanked him again and hung up, looked around her depressingly empty apartment and headed for Mullen's. Had a couple of glasses of wine and a long conversation about jack shit with Paul behind the bar, which was about all she had left to do.

Nothing had gone right since the court vindicated Lieutenant Saganowski and killed her career – itself barely two years old. Maya was twenty-three and already done. The sources Maya had used in the story accusing the lieutenant of massive corruption had turned out to be less concrete than she'd thought. Certainly not enough to convince a libel judge, anyway. Part of her liked to believe he'd been bought off too. Better that than having made a mistake writing the piece in the first place. 'Maybe it'll work out,' she'd told Shaun during one of their increasingly brief good moments at the tail of the hearings. 'The case isn't lost yet. They've not proved it's hurt her reputation, so the damages might not be too bad. Make an apology, suck up the legal costs, move on.'

'Bullshit,' he'd said, waving his wine glass like a judge's gavel. 'You're fucked, Maya. They're going to nail you to the wall. You should quit the news, come work with me in auditing. We got our shit together. I could get you an apprentice post; you're pretty smart, the company'll take you. You could really make a name for yourself. And we'd be workin' together, too.'

She hadn't told him then, but she was already having about as much of Shaun as she could take. She'd changed the subject and the evening had ended in the regular argument about nothing much and some brief, lacklustre make-up sex. Two days later the *Tribune* told her to clear her desk, and she'd taken the opportunity to get clear of Shaun too.

Dirty snowmelt seeped through the toes of her boots, the suede like an icy wet compress. No pay cheque, most of her money gone on legal fees, little chance of being able to afford a new pair for the rest of the winter. Maya cursed her luck, the city, and the world. Then she saw Dominic.

She'd known him at college as a grungy would-be photographer with a languid smile and a slow-burning loathing for authority. They'd gone out for six fun months, and she'd loved him, fallen good and hard. Then he'd left her, broken her heart, and they'd drifted out of touch until a few weeks ago.

They'd met again on the subway, Maya running late following another fruitless meeting with her attorneys. She'd heard the shrill alarm sound, the doors of the D Train about to close and a half-hour wait for the next one beckoning, and had run for it. Jumped through as they hissed together, and collided with a stranger in tan suede and black canvas pants. She had been a couple of words into her apology when recognition sparked and she'd said, 'Dominic?'

A voice from only two years in her past, but it might have been another lifetime for all that had changed behind it. 'Maya? Jesus, what are you doing here?'

'Going home,' she'd said. Felt herself scurry for the safety of small talk and hated it. 'How about you? How've you been?'

'OK. Just out for a wander. You know, get lost a little, shake off everything "real world" for a while. Sometimes it's nice to get away.' He had shrugged. 'I've been following the case in the papers.'

'Oh.'

'It must be hard; Lieutenant Saganowski's a bitch. At least,' he'd added, 'that's the way she sounds. I thought about calling you, but I guess I didn't know if you'd want to hear from me. Listen, do you want to go get a coffee or something? Catch up properly? I don't know if you're free, but I'm not doing anything right now and it'd be nice.'

Coffee was a little café off Adams Square and snow speckling the glass. The place smelled of roasted beans and cold damp evaporating from people's coats. Dominic had been friendly, warm even, all the way, but always guarded, his face never completely relaxed. 'Like you became a spy or something,' Maya had told him.

'Ha! I sometimes think of it the same way.'

'Work?'

He'd nodded. Sipped his espresso, looked about ten years older than he was. 'It seemed sort of cool when I started. When they first offered me the job. And it is. But it can get pretty heavy at times. It's certainly a long way from what I figured I'd be doing. Have you had that feeling at all since we left college?'

'You mean aside from this court case?' Maya had said. He'd laughed. 'Now and again. I mean, I didn't get to do much of the hard stuff until Saganowski, but some of what there's been has been tough. Did you hear about Chalienski?'

A ghost of something there on Dominic's face for a second, and it was gone. 'Yes,' he'd said. 'I remember.'

'That was my first big call-out with one of the senior journos. Heavy stuff. But I don't regret it. What is it you do at . . . Daedalus Venture, wasn't it?'

'Junior dogsbody,' he had said. 'Did you see *The Devil Wears Prada*?'

'Bits.'

'Well, that's me, and Amanda's Meryl Streep. It's more

serious than that, what we do, but the relationship's not a million miles wide of the mark.'

'You could quit if it's that stressful. We're still young, life ahead of us, blah blah blah.'

A smile then, and she'd seen a flash of what she'd once loved. 'Better to be happy than rich, damn the career and choose life, et cetera? It's not that it's stressful – most of the time it's not, although sometimes there's a lot riding on me – but . . . well, I *can't* quit. You just don't. Not where I am.'

'You enjoy it? This mysterious dogsbodying?'

'No. Yes. I don't know. It's like if a friend persuades you to try cliff-diving and you jump off the edge. You won't know whether you like it, not for certain, until you hit the water and find out if there are rocks there or not. Until then you've just got the fear, but you can't stop falling. Maybe you'll be OK and find you like the rush. Maybe you'll climb out of the sea and swear you'll never do it again. Or maybe you'll smash your skull open and die.'

Without thinking about it, she'd reached across the table and taken his hand. Said, 'And you're still falling? Still undecided?'

'If the metaphor holds, yes.' An embarrassed shrug. 'I made it sound worse than it is. And it's a long way until I'll hit the water, so maybe I'll just get used to it before then. But thanks for the sympathy.'

'I don't get why it's so bad. You haven't exactly gone into details.' Realised, as she'd said it, how true this was. On the train, the walk here, everything, he'd said the bare minimum about his job. Dodged almost every question, turned them around on her. And she'd wanted to know why.

'I can't,' he'd said. 'It's not easy to talk about it. It puts me in a difficult position. Tell me, do you remember everything I used to say about the corporate world? Big business? People in suits and offices?'

'Sure.'

'It was all true,' he'd said. 'All true and worse.'

The tinkle of the bell above the door. Two serious-looking men in long dark coats and matching scowls. They'd stood just inside the café and stared at Dominic. He had looked at Maya, sad. 'Fun while it lasted.'

'They're here for you? Who are they?'

'Doesn't matter.' He had nodded at the men and stood up. Had leaned in close to kiss her on the cheek, and as he did it she felt him slip something inside her coat pocket. Said, 'It's been lovely seeing you again, M. Talk soon. Take care.'

'Take care,' she'd said.

A last unhappy glance sidelong at her as he had walked through the door, and Dominic was gone into the night. She had waited a few minutes before she had checked her pocket. In it was one of Dominic's business cards, but on the back he'd written a different cell number in ballpoint. Beneath it said: *Private no. Don't use the other ones.*

He wasn't off work this evening. He wore a suit like it was matte black body armour, held a sleek dark case in one hand and had four guys with him like Secret Service. Walking out of the Bastion Building like he was the CEO of Earth. Maya couldn't tell whether any of the people with Dominic were the ones who'd come to collect him from the café.

'The business suit is the SS uniform of the modern world,' he'd told her once, back in college, after an evening of too many mojitos and some light Moroccan grass. 'It excuses the actions of the wearer, allows them a moral detachment, safety within the collective body, an indulgence against any sins they commit because the culprit is, in some way, not *them*. It's the corporation, the hedge fund, the bottom line, the bureaucratic machinery, the government department, *whatever*, that's responsible. They're merely the vector for the action. Anonymity, hangman's hood. Whichever way you want to think of it.'

So much faux-intellectual student bullshit, pompous moralising about the world in general, but it had been genuinely meant; Dominic had been a lot of things, but never a fake. Obviously he'd ditched his student ideals in order to join the working week, and the strange career he'd now embarked on. She'd seen something of it when they'd met up before, but now, watching him on company time, she saw a clear projected coldness in his manner, and that same fear again. They jarred with what she knew of the private man, and the guy she'd loved in the past. Like seeing his twin, a perfect replica on the outside but wholly different within. An unsettling double from a parallel universe.

She watched Dominic walk towards a waiting Mercedes. If he saw her he didn't let it show. Maybe he couldn't, not while he was on duty. Then, beyond him, she saw the hooded man step out into the lines of near-stationary traffic. When he reached the middle of the road he raised his right fist in what looked like a silent salute, and exploded.

TWO

She came to, aware, through a heavy grey veil, of the sound of screaming. In her mind, Maya pictured the source of the noise as a single wounded animal fleeing into the distance on some African plain, blind with panic. The sound took a minute or so to fade, and by then she'd picked out other individual noises: the frozen-rain tinkle of falling glass, the fairy-bell ring of metal fragments, faint moaning and, here and there, hollow terrified howling. People in agony. Other senses returned, but slowly. The smell of smoke, rancid half-burned plastics. The taste of hydro-carbons, and a crushing pain in her chest. It felt as if there was something on top of her, making it hard to breathe, but when she fought to push it off there was nothing there.

Opened her eyes.

Green Street was gone. She was lying where she'd been thrown by the blast against the corner wall of a clothing store. A few yards to either side and she'd have been tossed through the shattered fragments of plate glass windows that, in those first fractions of a second, would still have been airborne, waiting like splintered crystalline spider webs to slice her to shreds. In front of her cars lay thrown around like trash, some flipped on to their roofs, others slammed hard and low into the traffic in front of them like steel and glass torpedoes. The wreckage formed rough walls at either end of the scene, a twisted metal hourglass with the pinch of the neck at the explosion's epicentre. Several of the vehicles were already on fire, reedy lines of smoke rising from fresh, hungry yellow flames, and more were leaking fuel.

The buildings on either side of the street were dark and broken, every window gone, most of their lights killed in the blast. Shards of glass fell like lethal rain from the upper floors on to the wounded and dead littering the sidewalks. The luckier victims had been picked up and thrown like Maya or pressed to the ground where they stood. The less fortunate had been ripped to pieces as the blast wave tore through them. All over, Maya could see dismembered body parts lying in bloody streaks on the ice. Only the centre of the scene was clear, a charred and shockwave-swept star at the point where the bomber had stood, now empty and quiet as a Zen garden.

The snow fell on in silence, turned a dirty grey by the soot, and for a time, with everyone who could run already fled, no one moved.

When breathing came more easily, Maya rolled on to her front and pushed herself gingerly upright. Her arms and legs were shaky and numb and her back was sore and pulverised where she'd slammed into the wall, but nothing felt broken. She stood and immediately her stomach turned. She staggered back, leaned against the building for support, but it seemed to be shuddering in the wind. Saw a severed hand lying palm up in the snow a few feet away and threw up over and over again until all she could do was dry-heave with tears in her eyes.

By the time she'd finished a few more survivors were moving, sitting up, dazed, or rolling in pain, clutching broken limbs and open wounds. No paramedics, no police, no one who'd run had yet returned to help those they'd left behind. Maya had never felt so alone or vulnerable, so unsure of the world around her. Then she saw Dominic.

He'd been blasted to the sidewalk right where he'd been standing. His neck was twisted at an angle that set Maya's stomach shuddering again, and there was something very wrong with the shape of his ribcage. The men who'd been surrounding him were gone; Maya could see one of them buried in the twisted front end of the Mercedes that had been waiting for them, nothing of the others. Closer to the bomber than she'd been, they hadn't stood a chance. When she had finally reconnected with someone who'd once been so precious to her, to have him snatched away in front of her after just a couple of brief evenings together cut her in a way that seeing the anonymous wounded and dead could never have done.

Then someone scurried, low and fast, out of the service alley beside a wrecked clothing store and ran to where

Dominic lay. Grey flight jacket, woolly hat. A young guy, his eyes hard. Maya saw the firelight glinting off a trio of silver crucifix earrings, the dark outline of a tattoo up the side of his neck. When he reached Dominic, he began to hunt, somewhat nervously, around the dead man. Then he seemed to find what he was looking for and rolled the body over. Maya tried to call out, to shout at the guy, ask him what the hell he thought he was doing, but her chest hurt and she couldn't force the sound through her throat. Tottered unsteadily towards him, unable to do a thing to stop him. When the guy stood up again, he had Dominic's briefcase in his hand. He looked at her, just for a second, and then he was running and gone.

Blue lights were flashing in the distance, reflecting dimly off the faces of the dead. All Maya could do was wait for the rest of the world to catch up with her while she waited in the blood-streaked snow, wondering why this had happened.

THREE

The van's back tyres screamed as it took yet another corner five miles an hour too fast for comfort. Garrett grabbed the oh-shit bar above his head and tried not to fall into McDermott's lap. The other cops were either concentrating on holding down their lunch or talking about what might have happened on Green Street. His shift was due to end in two hours and he'd been planning on taking Emi someplace nice, but emergency measures were in force and he'd be stuck at work as long as he had to be.

'There could be more bombs,' McDermott said. He and Garrett were the only officers in the back of the truck who'd been on the force long enough to be out of diapers, although if they gave it another few years, McDermott might be back in them. By a certain age, most people had either been promoted upwards out of the uniform division or else had a desk job that allowed them to take it easy and work on their beer guts. McDermott was pushing fifty and still on the beat for reasons he refused to discuss.

14

Garrett had been a detective sergeant six months ago, and looking maybe to the chances of promotion to lieutenant another six months before that, not that he'd been sure he wanted it. But still, he'd been high rank material just shy of his thirtieth birthday. His fall had been spectacular, and he didn't care. 'Howie Bruford at the Sixteenth said they'd had another explosion reported just before we left. Could be we're headed right into the middle of a shitstorm here. Could be the whole damn city's under attack.'

'Howie Bruford was convinced that crazy woman on Lexfield Street was telling the truth about a guy trying to get into her house, despite everyone telling him to forget it because she was a known nut. So convinced that he crashed in there one night thinking she was in danger.'

A broad grin. 'And he gets down into her cellar . . .'

'. . . and finds she's made a papier mâché model of him, along with a half-dozen other cops from down the years, and she's lying in front of it masturbating with a dildo shaped like a nightstick, and when she sees him she demands he give her a sample of his "righteous seed" or face a trespass rap.'

Laughter, and Garrett noticed that conversation in the rest of the van had stopped. He glanced towards the front, saw that Sergeant Patching was trying to begin the briefing. McDermott looked at Garrett, shrugged, and waited for the sergeant. Garrett muttered, 'Howie Bruford,' chuckled, and wished he had a cigarette and a drink. That he wasn't on call-out to a potential bomb site.

'Something you want to share, Garrett?' Patching said, full-on schoolteacher.

'No. I'm done for now.'

A difficult silence, then the sergeant said, 'OK. Refresher time. We're still trying to get a handle on what's happened and what exactly we've got to respond to. The initial explosion was reported roughly fifteen minutes ago. We have a few people at the blast site, but there's no security perimeter around it as yet, and we don't know how many civvies are still in the zone, how many are wounded or hiding, or who needs protecting from what. Traffic's screwed into the area and everyone's having a hard time getting on site. We've already had calls about looting, criminal damage, and panic turning violent, particularly towards anyone who "looks like a bomber". Usual disaster mess, just worse.'

Muttered comments. 'Fucking civvies,' McDermott said, tapping Garrett on the knee.

'Our job in those situations is to keep the peace, restore order and, if necessary, make arrests,' Patching said. 'Try to hold off on that if you can because we can't ship people back for processing and we've got nowhere to keep them at the scene. In addition, there's been a mass of reports of suspicious behaviour and worse, most of which will turn out to be trash. In those cases, all we need to do is talk to the witnesses if we can find them, see if the individuals in question are still in the area, and if so either restrain them or seal off their location, prevent escape and wait for SWAT.'

'We got any word yet on how far we can go to "restore order"?' one of the other cops asked. Jaw like a rock. He looked like a college running back. Garrett decided he despised him. 'This a softly-softly thing, or we shoot looters?'

'Exactly as you would on regular patrol. This isn't martial law and the disorder is not likely to continue for very long.'

'Shit. Someone blows up half the city and all them people think to do is grab themselves a new TV or an iPod. A bullet might teach them a lesson.'

'If you genuinely think a TV is worth killing someone over, you're worse than them,' Garrett said.

'People act like animals, they should expect to be treated hard.'

'You're an idiot.'

'That kind of talk, I guess you'll get to see if they can find someplace lower they can bust you than patrol, washout.'

No humour in it, only contempt. Garrett smiled at the jock since he was too far away to punch. 'I suppose they could always make me partner up with you.'

'You shut your fucking mouth.'

'That's enough,' the sergeant barked. 'Both of you.'

'You're an idiot, kid. People are freaked. You get it? Someone blew a big hole in the city and shit always gets crazy for a while whenever something like that happens.'

'Garrett! You, McDermott, O'Connor and Stringer, you're our first deployment. It's an unfinished commercial unit. Phone call from a woman who works across the street saying she saw four men, possibly heavily armed, gaining entrance to the building shortly before the bombing. We don't know if they're still there or if she was just blowing smoke, but your job is not to engage. You secure all exits, call it in to the ERC and wait for SWAT. They'll handle the sweep and clear. If someone comes out, you deal with it, but you do not go in. Understood?'

'How long till SWAT are available?' McDermott said. 'Shouldn't they be first response anyway?'

'We're hauling in every tactical unit we can from across the city, but it's taking time and it's a bitch to organise. NCPD has dozens of reports like this to deal with already, plus the explosion site itself. It's a question of prioritising. They'll get to you when they can. Regular backup might be available, but don't count on it. ERC will keep you updated. And Garrett, don't fuck this up. You're running out of second chances.'

Garrett knew he was right, and said nothing.

FOUR

The van slewed to a halt and McDermott threw open the back doors. Jumped down, said, 'Pierce Tower?'

'That's right,' Patching said. 'Four men, through the front entrance. Be careful.'

Garrett climbed out, the two other cops behind him, and the van roared away. The night air hit him, cold and sharp. Lights were on, smoke swirled down in flurries, and aside from the cops the street was empty and silent. Cold and clean and beautiful. Three blocks away, columns of smoke twisted upwards through a thin haze, silhouetted against the glowing Newport City. Their tails were lit from beneath by flickering orange firelight.

'That must be the bomb,' McDermott said. 'How big do you think it was?'

'Big enough. No one's around. It's even scared off rubberneckers. I wish the city was this empty more often.'

'You'd have to be pretty keen to freeze your balls off in this weather just to see some body parts.'

One of the other cops, O'Connor, pointed across the street. 'That's the building.'

They looked up. An eight-storey concrete shell, most of its windows not yet glazed. Scraps of scaffolding, sheets of clear plastic covering holes. Dark and dead and empty. It looked down on them with eyes like open graves.

O'Connor glanced at the two older cops. Said, 'You, uh, want to take the front or the back?'

'You two watch the front,' Garrett told him. Felt something like sympathy. Not what the kid could've expected to encounter when he was in the Academy, he figured. 'We'll check the side and the rear for exit points. Keep on the radio and we can decide on a plan when we know the score.'

'And try to stay out of line of fire from the windows,' McDermott added. 'Just in case by some miracle this call was genuine.'

The fourth cop shook his head. 'We're three blocks from a bomb site. Of course this could be genuine. Didn't you say in the van there could be more shit for us to deal with tonight?'

'I said more *bombs*, because I heard maybe there were more went off than just Green Street. But a thing like this always brings with it a thousand other reports worth nothing. You look funny walking down the street and someone'll call it in. People get wiggy. SWAT'll probably find a maintenance crew inside.'

The other cop said nothing, just followed O'Connor

across the street and up to the wall beside Pierce Tower's temporary main entrance. Guns drawn, they hunkered down with their backs against the stone. Garrett and McDermott were less hurried; Garrett, for all their advice to the junior cops, simply didn't feel a genuine sense of threat. If you ignored the smoke rising from Green Street, this was just another empty street on another quiet night. He followed McDermott into the service alley beside the unfinished building, gun out but held down. The gap was a wide commercial one, big enough for a decent-sized truck. There were huge bags of construction material, pallets of wood and steel beams, and other building industry stuff stowed neatly at its sides.

When they were safely away from the other cops, McDermott said, 'So how is Emi?'

'She's OK. Considering.'

He nodded. 'How long now?'

'Not long,' Garrett said. McDermott knew the truth about what was wrong with Emi, that she was dying and no one could stop it. Got it out of Garrett one drunken night at Dewi's Bar when Garrett was deep into a bottle over the fact he was bound to lose her to what they called 'the Curse'. 'Still long enough for me to fix it.'

'No one's managed it yet, the way you told it.'

'Maybe no one's needed to like me.' He pointed to the building, a gap in the plastic-draped stacks. Said, 'Side door here.'

The door was plain, looked pretty solid and had a five-digit keycode lock. McDermott walked up, gave the handle a try. Shook his head and said, 'Locked.' Over the radio, 'Side door's locked. We'll check the back before we sit on it. Get the lie of the land. Anything from ERC on SWAT yet?'

'No.' O'Connor. 'No ETA yet.'

They carried on down the alley. McDermott made a perfunctory show of shining his flashlight into the spaces between bags and crates. Said, 'Look, Charlie, I'm your friend. I really hope Emi makes it and you guys live long and happily together.'

'I don't need to hear this, Mike,' Garrett said.

McDermott ignored him. 'You've got to face the possibility that she *won't* make it, and you're going to have to cope with that if it happens. I've got two years to go to my twenty and that means I don't have to give much of a shit about anyone any more. No one boots a cop this close to finishing unless he rocks the boat for everyone else. I got my retirement fund set up; got my half of that thing I ran with Scott Broyne ten years ago when we were in the Twelfth. You don't have the luxury of either, and they can't bust you any lower. If you get any more screwed up over Emi they're going to kick you out.'

'I told you I don't want to hear this, Mike. I don't give a shit about them either.'

'And if they kick you out, who the hell am I going to talk to for the next two years? New intake gets shittier every year as it is. You're a miserable fucker, but at least you're not a complete dick.'

Garrett smiled despite himself, hunched his shoulders against the snow and lit a cigarette. Broke a dozen regulations by doing it, but who gave a rat's ass for regulations in Newport? They could stop him smoking on the job when they stopped everyone else taking cash or favours on the side. The truth was, he knew McDermott was right, and that was why he hadn't just upped and quit. He might have fallen into playing a strange game of chicken with the NCPD, almost daring them to fire him, but he couldn't bring himself to just walk away. In the shabby core of his soul he was certain he'd still be here a year from now, and police work was all he knew. Some part of him still believed he could do some good for the city, and he suspected that it was that part of him, most of all, that Emi loved. He didn't want to lose it, even if he lost her.

They had taken Garrett off the Curse eight months before, in early summer. 'You're losing your focus on this, Charlie,' his supervising sergeant said. 'Even if you hadn't started sleeping with one of the victims – which would be enough to see you moved to something else, if not up on disciplinary—'

Garrett was tired. Hadn't slept more than a couple of hours the previous night between seeing Emi and starting his shift. 'Come on, Sarge. Put me on review for that and you'd have to have most of the department on felony charges, the things we all do. Don't be ridiculous.'

The sergeant let that slide with a nod. 'Even if you hadn't done that, you've been getting out of line, interrogating victims, spending police time and resources chasing up nothing.'

'I should've known we weren't supposed to investigate crime. Shit, what was I thinking?'

'The Case isn't regular crime, and we can't treat it as though it was. You know that.' That's what it was in office jargon, and in all official documents, 'the Case'. Lieutenant Saganowski had made it known that anyone referring to a 'curse' in regular police paperwork or within earshot of non-involved officers would be suspended indefinitely without pay. 'Acting like you can solve it by shaking down anyone you think stands to gain from it just risks bringing the Case into the public eye and upsetting a lot of people we'd like to keep nice. Like Mr Seebold last week.'

'He's a—'

'I know that as well as you do, but that doesn't justify verbally attacking him in his own fucking office, Charlie. In front of three witnesses.'

'Two years ago his company tried to buy up a swathe of Willow Heights to clear land for a product development facility and industrial park.'

'For cosmetics.'

'Cosmetics means safety-testing and bioscience. He could be involved with the Curse.'

'He *is* involved with a senior officer who is to remain nameless, and this senior officer is real fucking unhappy with you. It has been made absolutely clear to me that any further harassment of Mr Seebold, without evidence, by this department will result in a number of sackings, including mine, and a massive lawsuit against all concerned. You, Charlie, are off the Case. Understand?'

Silence, then Garrett nodded. Said, 'Sure. Is that all?'

'When was the last time you got any sleep? You look awful.'

'Last night.'

'How much?'

'I'll be fine.'

The sergeant shrugged, shook his head. 'Whatever you feel for her, you need to start taking better care of yourself. You let this get on top of you and it's only going to end badly for you. And Charlie, if I find you having anything more to do with the Case – in any capacity whatsoever, up to and including eavesdropping on other detectives' conversations in the shitter – you will get busted straight down to patrol, if not out of the department altogether. Clear?'

Garrett said nothing, let the door clatter shut behind him. That evening, he told Emi why he wouldn't be at groups any more. She was quiet for a while, and he saw that she was glaring at him.

'This is great,' she said, at last. 'Not only am I going to die, but my boyfriend is bent on ruining his own life too.'

'I'm trying to help you, Emi.'

'By getting the sack?'

'By finding out who did this to you and making them take it back.'

'It doesn't sound like you'll have much chance of that now, does it?'

'Maybe I've got more than I had. You don't know how it works. How the NCPD *is*. We're not *investigating* the Curse. Not like you'd expect for something this size. We're *containing* it. Sure, there's lip service paid to obtaining information from victims and trying to establish patterns, but there are more active investigative personnel on the fucking Mallon murder than there are on this.' Heidi Mallon, not-quite-prom-queen high school graduate, had been found in pieces near Faemac Park the month before. 'You know why? Someone's gone to Saganowski and said keep a lid on this for us while we play around with it ourselves, or keep it quiet while we find out where Mad fucking Cousin George has hidden his lab and quietly stop him doing what he's doing. A pile of cash swaps hands and nothing changes.'

'I know how Newport works, Charlie. I've been here long enough.'

'If all I can do is look at this unofficially, maybe I can do it with more freedom than I had before.'

'Or maybe you'll just spend all our time chasing shadows and I'll still be dead.' Awkward silence. Emi sighed, stood up. 'I'm off to groups. Adam wants to take me for coffee afterwards. There's supposed to be a short-term arts post at NCU opening up and he knows some people there who've lectured at Bryant. It might be a nice job for a while. I'll be back later on.'

'I'll be waiting,' he said.

A smile, still hurt and angry, but a smile. 'Good,' she said.

Garrett and McDermott approached the small service road at the back of the building, trade and delivery access for the adjoining blocks, underground parking lots and the billowing grey boxes of heating units. Pierce Tower had two rear doors, one a fire exit, one a rollup commercial entryway. Nothing out there but snow.

'You want to check them?' McDermott said.

'What's the point? A fire exit's a fire exit. One-way. No one's going to be able to sneak out the other one either.'

'Cover both from here?'

'We wouldn't be able to see anything from that side door. Too much clutter in the way.'

'Fine. I call the side; less snow. You stay here, watch these two and freeze your ass off.'

Garrett shrugged. 'You can come warm it up for me when SWAT get here.'

'You hear me screaming for help, you come get me.'

'Got your back, chickenshit.'

Garrett found himself a sheltered spot against the wall, tucked between a drainpipe and a snow-covered steel housing, and waited, smoking. Occasional squawks on the emergency wideband, undirected radio traffic from the rest of the city. Chatter from dispatchers and responders, reporting conditions, traffic, situations cleared and those still unresolved. Cops, paramedics and firefighters reassuring one another over the ether that they weren't alone. They'd reached the blast site on Green Street, talk of dozens dead, many more injured. Buildings shattered, vehicles tossed around like litter, fires from spilt gasoline and broken gas pipes. Nothing about further explosions so far, but there'd been several scares, stampedes, some enterprising looting. Bomb squads were out at dozens of suspect packages and vehicles. No word yet on who might have been responsible or what they wanted, whether there was more to come.

In the shadowed dark, radio ghosts dancing quietly in his ear, he thought about Emi, and how long it would be before he'd see her tonight. Smiling as he came in, that shy little way she had, so fragile at first glance but showing no signs of fading as the day drew closer. The opposite, if anything. She'd clouded everything else, growing larger and larger in his mind until, soon, she would outgrow the space available and, suddenly, she'd be gone, a bubble become too big and burst, and he'd be alone again. It wasn't as though there'd been tinkling lutes and fairies dancing through their time together; Garrett had just never met anyone with whom he'd been able to *talk* so much, to share such a large part of himself without worrying about being hurt or embarrassed further down the line. And it was the same for her. He'd wanted to take her to the Phoenix tonight. Childish, an evening in a bar-cum-amusement arcade, but fun, and trying to burn as much joy into Emi's remaining time as he could was about all Garrett wanted to do. If this stakeout ended soon enough, maybe they could still go. Pick up something to eat on the street, have a few drinks, act like teenagers for a night. Hide, as McDermott had implied, from the truth for another day.

Garrett's hands and feet had gone cold and numb by the time the side door exploded in a thundering gout of shattered wood and steel.

FIVE

Gunshots from somewhere on the other side of the building. Garrett's ears rang from the blast and the alleyway was full of smoke and dust. Air like hot sand at the back of his throat. He was aware of O'Connor over the radio, shouting, and he could see a shape on the floor, a silhouette against the clearing cloud: McDermott, lying very still indeed. Garrett reached for his gun, told his legs to get him up and moving.

Then the dead man stepped out of the back door. Tall and neat, a long black European wool coat and a scarf blowing in the night breeze. Jason Blake, looking very lively for a guy who should've been dead three months before. Garrett thought of McDermott in the alley, Emi dying from the Curse, Blake still alive. Blake, who'd somehow beaten the Curse. Who could hold the key to saving Emi. Garrett raised his gun, realised that he couldn't – wouldn't – use it and risk losing the secret, and lowered it again.

Blake stepped off the loading dock and hurried across the back street, into the night. Garrett stared for a moment in

McDermott's direction, guilt cold and ugly in his chest, and then gave chase.

He'd first seen Emi on a cold, wet night at the support groups. She'd come in out of the sleet, hair in sodden ringlets, eyes wide behind smudged makeup. She looked like a bird, twitchy and uncertain. Garrett had found her a towel to dry off. He didn't know if it was her first visit, or whether she'd come before on nights when he wasn't on shift. She sat in the circle of chairs and said very little except to tell people her name.

When he walked into Wide Blue Nothing later, she was there again. He'd only called in on the spur of the moment. It was a bleak night and he'd decided that he wanted something warm before heading for home. Wide Blue Nothing was a riverside curiosity, a soup and sashimi restaurant and bar owned by Ted Bellion, a fat Irish American with a shaven head and a white walrus moustache. The symbols on the sign out front looked like kanji but as far as anyone knew weren't any genuine language. Ted had borrowed from a grab-bag of Pacific Rim cultures to make his place – Japanese, Korean, Chinese, Maori, Filipino – but gleefully, with a kind of innocent and knowing love, not crass or tacky. He knew about the many old ethnic divisions and happily ignored them all. There was a twelve-foot-square video wall at one side, showing an endless and seemingly unrepeating melange of jump-cut movie footage, anime and live-action, clips of no more than a couple of seconds at a time. Another, on the opposite, showed slower footage of clouds, waves on the Pacific shore, wind in the grass.

Emi was between the two, sitting at the counter framed by the soft turquoise neon glow of the lights above. Her hair like hazy dark fog, a shadow that shifted and swayed as her arm moved; writing, it seemed. Her eyes were locked on the paper, glittering in the first gleam of sunlight over Kiribati, the blue flash as Mikoto Misaka triggered her lightning field. The soft muddy glimmer of *In The Mood For Love* tracing the line of her cheek, the curve of her neck. As Garrett came closer he saw that she was drawing on a napkin with a black marker. Simple, sweeping lines, spreading where the ink soaked into the paper. The man behind the counter, the shapes of those sitting in the restaurant. Stark and simple, like sumi-e brush paintings, but they captured the movement and feel of the Nothing with grace. The look on her face as she drew, calm, lightly smiling, at ease, so different from how she'd been at the group and how withdrawn she'd been in that circle of strangers. It was an expression he would come to see many times, settling across her features as she slept beside him in the dark. The same peace like death, breathing softly, as the thin slow light bled across the eastern horizon, touching the windows of her apartment with dim gold.

'You're an artist,' he said and immediately hated himself. 'Sorry, that was really stupid.'

'And you're a policeman.' She smiled. 'Checking up on me?'

'No, I just come in here sometimes if I want something to

eat after the group meetings. I saw you here, and . . . Anyway, I'm Charlie. Is it OK if I sit here?'

'Of course.' She moved some more napkins aside, and Garrett saw they were all covered in similar sketches. 'I'm Emi. Though I suppose you must know that. Sorry.'

'These are great. I can't draw for shit.'

'They're just to fill in the time. I mostly work with oils.'

'So you *are* an artist?'

'And you *are* a detective.' She laughed. 'Don't take offence. I'm just being silly. I'm a painter, mostly.'

Their evening together became night, became morning, and a ferry trip across the harbour to the street market in Anchorhead. Gulls wheeling shrill overhead, and the cotton-strand hair on the wooden dolls Emi liked tousled in the wind. She held his hand as they walked from stall to stall and the air smelled like rain. That evening, she told him about Jason Blake.

They broke across a wide avenue lined with white-shrouded trees, nothing moving on the road. Everyone who wanted to flee the bomb site had done so; anyone who wanted to see what had happened was doing it on foot. Blake dived into a high alleyway between office buildings, dusted with pristine snow. Garrett thought that some of the flakes now falling were tinged grey with smoke or dust from Green Street, but, running, he couldn't be sure.

Quiet laughter echoed from the walls. Blake was enjoying himself.

* * *

Emi had taken him to the Garden of Song, a strange little park in the heart of Newport that Garrett figured he'd always known about, but never visited. The whole thing was capped by a layered network of struts and cables, like a circus big top made from spiderweb. Designed, Emi said, to baffle and trap the wind, never leaving more than a breeze to disturb the park, but still allowing light and rain to fall within. The air was guided through steel channels which piped and whistled, while the cables vibrated under the dissipating energy, thrumming and warbling, the concerto of an unearthly invisible orchestra in the sky. While the park sang, they talked: about her childhood in Hokkaido and his here in the city, past romances, and about the groups and the Curse.

'I saw a guy from the groups for a couple of weeks,' she said. 'Just when I first started coming. It didn't last at all. Silly, really, but it's surprising how it feels to be with someone who knows what you're going through. That's why I changed what day I come; I think the meetings are awkward enough without adding extra.'

'It happens a lot.' And it did; Garrett had come out of meetings more than once to find people screwing in the parking lot. 'Who was it?'

'Jason Blake.'

He'd known Blake. The guy had started coming to meetings a month before, stuck it out for a while, then vanished off the radar. The Clocks – a term he felt bad even thinking while he was with Emi – usually fell into three camps. Some were upset, devastated at their bad luck and traumatised by the knowledge that they were going to die. Some accepted it and got on with what life remained to them. Others were angry, wanting revenge, but invariably lashed out at random for lack of a single figure on which to focus their ire. Blake was always calm when Garrett was there. He never raised his voice, but he was cutting and provocative. A troublemaker, and a smart one at that. Garrett had been glad when he'd stopped coming. He couldn't parse the notion of Blake with Emi at all.

'Blake? Why?'

Emi smiled. 'You're not jealous, are you, Charlie?'

'No, no. I just can't imagine what anyone would see in him. I thought he was a nasty, manipulative shit-stirrer myself.'

'He is, I think. Like I said, it didn't last. He's very tightly wound, very angry, deep inside. But he was clever and charming, and . . . vulnerable.'

'You're kidding.'

'No. No one becomes like that unless they've been hurt, and I think he felt as though he'd been betrayed in some way.' She shook her head. 'It was a mistake, but maybe there's just something very tempting about looking down into darkness, so long as you're careful not to fall in. I think Jason was hurt by our split. Whatever his failings, he had genuine affection for me. I don't regret it. All things have their consequences, and I like where mine have led me now.'

And back then, so did he.

Now, with Emi's days almost run down, less than a fortnight to go and the clock ticking harder and harder, part of him hated the fate which had given him something so valuable to lose, and no way to prevent it because the Curse was incurable. Except that Jason Blake should have been dead himself weeks before, yet here he was, and whatever had saved him could save Emi too.

Turn at the end of the alley, nearly slipping, then over a fence and into a silent construction site. Blake skidded down the side of an earth ramp leading into the base of the dig, then up the other side, Garrett following, his muscles burning beneath his tactical gear. Up a sloping wooden plank beyond, on to a line of scaffolding, the distance between them slowly growing. Footsteps pounding hollow on the damp boards and the distant flare of halogens like stars.

Blake made another hard turn, and when Garrett followed he saw him trotting nimbly along a steel I-beam, part of the frame that spanned the whole proto-building. Garrett looked down to the frozen earth twenty feet below, swallowed hard, and stepped out on to the metal. Wobbled and swayed, forced himself to continue, slow and unsteady. Didn't look up until he was across, heart thumping, and by then Blake had reached the fence at the far side of the site. A van was there, waiting, engine running. There was a faded logo and the last remnants of peeling text alongside. Garrett stared, trying to hold the design in his memory, as the van's side door slid open and Blake jumped inside. He looked back for a moment, waved to Garrett, and was gone.

SIX

It was a week after their first, unexpected reunion that Maya saw Dominic again. A phone call, late, from the private cell number he'd written on the back of his card. She was at home, trying to shake off a near-argument with Shaun over nothing very much while they watched a movie.

'Sorry it's so late, M. Are you free for a while? Just to talk.'

She glanced at the time, at her boyfriend. Said, 'Sure. Where?'

'I'm at the end of your block. I'll get the cab to drive down and pick you up.'

'Two minutes.'

Shaun looked at her as she hung up. 'What's going on, babe?'

'Work,' she lied. 'Late call on a story and it's one of mine. Gotta go. I'll be back in a while.'

Grabbed her bag and was gone, and, she found, glad of it. There was a cab idling at the kerb when she came downstairs. In the back, looking tired and drawn, Dominic.

He gave the driver a street address and smiled at Maya.

'How'd you know where I live?' she asked.

'I looked you up in the phone book.'

'I'm not in the phone book.'

'It wasn't a regular phone book. Did I tear you away from anything?'

'Nothing important. Where are we going?'

'To get a drink. To carry on that catching up we were doing last week before we were interrupted.' He turned, stared out the rear window for a few seconds, then settled back in his seat.

'Worried we're being followed?'

Maya had meant it as a joke, but he shrugged. 'I should be free of them but you never can tell.'

'For real?'

'How do you think they found us at that café? Amanda likes to know where her people are at all times, especially when things are tight. Can't have anyone going off the reservation if something's about to go down. You never know who else will find them.'

'Won't she be unhappy if you've given her the slip? Especially to meet a reporter. At least,' she added, 'I'm still a reporter for another few days. Probably not after that.'

'Maybe, but she needs me right now, so she'll have to put up with it.'

'So what is it that's "going down"? Some kind of major deal?' She smiled. 'I never thought you'd go into mergers and acquisitions when we were going out.'

'Not here. Drinks first.'

They drove.

'What would you do,' Dominic said, later, in a dirty hole of a bar called Warriors, 'if you found out you had inoperable cancer?'

She looked round at the scattered clientele of alcoholics and rednecks, the faded, sticky posters of sports cars and old cigarette ads plastered to the walls, the gap-toothed, thirty-something meth addict tending bar. Said, 'Is that your way of saying it's happened to you? Or that it's happened to your boss?'

'Neither. It's a hypothetical. What would you do?'

'Party hard and die in pain, probably.'

'And what would you do if there was some hope of a cure? You'd want to live, right?'

'Sure.'

'Well, now imagine that your cure for cancer was in the hands of some really fucked-up people, and if you didn't get it someone else might and they might not let you have it. That's the kind of process we're going through at work. Why things are so touchy right now.'

'You're trying to, what, buy a cure for cancer?'

'Not necessarily.'

'But it's that kind of—Wait, not *necessarily*? You mean it could be?'

He flapped, looked away. 'I was continuing the analogy. Forget it.'

'You always were a lousy liar, Dominic. You, or rather

Daedalus Venture, have almost got your hands on a cure for cancer.'

'Not directly.' He sighed, finished his drink and went for another. When he came back, he said, 'Did you ever learn about Hero of Alexandria at school?'

'Who?'

'Ancient Greece. He built a brass sphere over a drum with water inside. When you heated the water, the steam rose into the sphere and escaped through two nozzles on the sides, causing it to spin. He was the first to figure out how to turn heat into mechanical energy but nothing was done with it – if it even could have been back then – and eventually Newcomen came up with the steam engine centuries later. This, this thing that we're talking about, this is Hero's sphere. The cure for cancer, or a million other things we can't do right now, is a steam train. Or maybe a car. Or a rocket. At best, this is just the start. It could get us nowhere – but it could be the first step, the breakthrough idea that puts us on the right road to unimaginable advances. And it's me negotiating access to it. There are others, too, who'd do anything to get it. If I say I'm in a race with Carl Wong Shan, Donald Glau, Harrison Valentin, Mary McGregor . . . Does that explain the kind of pressure I'm under? And they're all just like Amanda, you know? That's why everything's so goddamn closed in and why I'm so desperate to escape, just for an evening.'

A tired smile, and he shook his head. 'That's more than I should be telling anyone, and I don't want to talk work anyway, so what say we leave it at that? And it doesn't matter about the job; I'm glad we've met up again anyway. It was a shame we dropped out of touch in the first place. I don't know what your situation is, or whether you're seeing anyone, but that's not important. It's not . . . well, it's nothing to do with it. It's just nice to see you.'

'You too.' She raised her glass. 'Your job sucks and my career's in the shithouse. Let's enjoy tonight, because sooner or later it's going to be tomorrow and the real world again.'

And they did, and it was.

SEVEN

They kept Maya in St Luke's overnight for observation, and wanted her to stay longer, but she left even though the only alternative was her crummy studio apartment. She had a lot of bruises and a possible minor concussion, but nothing to hold her there. Told herself she shouldn't be taking up valuable hospital resources and time, but the truth was that she just couldn't stand the feeling of being surrounded by injured and dying people. St Luke's had admitted the first wave of the wounded from the Green Street bombing, and while Maya was kept away from the main wards and certainly a long way from the critical care suites where the worst cases were held, she'd spent most of the night imagining them lying in their beds or strapped to gurneys, the missing limbs and the blood and the white of shattered bone punched through flesh. She hadn't told the doctors that, though.

The police took an initial statement from her a couple of hours after she arrived, the air inside St Luke's one of palpable nervous activity, emergency treatment under disaster protocols the hospital had trained for, but never had to activate before. Every TV screen in the place showed live news coverage of the bombing and the aftermath, national networks as well as local. They gave Maya a room without one. She told the cops what she'd seen in the calmest, most detached journalist's voice she was able to summon; then, when they left the room and she was alone again, she cried uncontrollably. The hospital asked if there was anyone they should call, someone who'd be worried about her or would come and stay with her, and the sad reality was that there wasn't.

Maya lurched out of the main doors into the cold of morning, and blinked at the distant media cordon on the far side of the parking lot where the TV press had been corralled out of the way of emergency vehicles and regular visitors. She had the card of a PTSD counsellor, a pre-booked appointment for that afternoon and a helpline number, a set of goodwill clothes, her personal effects in a plastic bag and a cab waiting for her.

'Gonna be more snow today,' the driver said as they pulled away. 'Gonna be real cold. That's what they say.'

'That so?' was all she offered by way of reply.

Someone must have briefed the driver because he said nothing more to her until he told her the fare. Even the radio in the car was tuned to an all music, no news AM station playing endless R&B on a Moebius loop of synthetic bass.

Inside, Maya changed into her own clothes, watched

herself make a cup of coffee like it was any other day, and then opened her laptop and began to type.

She saw the evening flood of people along Green Street, normal people with normal lives, making their way home, going shopping, going out. Breath and car exhaust steaming in the glow of the streetlights. Alive.

She saw their final positions superimposed on an image of the scene that existed only in her mind. The bodies of those closest to the blast, of whom little but fragments would ever be found; those further away, or more sheltered, unconscious, dazed, screaming in pain. The neon extinguished, the only light bleeding from the surrounding city and the scattered fires in the street.

She saw Dominic Wheeler coming out of the Daedalus Venture offices, the case in his hand, the minders with him. Saw that unfamiliar tension in his eyes and his walk. Saw him again, down and broken, the guy in the flight jacket rolling his body off the briefcase.

And most of all she saw the bomber. The nature of what he'd done had etched every detail into her memory like diamond. The dark glitter of his eyes. The shadowed outline of his chin, and his mouth pinched firm with resolve or fear. The steam blowing from beneath his hood. His hands wedged in his pockets until the time came and he pushed the switch on his detonator. The explosives strapped to his body beneath his winter clothes. Tiny details: the scuff marks on his shoes, the low awkward hang of his pants where they were just a shade too big for him, and there, when he'd raised his hand in his final salute, the jailhouse tattoo of an hourglass on the inside of his wrist.

Forty-eight people were confirmed dead in the bombing, a further one hundred and seventy-plus were injured, and Maya would never forget the man who'd done it.

When she'd finished typing, she called Kevin McMahon. 'I wasn't expecting to hear from you this soon, Maya,' he said. 'Paper's busy as hell as you can probably imagine.'

'The Green Street bombing,' she said.

'No shit. What can I do for you?'

'That's what I meant, the bombing. You want a piece on it?'

A sigh. 'Maya, we've got just about every staffer covering it already. I don't see what—'

'I was there, Kev,' she said. 'Right there when it happened.'

'Jesus, Maya . . .' McMahon paused for a moment, tone suddenly turned sensitive. 'I didn't know. I haven't had the chance to scan the list of names they've released so far. Are you OK?'

'I got out of the hospital this morning. I'm OK. Got lucky, no serious injuries. But I saw the whole thing. You want the piece or not?'

'Send it over,' he said. 'Let me have a look at it.'

They accepted the story for the next day's edition as a piece of eyewitness op-ed. Kevin or someone else excised all but the scantest description of the bomber, but left Dominic's name and everything else alone. Maya figured it for a police thing and didn't ask him about it. Even a department as crooked as Newport's had to take something like Green Street seriously, especially with the Feds on it too.

'What would you like to talk about?' the counsellor asked her that afternoon.

Maya had expected, perhaps hoped, to respond with a long, tearful and ultimately cleansing exploration of her shock at the physical carnage she'd been surrounded by. Instead she found herself talking about Dominic. About how they'd met at college, how her grades had taken a nosedive while they were together because she'd been too busy doing other things to study, how she'd loved him, or thought she'd loved him, even as it all just seemed to end for no readily apparent reason. About how unsettling and hurtful it felt to have someone from her past resurface like that, and with him, maybe, some of her old feelings for him, only to have him snatched away for ever. As though the universe had taunted her with some doomed glimpse of reconciliation and an alternative future together.

She Googled Daedalus Venture again when she returned home. She'd done it before, after that first meeting with Dominic, after the men had come to take him away. Searched for more information on Amanda Kent, his boss, but drew little apart from a bunch of entirely unhelpful puff pieces for business mags. Nothing about Daedalus, and that in itself was strange.

'Why do you want to know about Amanda Kent?' Terry Wagstaff asked her when she tried his number. He sounded as if he'd be happy for an excuse to turn her down; Terry hadn't liked her even before she was sacked by the *Tribune*.

'Come on, Tel. I've got a prospective piece on one of her people that's come my way but I don't know jack about her. You've been business editor at the *Mail* for forever and you know more about this kind of thing than anyone else I've ever met.' Terry was a jerk, but he was famous for having an ego that even a beginner could play like a concert pianist.

'OK, but I can't tell you much. As far as I know, she's an investor. Moves money around to wherever looks like a good bet but doesn't make a big deal about it, rather like George Soros would be if he was an incurable introvert. On a different scale, of course, but I'm sure you get the picture. She's a member of all the right circles, but I'm not sure I've ever heard anything specific she's actually *done*. All I know is that she's widely respected and apparently very successful.'

Maya thought about Dominic's briefcase and the young guy, barely out of his teens, snatching it. Nothing else taken, from Dominic or, as far as she'd seen, anyone else. The looting all well away from the epicentre. 'She's never dealt in hard currency, precious stones, physical goods, then?'

'Good lord, no,' Terry said. From his tone, he clearly considered it beneath her. Like she was royalty.

Not long after she put the phone down, a man introducing himself as Harrison Valentin called her and said, 'Miss Cassinelli, I would very much like to discuss Dominic Wheeler with you, in person.'

'Why?' Then, 'Hold on, how do you know I know Dominic?'

'I've read your article for tomorrow's paper.'

'Excuse me for saying, but that's mighty creepy of you. How did you get to read that? More to the point, why shouldn't I hang up on you?' Knew, as she said it, that she wouldn't. Not someone Dominic had mentioned in the same breath as his employer just days before he died.

'As it so happens, I have an association with the *Post*. Of sorts. Friends in high places. I also have an interest in Mr Wheeler and what happened to him, and to everyone else on Green Street, as I believe do you. I have a proposal to put to you. We could be of great service to one another.' A grin she could hear, teeth sharp and bared.

EIGHT

Eleven months before the Green Street bombing.

Leonard Hume shrugged out of his coat and tossed his keys on the hallway table. Sighed at the pictures of his kids next to the mirror. He'd been Cursed a month before. Hadn't believed it at first, but the police had taken it seriously, and once he'd been to the support group he understood how real it was. At first he'd felt hopeful: that if there were this many people affected, and the cops were on the case, someone would find a cure for it before his time ran out. But then he'd seen the same hope dead in others, further into their allotted time, heard how little luck the police had had in cracking the case, and felt his optimism die too by degrees. More than anything, he was certain he didn't want his kids to grow up without their father. The idea made him feel ill. He had to make it somehow.

'How did it go tonight?' Sarah, his wife, standing in the living-room doorway. She was a slight woman, had been a bank worker when they'd met. Surprisingly strong, though. She'd cried when he'd told her how long he had left, but while the pain was clearly still there, she seemed to have mastered it, pushing a consistent line about the hopes of a cure and making the most of their last year together. Even around the kids, she had held it together. So far.

'OK, I guess.' They hugged for a time, then he moved past and dropped on to the couch.

'Aren't the meetings helping at all? You could try something else.'

'No, no, the group's fine. I just . . . you feel powerless, you know? And you see all these other people who are just as powerless as you, and half of them have given up and accepted it.' He shook his head. 'But I heard tonight that there's maybe another group I could join.'

'A different support group?'

'More than that. More active, like a pressure thing. To try to force people into doing something for us.'

'They're going to push for a cure for the cancer, then?' Sarah said. 'Or is there a drug treatment for it they haven't licensed yet? I read this story in *Newsweek* . . .'

That was the lie he'd settled on. Cancer. And as much as it hurt to keep the truth from his family, he'd found that if he repeated the lie often enough, in his head it sort of became the reality. Like he'd given the truth a nickname, so that it was barely a lie at all any more. He didn't have the heart to interrupt Sarah, talking at length about a cancer treatment – useless to him – that a group of patients had apparently managed to swing past the licensing authorities after a media campaign.

He tried to remember everything the guy, Jason, had said about his pressure group or protest group or whatever it was, but half of it had been rhetoric. A recruitment pitch. He certainly wanted more done for the Clocks, and that had to be better than the limited official efforts to save them all. If Jason's people could force change or make the authorities see how devastating the Curse was, it could only improve Leonard's chances of seeing his children's birthdays next year.

He slipped one hand into his wife's while the other fingered the card in his pocket that bore Jason Blake's phone number.

NINE

A half-drunk pint of Rolling Rock and another likely to follow hard behind. Moisture gleaming on the side of Garrett's glass and a bubble of quiet around him. The Vines was busy, night rolling on, but no one much bothered him. Up on the makeshift stage at the far end of the room, a heavy-set transvestite in a red garter belt calling himself Heavenly Kevin was murdering an already wounded Barry Manilow number. Garrett wanted a smoke, but not badly enough to stop drinking.

He stared into the mirror behind the bar, remembering the long grey-lit table he'd sat in front of that afternoon. Lieutenant Saganowski, Lieutenant Morgan, two suits he didn't know, probably from the OPC, all of them with flat, dead eyes.

'You left your post,' Saganowski said. 'You left it and Officer McDermott died from his injuries. If you'd rendered assistance, he might still be alive.'

'That's speculation,' Morgan cut in. 'We don't know that.'

'That's irrelevant.'

'Officer Garrett was in pursuit of a suspect.'

'He didn't radio it in. He didn't call for backup. He didn't even report the explosion at the site or summon help for Officer McDermott. He hasn't been able to tell us anything about this suspect.'

Garrett said nothing. It went that way for a long time.

'Trouble, Charles?' Back to the present, and the bartender, Marcel. A tall, elegant man whose parents had fled war in the Côte d'Ivoire when he was a child.

'Why do you always call me Charles, Marcel? No one does that.'

'Your parents did. I've always assumed they were people of intelligence and decency and so they must have had good reason.'

'Dad got his kicks cracking skulls on Union Plaza with the Seventh and Mom was a Vicodin ghost. I wouldn't set much store by their opinions.'

Marcel shook his head softly. The movement was like the mating dance of a stork. 'Painful memory, Charles?'

Guilt, but he didn't say so. Both parents gone from Newport: Dad retired to the back woods of the New York state, Mom dead from suicide, or cancer, depending on how you looked at it, when he was a child. They'd had their faults, but Garrett knew he was painting them, and in particular his mother, worse than they'd been for a quick shot of sympathy, and it disgusted him.

'No one has claimed responsibility for the bombing yet?' Marcel said, steering the conversation away. 'That's what the news says, but only a fool trusts what they see on the news.'

'Not as far as I know. But I wouldn't know now, would I?'

'Ah, trouble at work.'

Garrett nodded. 'A friend of mine was killed on the night of the bombing. I'm on suspension pending an investigation for negligence in the line of duty. Some shit like that.'

'A good man?'

'He was a cop.' In Newport, that generally meant 'no'.

Lieutenant Morgan, talking quietly to him after the meeting. Face like an eagle who'd just eaten a particularly sour lemon. 'I don't see why you can't tell us what it was about this suspect that made you pursue him,' he said. 'You're not an idiot, Garrett, though you're acting like one. You didn't shoot, you didn't shout a warning and try to apprehend him. You didn't call it in. Saganowski is ready to nail you to the wall. I can help you, but only if you give me something.'

'There's nothing to give.'

Long silence. 'McDermott was a belligerent jackass, but he was one of us. Tell me you left him to die for something. Tell me there was a reason.'

'There was a reason.' Garrett didn't go any further. Didn't want to. The memory of trudging back through the snow to the office tower was too fresh. The scene taped off, and behind the fluttering plastic the still, lifeless form of his friend. Blood in the emergency strobes. The guilt like a rock in his gut. The lieutenant waited. Eventually, Garrett said, 'Is that all? Can I go now?'

Disgust on Morgan's face as he waved Garrett away.

'Your woman,' Marcel said, and for a moment Garrett thought he was back at his interrogation. 'This has something to do with your woman. I must say, Charles, your unwillingness to back down from a doomed cause is admirable.'

Marcel thought Emi had cancer. 'Thanks.'

'Admirable, but foolish. Excuse me.' A faint smile, and he moved away to serve another customer.

O'Connor had been in the locker room when Garrett picked up his stuff. Felt it as soon as he walked into the room. Hostility like a leaden fog. He knew it from the job, at the sites of call-outs and riots. Not inside the precinct. Casual indifference or contempt, maybe, but this was ugly.

'You're a fuck-up, Garrett,' O'Connor said. 'You've been a fuck-up for a long time, but last night you could've got me killed as well as McDermott.'

Garrett, clearing out his locker, felt movement behind him. Three or four of them, a knot tightening. 'I just went through all this upstairs,' he said. 'And you didn't know McDermott from a hole in the ground. He was my friend.'

'I don't give a shit about McDermott.'

'Feeling was probably mutual,' he said. Tossed the last couple of his things in a bag.

'I care about *me*. You didn't hear me shouting over the radio? Saying we were pinned and needed backup? And what did you do to help, huh, Garrett? You ran. Probably heard someone opening a bottle down the street. You're a fucking liability to us all. We'll all be better off once you're gone. Now, you gonna apologise to me?'

Garrett, looking at the gym bag absently. 'What for? You're still alive.'

'Guess you're not getting it.' A hand pushed him in the back. 'Turn around. I want my apology, you sack of shit.'

Garrett turned, saw the four of them. He swung the bag like he was hauling it on to his shoulder. Slipped the loop of the shoulder strap over O'Connor's head and yanked it round and back, hard. Slammed his face into the locker door and dropped him, yelping and bloody, on to the floor. Looked at the others with a flat, empty gaze and said, 'Get the fuck out of my way.'

Something in the way he said it, because they did.

TEN

By the time Emi arrived in the Vines, Garrett was drunk. Her hand soft on his shoulder, and her voice cool in his ear. 'You started without me.'

'Disappointed in me?' He threw an arm round her waist, grinning. Knew he was acting the lecherous barfly, but enjoyed it anyway.

'No.' She leaned into him, kissed him on the side of the head.

'Sometimes I wish you were.'

'My silly Charlie.' Sadness, there. 'Where are we going tonight?'

'Whaler's Wharf,' he said. 'I'll buy you dinner at the Shark, and then I'll win you a glittering necklace at skeeball. My skills are legendary. If you're lucky, I'll teach you how to play.'

'My hero. Should I swoon?'

'Have you ever had the Shark's grilled monkfish?'

She shook her head.

'Then you'll swoon regardless.'

* * *

The Shark had originally been called something else: the Shark's Mouth, or the Shark's Fin, or Head, or Eyes. The Shark's Balls for all Garrett knew. Some time before he was born, one of the big Atlantic storms had blown in, worse than normal, and taken half the sign on the restaurant's roof with it. It stayed like that for a while, and by then it was just the Shark, and never went back to being anything else.

The snow had started again at some point after he'd reached the bar. It drifted down on them now in slow fat flakes as they walked to the wharf, drifts of static against the hard black sky. Emi, talking about her ideas for what she knew would be a final exhibition, something to leave behind her when she was gone. Her arm wrapped round his, tucked close for support on the slippery streets. Garrett felt himself sobering up and wished he wasn't. The alcohol gave him a warm comfort blanket, a barrier against reality that allowed him to pretend that life was normal. Without it, he could feel the dwindling supply of their time together crushing harder and harder against his heart.

'They suspended you,' Emi said, and he realised he'd lost track of their conversation.

'Yeah.' He shrugged. 'Probably fire me this time.'

'You should have told them.'

'If they know it was Blake, and they find him first, he might get shot, they might not ask the right questions, he might not tell them the cure. And I wouldn't know, because they kicked me off that case, didn't they? So let them fire me. I want to know. I want to keep you alive, Emi.'

A wry shake of her head, and she tightened her grip on his arm.

The fish was good, a bottle of wine and an hour or two in the gloomy soot-marked interior of the Shark. Later, they played skeeball in a rattling arcade further down the wharf. Garrett had drunk too much to be any good, but he showed Emi how to play anyway, then bribed the kid at the counter ten bucks to let him take one of the shit two-dollar necklaces from the prize rack. Emi, laughing as he slipped it round her neck with great ceremony. Smiling with her eyes shining as she admired herself in the unlit glass of a closed storefront. The same smile, much later, as they lay together in the quiet dark of Garrett's apartment, Garrett feeling her breath against him, wrapped in each other's warmth.

In the tail end of night, Emi stirred against him, said, 'Come for a walk along the waterfront with me.'

Distant light stirred the darkened sky beneath the thinning blanket of cloud and the far horizon was shaded a murky purple. They walked through the quiet by the icy river, Emi talking quietly about her family, stories from her childhood. The port authority lights flaring harsh and white in the distance and the faint glimmering chaos of Port Blackwater across the river.

And there it was. The same logo he'd seen on the truck, painted on the cabin of a fishing boat slowly steering out of the twisted waterways of the Port. He held Emi, and watched it over her shoulder as it weaved through the mass.

Eventually it tied up behind one of the permanently moored vessels there and a couple of men crossed to the other boat. A boat he knew; six months he'd been stationed in the Port and he'd visited it himself. Home to a low-rent explosives guy they called Roadblock, a man the NCPD figured had worked for hire on the robbery circuit before he retired. But then came the memory of smoke rising from Green Street and McDermott lying dead in the snow, and maybe, he figured, Roadblock hadn't retired after all.

ELEVEN

K:Max was a restaurant designed along carefully acultural lines to be somehow both intensely chic and fashionable and at the same time wholly artificial. It was, Maya reflected as she waited behind a couple whose clothes must've cost more than she earned in a year, the dining equivalent of a high class airport lounge. An elite transitory space with absolutely no defining features a visitor could use to pin it to a specific place or era. Soulless and exclusive. About as far from her tiny apartment in Dartwell or the all too real destruction on Green Street as it was possible to get. The woman at the maître d's desk said, with all the charm of liquid nitrogen, 'Name?'

'Maya Cassinelli. I'm here to meet Harrison Valentin.'

The woman scanned a list on the touchscreen built into the desk. Said, 'Yes, I see.' Without glancing at Maya, she added, 'We normally insist on a minimum standard of dress.'

'I'll try not to hold it against you.'

'You understand, we have a certain . . . image to maintain.'

Maya, in another stubbornly picked pair of unsuitable

suede boots, jeans, and a plain cotton shirt under her coat, felt her anger rising. Said, 'And if you feel that turning away an injured survivor of the Green Street bombing with an invitation to be here, in front of your customers – a loud, vocal survivor . . . a loud, vocal, *journalist* survivor – because she happens not to be wearing a pants suit or a dress is going to be a successful way to maintain it, you go ahead. After all, I wouldn't want anything to fuck up your image, would I?'

The woman looked at her, summoned a minion and instructed him to take Maya to Mr Valentin's table. The man led her through a low-lit formation of black marble-topped tables arranged with the care and precision of an ancient stone circle to a small booth against the far wall. Offered, with Soviet efficiency and warmth, to take her coat; she declined out of sheer bloody-mindedness.

Sprawled in the chair opposite was a man perhaps ten years older than her. An artfully untidy spray of blond hair, an equally carefully creased blazer and a bright pink shirt, ice-pale blue eyes and a smile like he'd attended the same classes as Tom Cruise. He didn't stand up, but extended a hand. No jewellery, and a chip of glass in a silver bracelet where his watch would have been.

'A pleasure to meet you, Miss Cassinelli,' he said. His accent was non-regional American, the hint of something long-buried in some of the hard vowel sounds. 'I read your article, of course. Very moving, very shocking. How are you feeling now?'

'I've been better, been worse. Bruises are ugly, but healing. They gave me pills to help me sleep. Don't do shit for the dreams, though. I'm told that's normal.'

The Soviet reappeared, soundlessly. Said, 'Can I get you a drink? Sir? Madam?'

'A Lost Coast Pale.'

'Mojito,' Maya said.

'Charmingly unseasonal,' Valentin said. 'What would you have asked for in the summer?'

'Mulled wine. What exactly is this about, Mr Valentin?'

'Well, now.' The smile again. He exuded sexuality, but in a weirdly directionless way. Maya didn't feel as though he was actually about to hit on her, but that he was, in a sense, constantly pursuing the entire world around him without really being aware of it. That, or it was just manipulation. Dominic had certainly feared him, said he was the same as Amanda Kent, and look at how she'd treated one of her own – held under escort, followed everywhere, a virtual prisoner. 'This is about Dominic Wheeler. And call me Harrison. I'm no fan of formalities. How did you know Dominic?'

'He was my boyfriend at college.'

'Lucky guy.'

She ignored that. 'We stayed friends for a while but then we lost touch, like people do. So I guess you could say I knew him very well, but a long time ago. How did you know him?'

'We had shared friends, so our social circles crossed. I

didn't know him especially well, but we had several things in common.'

'Such as?'

Harrison laughed. The Soviet returned with the drinks, asked if they were ready to place their order. Harrison dismissed him with a shake of his head. 'Your health,' he said to Maya. 'If that's not terribly inappropriate.'

'So?'

'Some of our work has been in similar fields. Recently, for instance, Dominic was involved with an unusual matter that greatly interested me. Before I come to what that was,' he said, holding up a hand to ward off another prompt from Maya, 'let me ask you a couple of questions.'

She shrugged. The mojito was pretty good. 'Your dime, I guess.'

'Do you want to know what happened on Green Street? To yourself and the others as well as Dominic?'

'I'd like to know who Dominic was when he died; he was a long way from the guy I knew, but beyond that, yeah, I want to know what happened.'

'And you aren't content to wait for the police report.'

'This is Newport City. People who wait for the police to solve everything generally die unfulfilled.'

He nodded, sipped his beer. 'And what would you say are your main obstacles to finding the answers you're looking for?'

'Connections, resources, a place to start. You name it. Dominic's employer wouldn't even give me the time of day.'

'I imagine that sort of thing would be more common for you as a result of the Saganowski case.' He raised an eyebrow. 'I, of course, checked you out before I contacted you. For what little it's worth, you have my sincere sympathy; the lieutenant's rotten to the core.'

'Which of course brings us to this meeting,' Maya said. 'A man like you, in a restaurant like this, and all your questions: are you offering me what I need to do this?'

The bright white grin again. 'Well, now. You're right on the money. I want to know what happened too, and I happen to be in a position to pay you to find out and allow you to slake your own curiosity at the same time. Specifically, though, your article said you saw someone looting Dominic's body. A terrible indictment of this city's attitudes to tragedy, et cetera.'

'Yeah.' Felt something, a sense that she was swimming out into deeper water.

'What did they take?'

'His briefcase.'

Harrison nodded. 'I have good reason to believe there were things in that case, presumably the things the thief was after, that would be of very great interest to me. I would like to know what became of the case and obtain the contents, if that's possible. I'm sure it'll come up in your investigations, since it seems a fair bet that the thief may have been in on the bombing. In return, I'm willing to bankroll your work for as long as it takes, within reason.'

'Cards on the table,' Maya said. Knew, even if he denied

it, that there would be a catch. Dominic had implied as much when he'd compared this man to his own employer. 'What the hell are you talking about?'

Harrison leaned forward, fixed her with his pallid blue eyes. Said, 'Tell me, have you ever heard of the Curse of Willow Heights?'

TWELVE

'Like all good curses,' Valentin said, gesturing with a forkful of some kind of many-legged sea creature, 'the Curse of Willow Heights is very much a human invention. Both literally and figuratively. It is at once part urban myth and part something terribly real.'

Their food had arrived. Maya was surprised by her appetite. Less so by the quality of the food; the pigeon something she was eating was excellent. 'I know Willow Heights,' she said. 'Not like it's the Levels, but it's not a great area. Knew a guitarist who came from there, long time ago. But I never heard of a curse.'

'I'm not surprised. The police have done a thorough job of keeping it under wraps. In most cases, not even a victim's immediate family are aware of the entire truth.' He devoured his strange little beast and speared another. 'The Curse is actually the effect, or some kind of after-effect, of a deeply peculiar and highly secret serial crime being committed by "person or persons unknown".' He made bunny ears with his fingers. 'The first cases appeared in Willow Heights but it has since spread to other parts of Newport, apparently at random. I have some contacts in the NCPD and they keep me updated.'

'What's so unusual about it?'

'Each victim is rendered unconscious and abducted or otherwise interfered with without their knowledge. When they awake, either having been dumped or, in some cases, back in the location where they'd originally fallen asleep or passed out, they find that the perpetrator has left a note on them that gives a date a year away, and says that on this day they will die, and nothing anyone can do will stop it. The victim, aside from anything incurred in the course of their abduction, is generally uninjured and seemingly unaffected. Careful examination might reveal a single needle mark, but nothing more than that.'

Maya raised an eyebrow. 'Sounds like a bad practical joke. Someone watched *The Ring* too many times.'

'Which is exactly what the police thought at first. They kept the matter quiet, though not as quiet as they do now, and investigated in a somewhat half-hearted fashion. Then, on the allotted date, the first victim, a man called Wilson Defort, collapsed and died while eating dinner with his family. The toxicology report revealed he'd been poisoned with massive amounts of botulin. Comparatively massive anyway; botulin's quite terrifyingly poisonous in minuscule doses. The police suddenly took the business far more seriously and put all the other known victims under surveillance, ran medical checks, CAT scans, the whole nine yards. The second victim died and they still had no idea how it was done.'

'How come I've not heard any of this?'

'As I said, secrecy,' Harrison said. 'The NCPD walled the whole thing off as soon as they realised the extent of the Curse. Cops on the case know the full version, but they're forbidden from talking to anyone else about it. Existing victims were mostly put into "protective custody" to try to control stories of their eventual death, while new victims are effectively sworn to secrecy. They usually tell their friends and families they've been diagnosed with a rare form of brain tumour. I'm told the NCPD threatens to withdraw any support for the victims and their families if someone talks about what happened. They, and by "they" I mean your old friend Lieutenant Saganowski, who's nominally in charge of the investigation even if she's not involved at the front end, feel that there's too much risk of massive copycatting by hoaxers. Not to mention mass public panic if people discovered that this was going on and no one knew who was behind it, or had a cure for the Curse.' Harrison paused, sipped his beer. Added, 'They're probably right. There's no medical test for the Curse; only the mechanical details, the nature of the note and so forth, can determine the likelihood of an individual case being genuine. It'd be chaos.'

Maya looked at him, not sure whether to laugh the whole story off. Harrison was infuriatingly difficult to read. On the other hand, she couldn't think of a single good reason for him to pick this, of all things, to invent. She ordered a second mojito, said, 'So how's he doing it? You said there was a needle mark – he's injecting botulin into the victims? Or don't they know yet?'

'Oh, they know now. Once it all became very serious, victims were under a lot more stress; imagine being told you had inoperable terminal cancer for which there was no cure, no palliative treatment whatsoever. When the first of them committed suicide, by drug overdose, the police examined the body in minute detail. Tissue samples, toxin screening, everything they could think of. When they examined his brain tissues they discovered microscopic sacs containing botulin bonded with the membrane at the blood-brain boundary.' When Maya shrugged, he said, 'The filter that decides what is and what isn't allowed to cross from your bloodstream into your grey matter. Highly specialised. Each sac had a kind of molecular clock of the sort used for nanoscale devices, computing and the like. Nothing complicated, in nature if not in manufacture, and all it had to do when it counted down was trip a kind of enzyme gate to release the poison. All on the same timer, of course. Once the sacs rupture, the victim's bloodstream is immediately laced with several times the accepted lethal dose of botulin.'

'They can't remove them surgically?'

'Far too small,' Harrison said. 'And while it might be possible to break down the poison or ruin the molecular clock in the same way one would deal with a tumour – bombarding it with radiation, primarily – to do so would mean bathing the victim's brain in radiation strong enough to kill them too. So far they've not found a way to remove the sacs or render them inert that wouldn't do for the patient as well.'

'All very interesting.'

'To say the least. The manufacture of the sacs alone is a technological feat most of the nanotech research sector would love to replicate. Clearly whoever's behind it is no regular citizen.'

'But what does it have to do with Dominic and Green Street?' As she spoke, part of the answer came to her. 'The bomber,' she said. 'He was a victim, wasn't he?'

'The police call them "Clocks". I understand that during the course of the investigation someone started referring to victims as being "on the clock" and the nickname stuck. And yes, you're entirely correct, he was a Clock. As you can imagine, they're unstable enough to make them ideal candidates to carry out that sort of atrocity.'

She thought back to the man's hourglass tattoo. The salute, the mastery of the fear of death it would have taken a normal man to kill himself in that way, a fear he'd already had to face because of the Curse. 'Jesus Christ,' she said. 'So why Green Street?'

'I'm not sure exactly why, but I suspect that Dominic or what he was carrying was, in some way, the target of the bomber or the people he was working with. I've heard that Amanda Kent has taken an interest in the Curse recently, and Dominic was a key part of her personal staff.'

'Could be coincidence.'

'The first time a Clock lashes out against regular society he happens to take out someone who's recently become involved with the Curse, and whose briefcase is the only thing known to have been stolen from the scene in the immediate aftermath?'

Maya shrugged, conceding the point. 'How did Kent know about the Curse? And how would the bomber or anyone else know about her?'

'I don't know the answer to your second question, and that's something you should look into, but the first is simple: I imagine she knows in the same way I do. I pay people in the NCPD and elsewhere to bring me information on anything that might interest me.' Harrison laid down his fork and pushed his plate back. Looked serious for a moment, and said, 'So, what do you say to our arrangement?'

'I get to back out any time I want,' Maya said. 'No strings attached. Clean break, everything as it is at that point, no terms or conditions. Understood?'

'Agreed.'

'And you give me as much information as I need. If you've got any leads, I want to know about them.'

Harrison grinned broadly again and spread his arms wide, welcoming. 'Marvellous! I do have a lead, of sorts. Or, at least, a likely first avenue of inquiry. Victims – Clocks – who've come forward to the police to say they've been told they have a year to live are encouraged to meet in support groups run by the NCPD. They're the only places where Clocks can freely share their experiences, hopes and fears with others. From the police's point of view, of course, they're a great way to compare notes and maybe come up with some kind of pattern, a description of the perpetrator, a place, something. I can get you into the groups under a false name; relatively easy as, like I said, there's no test to prove you're a Clock. Go to the groups undercover, find out what you can. The bomber will have been there, people will have known him. They may know who he was associated with, what he'd talked about. Take it from there. It'll be easier than trying to crack Amanda Kent's organisation, trust me.'

'What if the cops identify me?'

'Saganowski?'

'Or someone who followed the case, or knows who survived the bombing.'

Harrison shrugged, a gleam in his eye. 'You'll have to chance it. Saganowski won't know you're there, and chances are the other cops won't know you at all. As for survivors, it's the dead who get the coverage in these things, not the wounded. Usually.' The gleam brightened. 'You're good-looking enough to get in the news, but there's no specific human interest angle. If you'd been pregnant or a decorated war hero . . . Don't worry about it. You'll manage.'

Maya broke eye contact, withdrew from Harrison's off-putting directness. She sipped her mojito, looked around the restaurant. Imagined that any of the people eating dinner here might be running on a clock, told to keep it a secret from those closest to them; days, weeks, months to live, and then a sudden death. Not a damn thing anyone could do to stop it happening, and no reason behind it that anyone could fathom. Nothing but the fickle whims of someone playing God.

And watching over it all, a rich man with a Cheshire smile who, she realised, hadn't told her what he wanted with the Curse. Nor what he'd do to her if she failed to help him find it, now that she knew its secrets.

THIRTEEN

In Chapel's dream, the four massive towers at the heart of the Levels soared in front of him. A hot, cutting wind blew past, bringing sun-bleached trash and the smell of festering weeds off the canals. He was back waiting for Scorp with a vanload of stolen weapons ready for a buyer and the hustler's itch that told him maybe this was a bum deal, like he shouldn't have jacked the load without knowing for sure where it was heading. As if there was any doubt; no one in the Levels except the Tower could possibly want such a lot of hardware at once. But it was a big score, could put him far up the ladder, maybe get him out and set for life. Besides, rumour had it things were strange in the Tower, maybe had been since the bad business a year ago. Chapel had had a peripheral part in that, and the uneasy feeling ever since that perhaps leaving for someplace new wouldn't do his long-term health any harm at all.

Then Scorp came sailing out of the sky to land on the splintered concrete in front of him, shattering on impact like a bag of frozen meat. Chill on Chapel's neck, the shadow of Sanctuary Tower growing over him, the broken black monolith looming behind him like a tsunami blotting out the sun, and its knives waiting in the dark.

He jumped awake, cracked his head on the low roof of the boat's cabin. Dropped back on to the dank sweat-smelling mattress in the frozen blackness and probed his shirt pocket for a cigarette. It was a stress dream, he told himself. Nothing more than that. It hadn't gone down like that in reality. Short Wilson had lifted the guns, come to Chapel to act as middle-man and find a buyer, and Chapel, desperate to move up in the world, hadn't pushed him hard. Contacted Scorp and gone to a meet, but they'd all been dead before he got there, and that's when he knew the Tower was involved. Chapel didn't even bother calling Wilson, packing his shit, anything. Just paid a kid fifty to take him to the Harwell Bridge and put in calls to anyone he could think of outside the Levels on the way, looking for a place to stay and a chance to start again.

Maybe he'd fucked up again, taking the briefcase. 3-Fall hadn't sounded too pleased with what he'd got, or that he'd done it. 'You got any clue the kind of shit that'll come down on us, someone puts you there, taking that?' he'd said, jabbing an unlit blunt at Chapel's face to emphasise each point. 'Green Street means *federal*, you understand? Maybe you can buy that off if you're Amanda Kent, but you an' me can't do squat. And just for some techno shit?'

3-Fall had thought for a while, just sitting, shaking his head, then told Chapel to take the case and get the fuck out of his sight – out of everyone's sight, away from Willow Heights, away from the usual places – for a few days while he tried to find someone who could tell him what they had and who might want to buy it.

So now Chapel was sleeping in a cramped, filthy boat in Port Blackwater, courtesy of a friend, and had been since yesterday. Cursing 3-Fall on the hour, every hour. Maybe he was growing beyond 3-Fall. Sure, the guy had given him a place to stay, get his ass settled and back in the game after he'd left the Levels, but it wasn't like he was big-time. He acted it, talking all heavy any time he figured there was someone needing impressing, but Chapel figured he knew a hustle when he saw one, and 3-Fall was pulling one. Chapel had some contacts now, maybe enough to strike out, go it alone. If 3-Fall wasn't up to it, he was going to have to look out for himself anyway. Always take care of Number One, right?

'Fuck, yeah,' Chapel said, in the cloying dank of the derelict motorboat. Outside, a thin, reedy dawn had broken at last, and the gulls were wheeling, shrill and howling, over the Murdoch.

FOURTEEN

They were there waiting for Garrett in the twilight morning as he left his apartment early, headed for the Port and Roadblock's boat. The car pulled up beside him and three guys swept out while it was still moving. One in front of him, two behind. Sharp-dressed, like Feds. Garrett saw a shoulder rig under the jacket of the first guy.

'Would you mind coming with us, Detective Sergeant Garrett? This won't take long.'

Felt the presence of the pair behind him like a weight at the back of his mind. Knew he couldn't do squat even if he needed to. 'Who are you?'

'That's not important. There's someone who needs to talk to you. Just for a short while.'

'ID?'

'Get in the car, please.'

He went. He didn't have a choice. At first he thought they might be OPR: suits from the Office of Professional Responsibility looking for cops stepping out of line – or, since this was Newport City and even the OPR was bent,

79

stepping out of line in ways even the NCPD found unacceptable. But they'd have shown a badge at the very least. It didn't seem likely that Jason Blake's people would operate like this; these guys seemed as if they were used to giving orders, acting official. Then he figured they might be crooks. Something organised. Except why would anyone in the rackets want him? Then he stopped thinking and gave up. The three men said nothing, gave nothing away. The one sitting beside Garrett in the back kept a watchful eye on him, while the other two had their gazes on the road. Garrett patted his pockets, fished out a cigarette, but the guy next to him shook his head and said, 'No smoking.'

For lack of anything better to do, he stared out the window. Told himself he was checking their route and didn't believe a word of it. They were heading into central Newport and the glass palaces of the city's core, walls of steel studded with knots of flat white rime that blended into the clouds, as though the eraser of a vengeful god was slowly wiping Newport away, one chunk at a time. Half an hour drifting through the slow-moving ice-bound traffic, and the car turned through a security gate and into an underground parking lot.

A ride up in an express elevator like being fired out of a cannon, and Garrett was shown into the sitting room of a vast penthouse apartment.

'Wait here,' the guy said, and left him alone in the room.

Huge floor-to-ceiling windows, a view down and along Petric Avenue, something vaguely imperial in the feeling of height and grandeur. There was a grand piano in the corner of the room, though it didn't look as though it got a lot of use. A dozen or so pieces of art – sculpture, for the most part. They looked extremely expensive and completely beyond Garrett's understanding.

'You must be Detective Garrett,' a woman said behind him. He hadn't heard her come in. 'I'm sorry if my people startled you at all. I'm afraid they're used to asking no questions and providing no answers. Discipline's a useful trait when you're working for someone in my position.'

She looked like she'd been carefully airbrushed and talked like a politician, no edges, the shape behind the words impossible to see. 'If you wanted a regular meeting, you could just have phoned,' he said.

'Sorry,' she said again. Eased herself into a Scandinavian armchair. 'With phones, one can never be sure who's listening. Would you like a drink? Some coffee?'

'Who are you, exactly?'

'My name is Amanda Kent.'

Garrett raised his eyebrows. He knew the name of course, that it belonged to someone stratospherically rich, living at a level far removed from his own humble orbit. 'So why am I here, Miss Kent?'

'Can I call you Charlie?'

'You can call me anything you like if you answer my question.'

'I know what you did on the night of Green Street, Charlie. The bomb was right outside my offices, and a number of my people died in the explosion, so I'm sure you can understand why I have an interest in what happened, including your role.'

'I let an old friend die so I could chase phantoms,' he said. 'That's what I did.'

'According to my reading of what you told the NCPD, you pursued a man who may have been involved in the bombing, at possibly great personal risk, and despite the fact that you knew there was no chance you'd get back-up in the circumstances. You have no medical training, and with the best will in the world you couldn't have saved your colleague. Instead, you tried to apprehend the man responsible for his death. By most ordinary standards, you're a hero.'

'Tell that to the supervisory board.'

'Hear me out, and I might.' She smiled.

A pause. 'Go on,' he said.

'I want to help you, Charlie. As I said, several of my people were killed in the bombing, and I don't like the way the NCPD have treated the man who, as far as I'm aware, has come the closest of all to catching those behind this atrocity. I want justice for the dead, but the NCPD seem to have taken completely the wrong approach. The case might be federal now, but I'm still not happy with things. I don't want the person responsible to escape.'

'You want me to find him, is that it?' Stopped just short of naming Blake.

'Don't you want to as well?'

'Yeah . . . but there's a difference between wanting and achieving. You're expecting me to deliver him to you rather than to the Feds, is that it?'

She looked shocked. 'Of course not. I want him arrested and tried. I want him handed over to the proper authorities. I know they've placed you on suspension; are you still looking for him, given the time you have on your hands? I imagine it's a hard thing to shake, as a policeman.'

'Maybe,' he said. 'It's not like I have any resources, though. Not likely to get anywhere outside regular channels, you know?'

'Of course.' A shift in her position, leaning back, softening. 'Tell me what you saw that night.'

So he did, the edited version he'd given in his statement, at least. Careful not to name Blake, or to give away anything about what he'd seen on the van. They were his trump cards. By the time he'd finished, Kent was nodding to herself.

'If you can find this man, or his friends,' she said, 'I'll see to it that you're restored to your proper role and rank in the NCPD. I have some sway there. I wouldn't want them to destroy the career of a good man.'

'I might not be able to. The Feds could pick him up first.'

'Try, Charlie.' The smile again. 'Just think about what I said, OK? I'll have Boris drive you back.'

FIFTEEN

Nine months before the Green Street bombing.

'I wonder what this guy does,' Jackson said. He was idly watching the black Mercedes slide through the traffic ahead. He was in construction, taking time off to work for Blake. Many of the Clocks had quit their jobs entirely, those with the savings or insurance to afford it, or a life they could maintain on welfare. No sense sticking with the daily grind if they didn't want to.

Clara, driving, had been in financial management. Now she was keeping them a strict half block behind the car they were following. Jason's current orders – discover the extent of Amanda Kent's empire, unofficial as well as official. See where her people went, who they met, find out what resources she had at her disposal. He was insistent that she was deep into the Curse, and that if they found the right way to hurt her they could force a cure from her or, at least, better treatment. There were enough of them working for Jason to provide plenty of cover. Plenty of eyes on the ground.

'Who knows,' Clara said. 'Probably nothing special. Sooner or later we'll know what we need to, I guess.'

'I guess. And then . . . I suppose we do something. I wish I knew what Mr Blake was thinking.'

'He said we can't just start off polite and work up. She'll bury us.'

'What do you think we'll have to do? How heavy we gonna be?'

She shrugged. 'As heavy as we need to be to make her listen.'

'Man, I don't wanna end up in jail.'

She shrugged again. Said, 'What we're doing now, what we've already done, is pretty much illegal. Once you start, backing out doesn't make it any better. You're committed.' Realised that it was basically true. She hadn't really thought about it, but once you'd joined something that set you against the normal rules of society, the fear of leaving – of being seen to leave by the group that you recognised as your own, your clan, bound by something deeper than blood or friendship or shared ideology – was greater than the fear of the consequences of what you did for them. Particularly, she thought with a brief chuckle that drew a glance from Jackson, since she'd be dead in a year. What could be worse than that?

'Is going to jail harder than having the Curse?' she said. 'You want a cure, you follow Jason.'

'If he's right.'

'He's been right so far. You know we can't go to the media – the NCPD and these rich types have the whole thing under lockdown. He's got sources. He knows things. We can't do anything on our own, but together . . .'

A smile, then, from Jackson. 'I did always want to be a secret agent when I was a kid. Sort of reminds me of that.'

Ahead, the Merc's turn signal was flashing. It was taking the turn on to Newton. Nothing that way but the bridge and residential districts. Clara felt her breath catch.

'He's headed to Willow Heights,' she said.

SIXTEEN

Roadblock jumped as Garrett kicked in his door, shards of wood and painted glass skittering across the boat's cabin. He'd been busy with something delicate and electrical at a workbench when Garrett made his entrance, a tangle of wiring surrounding a narrow cluster of plastic tubes. Garrett was only a stride into the cabin when Roadblock threw a smoking soldering iron at him and sprinted through the door at the back. Garrett ducked, felt lead vapour sting his throat. A crash from up ahead. He ran in pursuit, opened the door to find a rack of galvanised steel shelving hurled drunken and twisted across the narrow passageway beyond, contents littering the floor. Roadblock was wriggling up through a hatch at the far end, feet kicking as he heaved himself through the gap. Garrett swore, turned and bolted back the way he'd come.

Up on deck, leprous patchwork layers of marine paint and a snarl of cables, washing line, hanging plants and wind generators. A path weaving between them that allowed access between Roadblock's vessel and the rest of Port

Blackwater. He was running bent over, hadn't bothered to straighten up and catch his balance. To the end of the bow, on to the rail and out, his outstretched arms slamming into the edge of the deck of the boat moored in front. Scrambling up as Garrett wove through the tangle behind him.

'Roadblock! We need to talk.'

No answer from the fleeing man. He finished his climb, slipped over the top and vanished. Garrett vaulted, hit the rail without breaking stride, and leaped after him. Flash of murky open water, then his teeth slamming together as he hit the other boat. Arms and torso thrown forward, on to the deck. He struggled for purchase, then was up and running again, aware of Roadblock ahead. The smell of charcoal and frying fish. Breakfast in the Port. A couple of narrow counter tops and seats made from empty plastic drums. Half a dozen customers, voices shouting. Roadblock grabbed a line holding the ship's boom in place, swung round on to the gangway down to the pontoon without losing momentum. Garrett followed, feeling the salt-rough fibre bite into the palm of his hand.

Down, now, into the Port's main thoroughfares. They weaved through knots of people setting out stalls or running morning errands, another day beginning on the water. Roadblock, twisting back to see Garrett, caught one old Haitian woman by the shoulder, sent her spinning to the floor, scattering a basket of what looked like junk to Garrett. He jumped over her, kept running. Sweating now and breathing hard. People moved out of their way, parting to let them through. This wasn't their business.

Hard left, across a quartet of narrow fishing boats crossed by rough planks. There were makeshift tents made from plastic sheeting at the backs of all but one of them. Along another pontoon, up again, the foredeck of a former dredger. Roadblock hit the edge and jumped, reaching for the rail on a small high-sided cargo ship streaked with rust. He missed, managed to snag its mooring line with his fingertips, clawed for purchase and hung there, winded. Garrett chopped his stride length, adjusted, made the leap himself. Hit the rail square-on and hauled himself over, on to the deck.

He looked down. Roadblock, dangling, knuckles pinched white. A thirty-foot drop into the water and the steel piles that punched through its surface, the remains of a jetty never finished. He bent down, within arm's reach of his quarry. Said, 'The fishing boat that visited you last night, Roadblock. I want to know about it. I want to know where Jason Blake is.'

'Fuck you, Garrett.'

'Tell me and I'll pull you up. I only want information, nothing else. You can go back to whatever you were up to. I don't care.'

Roadblock was sweating hard, teeth gritted. 'Can't tell you that. I can't.'

'Try.'

He shook his head. 'Rather take my chances. Swim for it.'

'You don't have much of a choice. What the hell did Blake

tell you that'd make you willing to freeze rather than talk to me? Is it really that bad?'

'You don't know him. He tells you something, he *means* it. I can't. What he'd do . . .'

'I could help.'

Another desperate shake of his head, and Roadblock let go. Sailed down, feet touched the water, spearing through the surface, looked like he might make it for a moment, but then his head hit one of the steel pillars with a snap like a pulled tooth. Vanished into the water, left Garrett with an after-image of something badly wrong with his skull, and never re-emerged.

'Fuck,' Garrett said. But maybe the situation was still salvageable. He walked back to Roadblock's boat.

The vessel had been a mess before he'd scattered half his crap to block Garrett. Garrett had first met the guy not long after joining the force, when he was part of the team arresting him as an accessory to an armoured car robbery. Back then, Ossie 'Roadblock' Taylor still had an apartment in a murky West Grayside tenement, along with a dozen arrests and a reputation, probably deserved, as one of the best go-to guys in the city for anything explosive, chemical or electronic. Some time after his arrest, and the inevitable release without charge, Roadblock had pulled up stakes, moved to Port Blackwater and gone into semi-retirement. Rumour had it he'd traded his services on a couple of jobs to a Salvadorean gang in return for the boat. Garrett had visited him in the Port once, during his posting to the floating settlement.

Some questions about a crime Garrett could no longer remember. He'd had a joint in his mouth, was hanging tomato plants in pots over the side of the hull. Been polite, and entirely unhelpful.

Garrett had no idea what the device was that Roadblock had been working on when he arrived, but there were two more tossed into a box by the side of the workbench. A mass of circuit boards and wire, a half-dozen gutted bluetooth units. Small plastic drums with ripped chemical warnings.

Further back, scattered in his flight from Garrett, drifts of paper scraps and pieces of what looked like junk. Garrett flipped through them, turning over yellowing receipts and bundles of notes in Roadblock's crabby hand and code-like abbreviations, looking for something relating to Jason Blake, and to Blake's current location. Hoping to see the logo again. He was disappointed. Likewise when he tried Roadblock's ancient laptop; nothing but some fairly tame porn and spreadsheets full of random numbers, no text. There were some saved documents but they seemed to be letters or emails from a niece in Central America and she didn't seem to have known about her uncle's career.

Garrett took one last sift through the clutter before giving up. Stared blankly at the boat's walls for a moment, wishing he had some way of replaying Roadblock's recent past, then hit the solution. 'Julius,' he muttered. If anyone would know who the dead man had been working with, and where Blake was, it was Julius.

SEVENTEEN

'Gentleman' Julius Poll styled himself after a Caribbean pirate from an earlier age. Garrett had first met him during his assignment to the Port. Garrett, inexperienced and still learning the subtleties of internal relations in the floating district, had run into trouble with a Haitian people smuggler and Julius, a fixer and professional go-between, not to mention Haitian himself, had found him tied to a chair, about to be dropped into the river. In return for some minor information, as well as to avoid the aftershocks of a police death in the Port, Julius dealt with the Haitians. He was based on an old tug he'd rechristened the *Adventure*.

He was sitting on deck under a sky-blue cotton canopy, cold be damned, bidding farewell to a group of half a dozen people when Garrett arrived. They were a motley collection: a couple of bomber-jacketed gangbangers, a pair of French-sounding girls with unlikely tans, and a man and a woman in matching suits.

'Mr Garrett!' Julius said, standing and extending a gloved hand. He wore a long imperial purple leather coat, a black cravat held in place with a Gucci tiepin, and a wide black hat. Rumour had it he was handy with a sword, had taken lessons to match the image. 'Long time, my friend.'

'How're you doing, Julius?'

'Very well indeed, lad. Very well indeed.' He laughed. 'I was going to contact you soon. Something a policeman might want may have just fallen into my lap, and I thought of you in particular.'

'What I need right now is information, Julius.'

'An item apparently taken from the scene at Green Street. Lot of interest in it, I hear. A briefcase or some such. No?'

Felt the distant stirring of old police instinct, buried and drowning under a dozen other things, some of them pressing. Ignored it. 'Maybe later. You know Roadblock?'

'The bomb-maker?'

Garrett nodded. 'Dead. Ran halfway across the Port and then dropped into the Murdoch rather than answer what I thought was a simple question about something I saw at his boat last night.'

A shift in Julius's posture, slight, unconscious. 'You killed him? That's not like you, lad.'

'I didn't touch him, Julius. He let go, hit his head on a steel stanchion on the way down. Even if he hadn't, the river's so cold I doubt he would've made it out without freezing to death.' Garrett shrugged. 'So I figured maybe you could help me.'

'Have a seat, lad,' Julius said. 'Coffee?'

'Sure, thanks.'

'Bosun LaBelle! Drinks, if you would.'

A girl a few years younger than Garrett emerged from the forecastle with a tray. She wore knee-high leather boots, a long fur-lined coat and not a whole lot else. Hair in ringlets, no makeup but plenty of jewellery. She put a jug of coffee and two cups on the table in front of them, smiled at Julius, then retired.

'Bosun, eh?' Garrett said. 'She had much nautical experience?'

'More than you, lad. Old man like me needs some company in winter.' Julius grinned. Slopped thick black coffee into the cup in front of Garrett, then pulled a small bottle of rum out of his coat pocket, dropped some in his own and offered it across. 'And something extra to keep off the cold, too.'

Garrett took it, poured a shot in his coffee. 'You're ten years older than me, tops.'

'Makes all the difference. So what was it you saw at Roadblock's boat?'

'Visitors. They took a fishing boat to his quay. It had a logo on the back, but no name. I tried watching where it went when they left, but I lost it when it hit the shipping channel; too difficult to track from the other side of the river with all the other water traffic.' He pulled out a sketch he'd done on the back of an old receipt and slid it across. 'I've seen it before, but I don't know where it's from.'

'How badly do you want to know?'

Beyond the canopy, snow began to swirl gently, a field of

interference overlaying the buildings on the far bank of the Murdoch. 'Name a price and it's yours.'

'OK, lad. We'll settle up later. Fact is, I happen to know a little about the people you're talking about. They've got an operation of some kind at Copeman Fisheries on Arcadia Wharf. The place ain't much to look at, but they've got plenty of people in there, and no fish, either. Moved in a few months ago.'

'Any idea what they're doing?'

'They've been real quiet about it. If it's drugs, I don't know who their buyers are. If it's people or weapons, they're dealing in very small numbers indeed. Frankly, lad, it's a mystery. There's probably two dozen or more in there at any one time and I have no clue what they're up to.'

Garrett finished his coffee. 'That's got to be something in itself.'

'Indeed. You planning on paying them a visit?'

'I—' Garrett stopped as his phone rang. Home number. Emi.

When he picked up, she said, breathing hard and panicking, 'I'm bleeding, Charlie. All I did was wash my face, and then I used the towel and there's all this blood . . .'

'Calm down, Emi. It's just a nosebleed.'

'What if it's not, Charlie? What if this is it? If he got the date wrong and it's happening early? I don't want to die like this, not alone. Please come home. Please.'

Garrett looked at Julius, who nodded, understood. He stared emptily away in the direction of the wharf, hidden behind a wall of boats and the drifting screen of snow. Felt himself struggle, tear in two. Felt the frustration of defeat, and Blake slipping from his grasp.

'Sure,' he told her. 'I'm on my way. Try to stay calm. It's all going to be OK.'

The first time Garrett saw Emi cry, they were in a restaurant near Malton Yards, a strange little place made up to look like patchwork wartime ruins, all plywood barricades and worklights strung from bare beams. The food kept to the survivor theme, and Garrett was regretting bringing her, like maybe it was an insensitive choice. They'd been seeing each other a couple of weeks, pretty much inseparable from the start of the second. There was a Portuguese family a couple of tables along, eight of them, and they all burst into song as someone came out of the kitchen with a cake and candles. Garrett turned to watch from the first couple of bars of 'Happy Birthday', applauded with everyone else when the song ended, and turned back to see Emi's shoulders shaking and her hand over her eyes. Sobbing, silently.

'It's my niece Masafumi's birthday next month,' she said after a time. 'She's eight. I need to go shopping for a present for her. It's going to be the last one she ever gets from me. Every birthday this year is going to be the last, including mine.'

Garrett felt lost, fumbling for something to say that might help and coming up empty. They both knew there was no cure.

'Come back in a year and those people could be here again, having their cake, laughing and smiling, but I won't be. How is that fair? Why do they get to live and I can't?'

'You could get lucky – they might get hit by a bus on the way home tonight.' It was weak, and she didn't laugh.

'When I was a girl all I wanted to do was be a great artist. After I'd stopped wanting to be a dragon-breeder or a princess,' she said. 'Now I'd give everything – my ability to paint, my livelihood, my eyesight, anything – to be able to come back to this restaurant the same time next year. It's not even like the food's that good.' Bitter laughter, and back to sobbing.

'There's still plenty of time for someone to crack it,' he said. Didn't convince even himself.

'Do you have any idea what it's like for that to be your only hope, Charlie? It's a joke. And every day you do something for the last time. You're constantly looking at things, trying to burn them in your mind because you might never see them again. Do you know how that feels?'

'No,' he said. Drank. 'No, I guess I don't.'

'Sometimes I wish I was dead already, and it was all over.' Silence for a moment, then she said, suddenly, 'I love you, Charlie.'

'What?' Taken aback.

'Sorry. I was being maudlin, and I wanted you to know that. I didn't want you to have any doubts. I'm sorry.'

'It's OK,' he said. 'I know it's difficult for you. I understand.'

'Good. Thanks.'

'And I love you too.' It felt strange, saying it. Especially there and then.

Later, they walked through Lord's Row market, the ragged plastic awnings on the stalls lit from beneath by strings of LEDs and coloured paper lanterns. Garrett told Emi about his mother, and her long, slow deterioration from disease when he was a child. How one day she just wasn't there any more. His dad, eyes flat and wet, telling Garrett that his mother was dead. That she'd taken her own life rather than face the last, awful weeks and months. Walked down to McCarthy Pond and waded into the water until it was deep enough to take her. The quiet, empty weeks that followed and the long return to normality afterwards. He didn't know why he was telling Emi, what he expected it to achieve or how it could help her, but it didn't stop him talking.

'How did your dad cope?'

'I'm not sure. He's never said much about it, except to say that he figured it was better she didn't suffer. He found it difficult the whole way through, so I guess it was maybe a relief that it was over.'

'Will you be relieved when I'm dead?'

'That wasn't what I meant.' Anger stirring. 'Don't act like it was.'

'Sorry,' she said, again.

'He used to take flowers down to McCarthy Pond every year on the day she'd died. Lilies. He'd set them floating, one by one, out from the edge. I always went with him, and

I don't think I ever heard him say a word. Never to the grave, always to the water.'

'Does your father still live here now?' Emi asked once they were back at Garrett's apartment, in bed.

'No. Dad moved away to this little town in New York State a few years ago, when he retired. Him and a buddy from work had their eye on a place there. I go see him a couple of times a year. Why?'

'I thought maybe I could talk to him about your mother. But I'm not sure I want to know how to cope with everything. I want to live. I want to stay here. I don't want to be flowers floating on water and life going on all around me,' she said, and cried until her sobs slowly changed to deep, sleeping breaths.

Garrett lay there in the tearful dark, thinking.

By the time he reached the apartment, she was sitting in an armchair with her knees bunched up in front of her, crying softly. A drift of scrunched tissues surrounded the chair. Some of them were dark with blood. The drapes were closed, the room gloomy.

'I'm sorry, Charlie,' she said. 'I'm so sorry. You were right, I guess. I just . . .'

He cradled her head against him, ran his fingers through her hair. Whispered without words.

'I don't mind dying,' she said quietly. 'I don't want to, but I've accepted it. It's going to happen. I just don't want to be alone when it does. I don't want to reach out in the last moments and find that you're not there. I don't want the last thing I see to be a stranger's face on the street or an empty room.'

'We know when it'll happen, Emi. We've still got a week. I'm going to fix it. You'll be OK. I've got a plan. I'm going to find Blake and he's going to tell me how he survived.'

Sadness, again. 'And most of our last week together you're going to be away, and I'll be alone while you chase around the city.'

'It's not going to be our last week together.'

Emi sighed. 'Stay with me now. Just for a while.'

He wanted to go, thought of Blake lurking in the Port, just out of reach. Said, 'I'm not going anywhere.'

Stayed there like that until she fell asleep. Garrett carried her to bed, surprised at how light she felt. Again the thought tugged at him to leave her there and find Blake, but guilt held him close. Instead, he went to the bathroom, rinsed his face under the cold tap. Told himself he'd need the cover of night anyway. Towelled dry, lurched back to the bed and lay down beside Emi. She shuffled back into him, spooning, and for a long time he stayed like that, trying to tell himself he could save her, and that he wouldn't get killed in the attempt.

EIGHTEEN

The support groups met in a boxing gym a few blocks from the Murdoch River. The building looked like it had been renovated in a surge of seventies post-*Rocky* optimism and allowed to slowly decay ever since. A public notice in a yellowing plastic sleeve on the door said that the place had closed and everything inside was the property of the business's receivers. The notice was three years old. Dirty snow was piled up in front of the building when Maya arrived, but someone had taken the trouble to grit the steps. That, and the tungsten glow of the lights inside, were the only signs that she'd come to the right place. Inside, a short corridor branching off to the locker room, and swing doors into the gym proper. The practice ring at the far end was cracked and frayed, the bright red dye of the ropes faded and streaked by decades of sweat. Heavy punch bags hung like meat, pendulous and swaying in the thin draught bleeding in through the high letterbox windows. The smell of coffee from the machine in the corner blanketed the lingering must.

A couple of the people gathered in knots by the circle of plastic chairs near the side wall looked over as Maya walked into the room. There were twenty of them in total. Three, she guessed from looking at them, plainclothes cops. The rest Clocks.

'Hi,' she said, quiet and a little hesitant as she reached the circle. 'I'm Eliza. They told me to come here?'

One of the cops checked a clipboard. 'Yes, that's right. I'm Adele. Help yourself to coffee if you want it, then find a seat; we're about to get started.'

Valentin had said he'd set her up with an identity as a victim; one of his people in the NCPD would add an entry to the system – name, a brief statement explaining how she encountered the Curse, more or less copied from all the other ones – and put her on the list of victims cleared to be at the groups. That was all there was to it, he'd said, and apparently he'd been right. The groups ran every weekday, and while Maya figured some people would go more than once a week, there had to be more who attended less frequently and, she guessed, many who never came at all. Which meant that if tonight's numbers were typical, there were somewhere over a hundred victims of the Curse, not counting those who'd already died.

Jesus.

'I'm Barbara,' the first Clock said once the meeting was under way. She was a soft, quiet woman in her fifties. Short grey hair, sensible shirt and slacks. 'And I don't know about y'all, but this ain't been a good week. It was Edwin's birthday, and it's hard for him knowing his wife's going to die. Harder still for me, not being able to tell him the truth why. It's a heavy feeling, lying to someone who loves you that much.'

Nods, and murmured agreement. 'But we go on, y'know?' she said. 'Everything's set now, all ready for the end. I'm glad I'll still be here for our last anniversary. I'm taking him to Antigua for a fortnight; he doesn't know anything about it. Janey and her husband and their kids are going to be with us for a week of that, as well. It'll be a fine goodbye trip. So when I'm not here in a couple of weeks, it doesn't mean anything bad's happened.' She smiled, sat down.

'Name's Johnny,' the next speaker said. Younger than the last, looked and talked pretty rough, pulling minimum wage somewhere without much of a home life, Maya figured. 'Guess I know most of you pretty well by now. Ain't had an easy few days. I got three months to go, and it don't look to me like the cops're gonna catch the guy or come up with some way I'm gonna make it. Got in a fight at Paulo's night before last, and I don't even remember what it was about. I guess I just got a lot of anger right now.'

Silence. No one challenged him, and Maya couldn't see anyone who looked disapprovingly at him. One of the cops stifled a yawn behind his hand. 'It's just . . .' Johnny shook his head. 'Why the fuck is it me? I never did nothing to deserve it. I ain't special or important or different. I

never pissed someone off so bad they got to get revenge.
I never did shit to anyone, and now I'm gonna die. Why
the *fuck*?'

The echoes of the last, shouted word faded around
the gym. Johnny stared into space like he was defying the
world to give him an answer. The guy next to him rested a
supportive hand on his shoulder as he sat again. Johnny
looked at him, then nodded in acknowledgement.

Another man stood up. 'I'm Tony,' he said. His voice
was already breaking. 'Hannah's pregnant. Jesus Christ,
Hannah's pregnant and I'm going to die three weeks before
the baby's due.'

A chorus of sympathetic comments, consolation as the
group broke ranks to tend to one of their own. Maya heard
Johnny say, 'That's fucking harsh, man,' and saw him give
Tony an uncertain pat on the back. The man who'd offered
a hand to Johnny spoke softly to Tony for a while before he
sat back down. She thought she heard the crying man say,
'Thanks, Adam.'

Maya, outside the circle and feeling more and more like a
fraud and an intruder on a peculiar private grief, took the
moment to assess the group. Men and women, black and
white, ages ranging from Johnny to Barbara, and from
the different styles of dress and speech she guessed there
was a similar spread in education and class. Valentin
had been right about this being no ordinary serial crime,
and she began to see why the cops had been unable to catch
the perpetrator so far. Pattern-matching was one of the first

stages of investigation; here, there was nothing. The Curse was like a disease, invisible and indiscriminate.

Once Tony had calmed down and everyone was back in their seats, a woman maybe five years older than Maya stood up. She was still wearing a brightly knitted hat and had a vivid red parka on the back of her chair. 'I'm Alice,' she said, smiling benignly. 'My experiences since the last time I was here have been very positive. Last week I saw Machu Picchu, so that's another thing off my list. It's really something, up in the clouds, on these terrifying donkey trails along the sheer sides of the mountains. I guess I had a lot less to fear than some of the other people I was with, huh?' A ripple of thin laughter. 'The next two weeks I'm helping deliver books and other things for a school in the Levels, and repairing and decorating the building. Guess you guys will see more of me for a while. I see we've had some new members since I was last here; I'm real sorry for you guys, genuinely, but I think you'll find that it's a big help that at least we've all got each other.'

Maya took that as her own cue to stand. Her nervousness was only partly an act. 'I'm Eliza,' she said. 'I'm . . . I'm new to all this. Still trying to get my head round it. Uh . . . uh, I guess that's all I've got to say right now.'

Waves, smiles. Some friendly, some disinterested, a few carrying something more. What, exactly, Maya wasn't sure. The Clocks had all seen one of the normal anchors to life – that you'd still be here next year – stripped away, and their conflicting emotions and expectations made them a difficult read.

When she'd sat down, another woman stood. She had the hair extensions, tan and makeup of a beautician, the voice of a cheerleader and the dark, haunted eyes of a murder witness. 'I'm Tammy. I had that dream again last night. The one about the Razor Gate.'

The atmosphere in the circle changed. Several people shifted to sit more upright, the cops seemed more intent, and more than a few people leaned back, shaking their heads. Johnny dismissed Tammy's words with an irritable wave of his hand.

'Excuse me,' Maya said. 'I don't know if I'm allowed to interrupt or not, but ... well, it looks like everyone else knows what you're talking about. What's the Razor Gate?'

NINETEEN

Six months before the Green Street bombing.

'Power in Newport City, maybe the rest of the country, is in the hands of the rich,' Jason Blake said. 'I'm not being vague or metaphorical. There is a group of them, the elite of the elite, right here in this city, who use their wealth and position to run things the way they want them. They control the cops, they control the media, they control everything. They call themselves the Foundation. It is they who have decided that the Curse is something to pursue for themselves, leaving all of you to die unaided, in secret. They've killed the NCPD investigation, whatever that was worth to begin with, and they've kept your stories – your existence as Clocks – out of the papers and off the TV news.'

Standing, watching him, in the back of the panel truck, were twenty of his followers. They were dressed in black military surplus, and armed. Most of them, he knew, were nervous. Loyal – he could see that in their faces – but regular people for the most part. It was the first time they'd done anything remotely like this.

'You know one of them,' he said. 'Amanda Kent. Thanks to you, to the things we've done together, we know that she's trying to claim the Curse herself, and we know who her people are and where they hide. I imagine she thinks that so long as no one can gain access to her secrets, to her computer files and her personal documents, she's safe. She's wrong. We don't need to know what the passcode on her luggage is, or what her stock deals are like. We just need to know where she is.'

In his head, he pictured the photographs and the plans they'd worked from when they plotted this. Every detail, one last time. No chance of screwing up. A small manufacturing warehouse on an industrial development near the Wilder Turnpike, bounded by parking lots and near-deserted commercial units. Up to a dozen people inside, half of them armed. Part of Kent's less respectable underground, dealing in all sorts of illicit goods ferried to and from the south. Enough inside to finance his own operation for as long as it took, including everything he'd need for the planned finale. Make it look like a gang thing, opportunistic, and she'd never know what was coming.

'The men in there aren't expecting trouble, and they're certainly not expecting us. They're not going to take a bullet for a pile of cash that's not theirs, not when they're outnumbered and outgunned. Kent and the others own this town. Their people are comfortable, their standards are lax. When we storm in there like we already own them, they'll roll over in a heartbeat. If they don't, we have a resolve that they lack. Most people fear death. You all face up to it on a daily basis. That gives you a strength that means you don't *need* to fear anything. If something falls apart, you all know that the worst it's going to get is how it already is for you. And then there's the prize.'

Drive through the doors while half his people crashed the back entrance, he thought. Catch them cold. Load what they needed into the truck and disappear into the Port, some of the stuff going to the bomb-maker, Roadblock, to cover the price of his services, the rest split up, sold, traded for everything they'd need to keep his war on Amanda Kent running to its end.

He smiled grimly at the Clocks. 'We pull this off tonight and we've got everything we need to make Amanda Kent, the Foundation, the city, notice us. To force them to acknowledge what's happening. To find a cure. To provide for our families. Do this, and we're almost home.'

Jason slapped the truck wall, dividing cab from cargo, twice. The engine thundered into life.

TWENTY

'Here we go,' Johnny said. 'Another fucking sermon. The Gate's bullshit. Just some crazy dead guy's drug memory that some people take like it was more than just a fairy tale.'

Tammy sighed. 'Thanks, Johnny. I think we all know how you feel about it.'

'Bunch of fucking alien abduction *bull*shit.'

She looked at Maya. 'It was a man called Roberto Moreno who first saw the Gate. When he was taken, he woke briefly from the drug they used to knock him out. He was being carried down a dark tunnel, lying almost flat, like he was hovering.'

'Like he was *tripping*.' Johnny.

'He saw paintings on the walls of the tunnel, but he couldn't see what they were. At the end of it, there was a door, or a gate, which he said looked just like a razor blade. It was bright red and made of steel. The gate opened, slowly and noisily, as he reached it, and light poured out. He was in a courtyard with buildings all around, and there were people looking down at him.'

Johnny had been right; it did sound like alien abduction nonsense. 'He didn't say it was red,' one of the other Clocks said. 'That came later. Moreno didn't say it was red.'

'And I thought he said it was the Gate that had pictures on it, not the tunnel. Like tribal designs of animals or faces,' another of them added.

'No.' Tammy shook her head. 'He saw the pictures in the tunnel. But you're right, it was someone else who said the Gate itself was red. I remember it having red along the edges, like a razor that had been used to cut someone. Like there was blood on it. It turned the light pink when it first opened.'

Maya glanced at the detectives. 'No one's ever found the Gate, then?'

'They've tried,' Tammy said. 'But it's hard; our description of it is a bit hazy and a lot of what we remember could be almost anywhere in the city. If there were more of us with the ability to draw what we remember, it might be easier, but I think only Emi has ever done that, and I don't think she wanted to paint it too often. I'm not sure she's really a *believer*.'

'She comes on Thursdays, doesn't she?' someone said. 'How much longer has she got?'

'Not long,' the man who'd been the one to offer Johnny a hand said. 'I haven't spoken to her for a while, but I know her date is due very soon now. She was trying to paint as much as possible while she can.'

Tammy nodded. There was a look of almost reverential awe in her face as she said, 'I remember her picture of the Gate. It was *powerful*. So much closer to the *feel* of the memory than anything I could have imagined. I was surprised that she included the writing on it, though. I thought it was only Mikkel . . .'

She trailed off into embarrassed silence. A couple of the other Clocks glanced away, awkward or ashamed. Johnny looked at Maya and said, 'I dunno what the cops told you, Eliza, but, see, not everyone handles this real well. Some people off themselves, some go on a drunk lasts months or spend everything they've got getting high, and Mikkel, well, a couple of days ago he blew himself and half the city to pieces. Couldn't take the pressure, I guess.'

'He killed all those people on Green Street?' His breath, cold fog in the night air. His eyes glittering under the hood. The salute, and the chaos that followed.

'They released the name to the news. Course, no one said nothing about him being a Clock. Just that he had "problems", like guys who *don't* have problems sometimes get the urge to kill dozens of people who've done nothing to them.'

Barbara nodded sadly. 'We didn't know him well. He stopped coming to the groups after a few weeks. I don't think he found them helpful. It seems to be the ones who feel that way who need them most. I feel sorry for him, as well as the poor people he killed.'

'Jesus,' Maya said. In any other surroundings, she realised, having a mass murderer in your social circle would be the sort of thing that drove you to need support groups in the first place.

'What you have to understand,' the man who'd supported Johnny said later, 'is that the Curse isn't like cancer or some other kind of terminal illness. It's not even like being on Death Row.'

They were standing at the side of the gym, drinking coffee from cardboard cups. The formal part of the evening was over and the group had split into loose conversational clusters. The man had introduced himself as Adam Nyberg, a research scientist, something to do with artificial intelligence according to his card, at Bryant University. He had four months left to live. Probably a couple of years into his thirties, but with a boyish geek charm that made him seem like a perpetual student rather than a member of faculty.

'You see, with terminal illness, there's the chance of a cure, a last-minute experimental treatment,' he said. 'Many people refuse to lose hope entirely for that reason. There's also the prospect of a painful death, or a slow deterioration in physical or mental condition, which some people fear more than death itself. With the Curse, there's no chance of a cure, and the end is nearly instantaneous. Either one accepts one's fate or one doesn't; there's no sliding scale of hope or fear involved. Inmates on Death Row generally have an outside chance of a last-minute appeal, and the actual scheduling of their execution can vary greatly. With the Curse, the end date is immutable. On top of that there's the secrecy involved, and the natural feeling that we haven't deserved it. It's a unique combination of psychological factors and it produces a wide mix of responses – from Mikkel's, to, say, Alice's, to those who give up well before their end. It's no wonder that people fixate on things like the Gate. I imagine it's rather like being a member of an isolated community who've apparently shared a disturbing religious experience. The vision at Fatima, for instance.'

'Or the Salem witches,' Maya said.

'Ha! Exactly.'

'You sound almost like you're enjoying it.'

Adam shrugged. 'I accepted what was going to happen a long time ago. I just want to get as much of my work finished as possible. I'd hate to be carrying any regrets when my time ran out. Since there's no point in worrying about the Curse on a personal level, it frees me to look at the subject with some detachment. It's a terrible, fascinating thing to be involved with. That's partly why I still come to the groups, as well as to help others who are new to it all.'

'So do you believe in the Razor Gate?' she said.

'Do you remember anything about it yourself?'

Maya caught herself, kept to her cover. 'No,' she said. 'Not a thing. It sounds . . . well, it sounds a lot like fantasy. The passage into the light, and all.'

'I'm in two minds. There's probably a grain of truth buried in the story. But the problem is, the story's been shared by so many people that it's become a kind of gestalt experience shaped by everyone's imaginations. We all rewrite our memories subconsciously to agree with others – if you and I see a car tonight, and you don't remember the colour and I'm convincing enough when I say it's blue, pretty soon you'll be remembering it as blue as well. Apply that on a wide scale, and you've got the Gate. The thing is, if I was wrong about that car being blue it's impossible to take the error back out of the system.'

'I don't really get why people are so fixed on it.'

'Imagine you'd met God. OK, so he didn't like you very much and he inflicted a plague of boils on you, but at least you'd met him. And all you had afterwards was a patchy memory of the experience. That's what it's like for those who claim they've seen the Gate. Somewhere beyond it is the person who created the Curse and gave it to them, who wielded the power of God over them. It's all they remember of something that completely changed their lives. It really is like part of a religious experience.'

He finished his coffee and tossed the cup towards the trash like he was shooting hoops. It missed by a yard. 'I'd better be going,' he said. 'That way I can get in a couple of hours' work before I go to bed.'

'What was Mikkel like?' she said.

'Quiet, unhappy and angry at what he thought was a very unfair world. I don't think he was like that before, though. Just an impression I had. Meeting him here at the groups was like seeing a ghost, a kind of emotional negative of someone who was still alive somewhere else. Very sad.'

'Where did he get the bomb from, do you think?'

Adam just shrugged and gave her an unhappy smile. 'Isn't that the sixty-four thousand dollar question? I don't know. And I wonder what the chances are of someone else doing the same. Good night, Eliza. It's been a pleasure. If you need any help with anything, call me.'

On her way out, she saw two of the Clocks screwing in a car in the icy parking lot like desperate teenagers. Making the most of the time available to them. She thought about Tony and his wife, and shuddered.

The news on the radio confirmed what she'd heard at the meeting. The Green Street bomber had been identified as Mikkel Thoresen, unemployed for nearly a year and recently diagnosed with inoperable cancer. The one estranged ex-girlfriend anyone had been able to track down said she was shocked he could have done something like that. He had no record of violent crime, but the reports carried a running undertone, the sort of 'he was always such a quiet neighbour' vox-pop normally reserved for the aftermath of serial killings.

Driving home, listening to the public's view of a secret world she was now a part of, snow speckling the windshield like powdered ash, she noticed the other car following her.

TWENTY-ONE

The car was fifty yards back, a low pale steel ghost behind the flicker of snow. It tracked Maya as she turned off Nevsky and on to the smaller roads leading away from the river. Accelerated to avoid catching a stoplight as she crossed an intersection, then throttled back into station. The weather and the hour meant the streets were quiet, traffic on foot or on four wheels both sparse. Another turn, chosen at random, and the car was still there. She couldn't think of a single plausible reason why anyone would be following her.

At the next junction she slowed heavily, indicated to turn left, taking it like she was afraid of spinning out on the slush. Her tail had reached the intersection too. At the point where she should have straightened up, come out of the turn, she cranked the wheel further over and dropped her foot on the gas. The tyres spun, squealing over the icy, wet blacktop, the back end threatening to fishtail out and leave her sliding. Then she found traction and the car slewed, speeding up, as she passed the other one and sped away, back up the road. A flash of a lone figure, no more than a shadow, behind the wheel. A man, but she could say nothing more than that.

He was quick, though, and a fair driver. Gunned the engine, used the slippery surface well to spin his vehicle and get back on her tail. By the time Maya had gone two blocks he was back where he'd been before. She thought about leaving a message on her own voicemail, something to say where she was going and what she'd seen of the guy following her, enough to provide a pointer for anyone who came looking for her if she vanished. But she knew the NCPD wouldn't look hard for her if she disappeared, and the message would be ignored.

Instead, she drew him into the heart of the city. The roads around Taft Center would be snarled until almost midnight, and even in the cold there'd be enough people about to give her an edge. Led him, block by block, the buildings either side slowly rising, lights studding the artificial canyon walls, into the cold glittering interior of Newport. The guy didn't budge, just closed the distance as the traffic became harder to read. When they hit the Center and the web of stoplights, Maya allowed them both to become wedged in the flow, cars either side and backed up behind. Then she stopped, jumped out of the car and stalked back to the other vehicle. Horns were blaring around her as she hammered on the driver's window and yelled, 'So what the fuck do you want, buddy? You going to explain why you've been following me?'

The window wound down. The man inside was probably in his early twenties, wearing a grey puffy vest jacket and a turtleneck underneath. Mousy brown hair and a thin nose, a distant hardness to his eyes.

'Nothing's wrong, Miss Cassinelli,' he said. 'But let's not make a scene of this. Let's pull over by the fountain in the Center. I'll explain.'

'Who the hell are you?'

'My name's Anton. I work for Mr Valentin.'

Wary and cross, she returned to her car, flipped the bird to a couple of other irate drivers, and did as he'd suggested.

'Mr Valentin wanted to make sure you remained safe,' Anton said. Maya stood with her back to the low stone wall of the fountain, her arms folded and her feet cold. No one was stopping to watch the water spray turgidly in the frosty air tonight. 'He told me to follow you and make sure nothing unexpected happened to you.'

'Like what?'

'Miss Cassinelli, you're looking into a matter which culminated in a man killing a lot of people on a city street. Mr Valentin considers the stakes to be very high indeed.'

She tightened her grip, drew her shoulders in a little more. 'I'm just trying to find out what happened to an old boyfriend.'

'Who worked for someone with immense financial clout, someone who may have been the target of a most indiscriminate hit. This is a dangerous business.'

'Maybe so, but I don't like being followed. And I *hate* being followed without being told. It makes me feel like people don't trust me.'

'That was not our intention.'

'Fuck your intention. I want you to stop tailing me. I'll look out for myself.'

'Mr Valentin said—'

Maya shook her head. 'Mr Valentin offered to bankroll my investigation. He did that because he knows what I can do and my doing it is useful to him. And I don't want to do it with someone breathing over my shoulder. You understand?'

Anton looked uncomfortable. 'I will tell him what you said,' he said eventually. 'I don't know if he will be happy with it.'

'He'll have to cope. Now I'm going home. Without you or your damn employer walking me to my fucking door.'

An hour later, she was in her apartment and angrily eyeing a glass of vodka when her cell rang. 'Eliza?' A man's voice, and not one she recognised. 'My name's Jason. I used to go to the groups. Couldn't make it tonight. Tammy's told me some of what you were asking about, and I might be able to help you. It's a shame I wasn't there. My job, you know.'

'Help me how?'

'I know things about the Curse, and I've found out some of the information the police keep back from us. I . . . I'd rather not do this over the phone. I'm working tonight at

Copeman Fisheries in Port Blackwater. Are you free right now? Short notice, but come by and I'll tell you what I've got. There's a lot of stuff that you need to know.'

TWENTY-TWO

Maya left her car a half-mile from the waterfront and took a cab the rest of the way. The river district was usually safe, but even if no one stole it there was no guarantee she'd be able to navigate the cluttered streets that radiated out from Port Blackwater like fat-clogged arteries. The lights of the harbour settlement gleamed in dull Technicolor projection on the heavy night clouds, orange and yellow flecked with just about every other tint imaginable, a shadow play of a disco somewhere in hell. Thin trails of smoke drifted up into the few lazy flakes of snow still falling. A couple of times she caught glimpses of the Murdoch River running sluggish, black and cold. No ice on its surface. Not yet.

'First time in the Port?' the cab driver said. 'You picked a good time; rest of the city might be shutting up, but the Port's open all day every day, right?'

'No,' Maya said. She could smell, or imagined she could smell, grilled fish, gritty acrid black coffee. Algae, river mud, photochemical pollution. See the slowly decaying drifts of packing waste and plastic netting and the shrieking clans of gulls that lived on them. 'No, it's not my first time there. I grew up in Port Blackwater.'

'For real?'

'Haven't been back in years.'

'How come you're going back now? Going to see the old place, huh?'

She hadn't gone back because there was nothing to go back for. Her dad dead and gone, and she'd taken so long and worked so hard to escape the place's gravity well that even going near it now made her wary, afraid of falling back in. The scent of whatever her dad had managed to pick up cheap from the market that morning, grilling in the tiny galley. The regular Sunday treat of lunch at old Thierry D'Croix's place, and the stew he always swore, in his broken mix of English, Spanish and some obscure Haitian dialect, was made from river rats, and maybe it had been. Sitting on mismatched plastic stools on the deck of Thierry's ancient tug, its surface protected from his customers' feet by tightly compressed strata of newsprint, a Burroughs cut-up catalogue of five years of history in half a dozen languages. Something she could feel, but was too young to understand, between her dad and Thierry. She knew then that her father had worked for the Argentinian government, knew now that he'd been in intelligence, but what that had to do with Thierry or why he'd ended up living in a floating refugee ghetto in America had been, and remained, a mystery to her.

'What was it like being a kid in the Port?' the driver said. 'I can't imagine it. Hell, I didn't even learn to swim till I was twelve.'

'It was different, but kids are kids, you know? Maybe it was smaller then, too. Grown over the last few years.'

Afonso Cassinelli and his baby daughter had arrived in the Port a handful of years after its 'founding'. A ramshackle flotilla of refugee boats fleeing civil war in West Africa and apparently aiming for Canada had made a navigational error somewhere crossing the Atlantic and showed up in Newport City harbour instead. Fishing boats, a couple of old tugs, a rusting freighter ten years past the date it should have been scrapped. This wasn't two hundred Cubans squeezed together in a Zodiac, or a cargo container with three dozen families who'd paid thousands of dollars for the privilege of suffocating to death at sea, but an organised flight to a better world. Conditions aboard were generally tight, but not inhumane. The authorities moved the boats to the storm-protected anchorage at Resolution Bay in the estuary, and gave the refugees the choice between staying on their boats after health inspections, or placement in block housing ashore while they decided what to do with them. Most stayed.

A few months later, more boats began to arrive. Refugees from Central America and Haiti, trying to avoid the camps of Miami by making the much longer and more dangerous trip up the coast to Newport. The city berthed the newcomers alongside the original arrivals. By the time they were given the right to stay, a certain critical mass had already been reached and the jetties between the clusters of boats and the shoreline were increasingly busy thoroughfares. Other, unofficial connections between vessels had sprung up, and the floating village had become a fixture. Botched city planning in the decades before, plans that spawned disasters like the building of the Levels, had left the city short on cheap housing and dangerously close to bankrupt. Newport City ran utilities out to the shoreside, gave incoming vessels basic sanitary and structural inspections, arranged a food stamp programme and quietly left the refugees be. Some managed to succeed in permanent visa applications or citizenship claims, but most stayed in limbo, stuck between a choice of menial illegal work in the city or making a living for themselves in the crowded confines of the Port. Maya held US citizenship thanks to the mother she'd never known, and even then it had been a struggle to escape. An address – such as they were – in the Port was death on an application for a regular job or a bank account.

'Sometimes I wonder,' she said, only partially to the driver, 'how many of us made it out. If I go back there now, how many of the kids I knew will still be there, or dead already.'

'I didn't think the Port was that dangerous. I never have trouble there.'

'It's not, usually, not in that way. My room, my cabin, was four feet wide and just over six long. In winter, in weather like this, condensation used to freeze on the inside of the little window I had, coat the glass with a sheet of ice. The nearest piped water was a standing tap at the shoreward end of the jetty, two hundred yards away. Some people boiled river water.'

'Holy Jesus.'

'My dad built a rainwater collector on the deck. It was cleaner, so long as we stopped birds getting into it. I was fourteen when I had my first hot water shower in a proper bathroom; my dad took me on vacation to Wheeler Forest. Our boat had a chemical head. Others just flushed straight into the water. Some people set up micro-treatment systems in old plastic tanks. There was a city waste barge, but that was just for trash. I learned to swim in the river. And to fish. There was no licensed medical care, and no emergency services in the Port. So if someone got sick – which happened a lot, and everyone lived so close together that any disease always spread bad – or had an accident, they might die when anywhere else they'd be OK. You see?'

It had been illness that finally took her father. Something long and slow and deadly that he'd done his best to hide from Maya. He'd refused to see a doctor onshore, insisting that crazy 'Brass' Velasco could do anything a city hospital could, short of surgery. 'And if I need surgery,' her dad had said, shaking his head, 'it's something that'll probably kill me anyway.'

Brass was a decent doctor, even if he only had one eye. He'd promised Maya he'd do what he could. Antibiotics, painkillers, other drugs she didn't know the names of, for something that looked like maybe it was tuberculosis, except it wasn't because nothing shifted it. Her dad had died in his own bed, on a cool spring night, breath faltering but, she'd thought, happy, and maybe that was OK.

Maya stopped the cab a quarter of a mile from Copeman Fisheries and walked the rest of the way. The air was cold and spiked with the smell of charcoal smoke and kerosene. The noise of conversation, competing traders' shouts in half a dozen languages, the rattle of metal and the soft low creak of mooring lines, washing across the water in waves like breaking surf. Along the jetties and the narrower steel and wooden walkways that criss-crossed between individual boats, clusters of people moved in streams, winter-wrapped shadows drifting through the scattered smoke and steam blowing from cooking pots and fire cans. Maya's foot hit the wood of the jetty, left the concrete wharf behind, and she felt herself pass through the strange invisible barrier that separated the Port from the rest of the city, from the rest of America.

Old, long-dormant pathways in her brain stirred at snatches of conversation she heard as she passed, words in languages she remembered from her childhood, phrases and accents that made up the fluid, ever-changing dialect of the Port. Unconsciously adjusted her stride, adapting to the narrower confines and the abandonment of personal space. Like crowded Japan, hundreds of unwritten rules and customs had arisen in the Port, codes of conduct and politeness to provide the illusion of privacy and isolation when the physical reality was lacking. Planes of codified behaviour overlaid on the bustling chaos like an invisible web, steering and guiding the occupants, and instantly marking out outsiders.

She saw the turn on to the pontoon at which her father's boat, her childhood home, had been moored, and made sure she cut the other way, across the deck of a former fishing vessel. Told herself it was the most direct route across the bay to Copeman Fisheries, but in reality she just didn't want to deal with the inevitable disconnect between her memories and the present. That boat would be part of someone else's life now, repurposed and reclaimed, the past gone and forgotten.

She wondered why Jason Blake had asked her to come to the wharf for this meeting. Sure he worked at the fishery, but if he wanted to keep the rendezvous quiet surely there were better ways than inviting her to a place she obviously didn't belong. There must be a hundred bars or cafés in the Port or ten minutes' walk inland. It was low tide, too; the air was muddier, the boats a little lower at their anchorages, the river running harder now it was no longer fighting the ocean. Not a time when boats would be unloading their catch. She hunkered further into her coat, walked faster.

Copeman Fisheries was a snow-covered two-tier corrugated steel warehouse unit on the edge of a cluster of other run-down commercial buildings that looked either abandoned or like they should have been. The painted logo over the doors by the waterside loading dock was lit by a single fizzing halogen spot that highlighted the letters COPE and very little else. Three more lights seemed to have burned out.

There were scores of footprints in the slush by the doors, wheel tracks leading into the cargo entry.

There was a guy waiting inside the door when she pushed it open. Stocky, huddled in a woollen hat and a bomber jacket. He looked like a thug for the Russian mob. Stamped out a cigarette as she shut the door. Said, 'I'll take you to Mr Blake.'

He had an hourglass tattoo on the back of his hand.

TWENTY-THREE

The fishery was a mess of cardboard boxes and tarp-covered wooden pallets under bare bulbs that hung from the support beams for the upper storey. No sign that it had been used for anything related to fish for a long time. Three vans, at least a dozen or more men like Maya's escort, none of them looking friendly. She heard others talking, somewhere further inside the building.

'So, you work with Jason?' she said. 'He told me he needed to see me to talk over some stuff, but I didn't know how busy you were here . . .'

'It's OK,' the guy said. 'He's expecting you. He asked me to keep an eye out.'

'What do you do here? I can't see any fish.'

'No, I guess not. Guess we don't have much to do with fishing here any more. Got more important things. Up we go.' He gestured at a galvanised steel staircase leading to the floor above. There were cobwebs hanging from the dusty wooden boards and streaks of rust at every point where the metal frame supporting them was bolted in place.

The stairs opened out on to a network of grubby rooms – offices, a locker room, store cupboards and something that had probably passed for a workers' break room when the place served its original purpose. It had probably been painted some time in the 1960s and never renewed since. Dingy, too; dim light the colour of piss and about as inviting. It stank of cigarette smoke and industrial cleaning fluid.

'I'm Eliza,' she said to her escort, trying to sound cheery. 'What's your name?'

He looked up at her, an expression that might have been withering pity or weariness etched in his eyes. Said, 'Alexiy. My father's from Minsk.' As though he felt the need to explain.

'Wow. Really?'

'It's not as exotic as it sounds. I've been there. It's a shithole.'

He guided her into a long, low room with a table to match square in the middle of it. At the far end sat a man in a leather duster the colour of fresh ochre and a bright red polo neck sweater. A couple of tattoos on the side of his neck, a crucifix and the tip of another symbol, both faded prison lookalikes, peeked over the collar. He had a neat sweep of black Slavic hair, square frameless sunglasses and pheromone chemistry that told of madness. The bad kind, the stay away kind, controlled and directed, tight as a laser. High cheekbones and an easy languid strength, a certain air that commanded attention, and he might have been attractive but for the instinctive chemical reaction that said *danger*.

Maya's guide pulled a chair out. She sat.

'I'm Jason,' the man said. He smiled, a schizoid half-grin that was anything but reassuring. 'I've got an offer to put to you, Eliza. And I sure hope you take it.'

TWENTY-FOUR

Garrett watched three men emerge from the fishery and head for the battered motor dinghy moored by the wharf. As the steel shutter rolled down behind them, he ducked underneath, praying there was no one waiting inside. One guy, muffled in a hooded parka, was walking away from the door with smoke that smelled like nicotine-laced road tar drifting behind him. Rows of pitted steel workbenches ran along this section of the plant, mirrored by hooked tracks above; this must have been the gutting and packing production line. Garrett scooted across the narrow aisle and hunkered behind one of the benches.

He'd said nothing about what he was planning to Emi when she stirred. Just kissed her, told her there was something he had to do, and slipped out into the night with a murmured goodbye trailing after him.

The frosty air smelled of wet steel and sweat. Muffled conversations filtered from the far end of the fishery, beyond a tattered set of plastic strip drapes shuddering in the draught. Garrett glanced quickly round the corner of the workbench, saw no one, and scuttled along the line. Heard voices, suddenly close, as he neared the drapes and threw himself against the wall beside them.

'Who was she, anyway?' A woman, throat sounding ragged.

A guy answered. ''Nother recruit. We missed Kent, so I guess more live bodies gotta be useful if we wanna try again. You got what you need?' Footsteps, and the rattling of a pallet-carrier's wheels, stopped. Garrett could feel them standing there, just beyond the drapes. A shift in the shadows playing on the edges of the plastic.

'McArthur's probably going to take an hour anyway. Never hurries when he goes to see the boat guy. You know how it is.'

'Tell me about it.'

'Home time?'

'Got that right. Ain't like he pays us for this.'

One set of footsteps moved off, the second waited a moment, then started again, the wheels rattling along in time. A woman came through the plastic drapes pushing a pallet-carrier loaded with heavy-duty steel boxes, unlatched. She was pushing forty, wearing a bright blue fleece jacket and a black woollen hat, and looked, Garrett thought, like she worked somewhere high up in customer services at a bank. Certainly didn't belong wheeling goods for a mass-murdering Clock.

She didn't have time to register his presence before he punched her square in the temple. She let go of the pallet-

134

carrier in shock, and he grabbed her in what he hoped was a sleeper hold, hauling her away to the side of the room as she scratched and clawed soundlessly at his arms. He saw that she had an hourglass tattooed on the back of her hand, between her thumb and forefinger, like several Clocks he'd met. Once she'd gone limp, he let her go, stuffed her in the corner, and carefully looked through a gap in the drapes. Crates and boxes, some covered in tarp, some not. A couple of vans. Movement. At the back, steel stairs leading up to a mezzanine office floor. If Blake was here, he'd be up there, Garrett felt sure. The lights were fluorescents dangling overhead, bright pools leaving only dim patches of shadow, and too many people in here to sneak past in the scant protection the gloom would provide. He could see what looked like the building's main fuse box, a block of grey steel plastered with electrocution warning decals, on the wall by one of the main entrances, too far away for him to shut down the lights.

Nothing for it but to front it out and hope. Garrett took the woman's hat, pulled it down low over his forehead. Tugged the collar of his coat up, lit a cigarette. Wedged his hands in his pockets, one of them clamped around his pistol. Thought of Emi waiting for him and strode out on to the main factory floor, eyes down like he had a job to do, which in a way he figured he did.

The few people whose field of vision he passed didn't bother him. He caught snatches of chatter, some of it end of shift stuff like any other job, some of it not. Two men were poring over a pile of photocopies – looked like newspaper clippings, maybe CCTV shots – on a stack of boxes behind one of the vans.

'That's the guy,' one of them was saying as Garrett walked past.

'That it? That case? What was in it?'

'Blake hasn't told me, and why would he? Doesn't matter. It was Kent's and someone took it from Green Street right before the cops showed up. We got the principals, right, but all they said was that the kid never brought it to them. Gotta still be in the Port . . .'

It was when he hit the stairs that Garrett finally heard the challenge he'd been expecting. A man, behind him, shouting, 'Hey! Who the fuck are you, buddy? What the fuck?'

Breathe in, out. Hand on the gun, the fuse box fixed hard in his mind. Garrett fired before he'd finished turning, and with a gout of sparks the building plunged into darkness.

TWENTY-FIVE

'**Y**ou recently found out you had the Curse, right?' Blake said. 'You've just started going to the support groups the police set up. Just found out how little help they can – or will – offer you. Or the rest of us. Like I told you, I hear you've been asking questions. I guess you want to know more about your situation, and how you might get out of it.'

Maya felt her heart quicken. Uncomfortably aware, now, of Alexiy behind her, the threat of the man in front. Exposed and isolated and alone.

'Questions,' Jason continued, 'that I and everyone else here have asked too. Questions like why no one's caught whoever's responsible. Like why no one's found a cure yet. Like why we've all got to lie about it as though the world would end if we told. Questions like who's best served by that – us, or a police force that doesn't want the rest of the city to know how badly it's running the investigation. Is that right?'

'I . . . I guess, yeah,' she said. 'You think they're deliberately dragging their heels? Why?'

'There are a lot of people who'd like to know how the Curse works and turn it to their own ends. Those people have money and influence and everyone knows how easy it is to buy the NCPD if you have those things.'

'The cops who spoke to me seemed OK.'

'They probably were. Policy on this investigation comes down from the top. Just buy out the ones running it, not the people at the front line, and you can do what you want. At least, that's how I'd do it if it was me.' That smile again, and he leaned forward. 'Which cops did you speak to exactly?'

Something cold passed across her, and the sudden fear that Jason Blake knew more than she'd like. 'I'm not sure,' she said. 'There was a woman . . . Philips? She explained to me what was going on. Then I was passed around a lot. I don't remember who it was took my statement. Then they handed me over to the support groups and I haven't spoken to them since. I didn't pay that much attention to their names, to be honest. I mean, someone tells you that, no joke, you're going to be dead in a year and they can't do shit for you, you don't take time to remember the name on the badge.'

'How did it make you feel?'

'How the fuck do you think?' she snapped. 'You invited me to come here. What's this about? I don't have time to burn, you know.'

'I might have a proposition you'd be interested in. But I've got to know if you're serious. This isn't for just anyone, is it, Alexiy?'

'Absolutely not, Mr Blake. You've got to be really committed to be a part of this.'

'How'd it happen?' Blake said.

'What?'

'The Curse. How did it happen to you?'

'What the hell's that got to do with anything?'

'I want to hear your story. If you really want to put right the wrong that was done to you then we can help one another and I can give you what you want. If you don't, then I guess this meeting was just a waste of time for both of us.' That smile again, and again Maya had the feeling he was playing with her, that he knew her for a phoney. 'What harm's it going to do? People share their stories all the time in the groups.'

'You tell me yours. You know a lot about the Curse but you haven't said jack about yourself. I'm not going to tell that kind of stuff to a complete stranger. I came here at your request and all I've seen is a bunch of guys doing God knows what and heard you ask a lot of questions. So what the hell, Jason?'

BANG as his hand slapped, palm open, on to the tabletop. 'Clock or not, no one gets to doubt my commitment and my sincerity. This is a delicate business and I'm not about to risk it for some newbie who could blow the whole thing if I don't make sure she's got what it takes first. You understand?' He leaned back, softened again. 'But OK. Since you gotta ask, I was in Kenton, on my way to a meeting with an old friend of mine, when I was taken. I was walking down the street, past a boarded up store, and I remember hearing a man's voice behind me. I think he was asking me the time. Then I don't remember much. It's like being drunk – I'm pretty sure I was awake for a while longer, but the memory isn't there. I woke up in a derelict industrial lot half a mile away the next day with a note on me saying I'd be dead in a year.

'The cops did nothing, Eliza. They took my story, just like they took yours, and they told me to be quiet about it, to tell everyone I had a brain tumour. But I know they were acting on orders to stall the "investigation", to do nothing while people died who didn't deserve it, so that those with an interest in the Curse could look into it themselves.'

'How do you know?'

'That doesn't matter,' he said. 'What's important is that I decided not to leave it in their hands. I took control of my own destiny, and the people you saw here all made the same choice. The cops won't do anything unless they're forced to. The media won't touch the Curse story because they're in thrall to the authorities. So we have to make them all take notice. To make our voices heard in such a way that they can't ignore us any more. It's that or crawl home and wait to die like the ones you see at the groups. Is that what you want, really?'

That confirmed it. 'You organised the Green Street bombing,' she said. 'You killed all those people.'

Jason Blake relaxed, shifted in his chair, like a snake easing its coils. 'I suggest you bear that in mind when you decide whether or not you're with us.'

Then the lights went out and someone started shouting, very far away.

TWENTY-SIX

Garrett shot twice more, muzzle flash strobing the darkness. Missed the guy who'd challenged him, heard him shouting, and more voices raised upstairs. He skittered backwards up the steps, feet ringing on the steel. An answering blast from down below. Garrett heard the metal beside him crack like a church bell struck by lightning. He sprinted to the top, threw himself through a door, lines and shapes forming in the dark as his night vision adjusted. Saw a fire extinguisher hanging in the corridor beyond, grabbed it and wedged it hard between the door handle and the wall, jammed into the plaster.

'Blake!' he yelled. 'Blake! We talk now or I'll burn down your whole goddamn operation!'

Someone moved up ahead and he fired twice, aiming low, shooting to wound.

More shouting, and then Maya heard gunshots, someone screaming. Blake had already gone, slipping quickly away without a word. She stood, said, 'Fuck this,' and headed for the door, picking her way mostly by memory. Found her path blocked by Alexiy.

'I'm sorry,' he said. 'Mr Blake wants us to stay here. This probably won't take long to sort out.'

'I'm not staying for this. What the hell?'

'I'm sorry,' Alexiy said again.

The lights sparked, flickered, and died again. Someone downstairs trying to get the circuit working. Alexiy glanced up and Maya drove her knee into his balls. Good, snapped strike, minimum windup. She felt the sudden movement rattle her tendons. Alexiy felt it more, and folded double, wheezing through gritted teeth.

'Sorry,' she said, and slipped through the door.

She'd taken one stride into the corridor, had enough time to register the narrow flight to steps on the far side, sound rising from the well, before she saw the man running at her out of the darkness, the gun in his hand.

Corridors subdivided the cluster of shabby rooms upstairs into a rough cross, bent into a hook at the far end. The guy he'd shot was thrashing and screaming at the junction as Garrett closed.

'Blake!' he shouted again. 'We just need to talk and then I'm gone. Blake!'

'And who are you?' The voice swam through the gloom.

'Charlie Garrett.'

A pause. 'The policeman? Ha! That's fantastic, it really is.'

Something he couldn't catch. The sense of movement by

the turn at the far end and a man's voice hissing, 'Get him clear. We'll deal with this.'

Hammering at the door behind him, the fire extinguisher shuddering against the wall. Garrett felt the moment slipping away from him, the chance dissolving in his hands. Blake was escaping through some back exit and the net was closing behind him. Desperation pulling at his heart, he ran down the corridor after his quarry. Didn't care, in that moment, how many people Blake had with him or what was waiting round the corner. He was so close he could *smell* Blake and the answer that could save Emi.

Three strides from the turn. Up ahead, a row of boarded windows overlooking the gutting shed roof. The sound of feet pounding down the steps round the corner. The door opposite the turn opening and someone stepping out. The metal-and-wood tearing sound as Blake's people finally kicked the fire extinguisher clear behind him. Two strides, about to collide with the figure who'd just stepped into the corridor. Flash of wide, surprised eyes, mouth like an O.

Then a *crack* behind him and a bullet struck Garrett square between the shoulder blades.

TWENTY-SEVEN

The running guy, staggering, smashed into Maya, his momentum picking her clean off her feet. She saw a white blur of gritted teeth, smelled cordite, felt his stubble against her forehead as they collided. They crashed into the plywood covering the window. It shattered wetly behind Maya, and then she felt gravity tug sickeningly on her gut and she was falling through the air.

She had flash images of smashing on to the concrete wharf, skull cracking open on the dockside, the guy's weight punching through her ribcage. Then they smacked into a corrugated steel roof. The man grunted as he hit. His shoulder drove all the air from Maya's lungs. For a moment they lay there, trying to breathe.

'Who the fuck are you?' He tried to move his gun, still clenched in his fist. Didn't have much success. 'You one of Blake's people too, huh?'

'No,' she managed. 'No. Trying to recruit me. Then you showed up.'

'Fuck,' the guy said. 'Fuck. Gotta move, fast.'

He rolled over, groaning, and helped Maya to her feet. Pulled her, staggering, over the ridge, down to the edge of the roof. She could hear voices near the broken window. They found a drainpipe. The man checked to see if there was anyone in sight and then slid down. Maya followed.

They scurried across a strip of empty concrete, into the cover of a cluster of old steel pallet boxes that reeked of decay. Shouts behind them, up in the window. Blake's people had discovered they'd escaped.

The guy pulled off his fleece jacket. Underneath he wore a bulky black polo neck and a shoulder rig. There was a ragged hole in the sweater, high up on his back. 'Fuck,' he said again. 'Feels like I've broken my spine. Is there any blood?'

'What?'

'The hole. Is there any blood?'

She glanced. Shook her head. 'No. What the hell's going on?'

'Someone shot me.'

'Really?'

'Police vest. Trauma plates and kevlar. Fuck, but that hurts.'

'You're a cop?'

'Depends who you talk to.' Shouting from the fishery. Orders, instructions. A search being organised to comb the night. 'Let's get out of here. You know the Port at all?'

'Some.'

They walked, stiff and sore, towards the waterfront and the jetties leading into the floating city. Once the fishery was a few hundred yards behind them and the feeling of danger had eased somewhat, the guy glanced at Maya and said, 'I'm Charlie, by the way. Charlie Garrett.'

'Eliza Begovic.'

'You look familiar. Do I know you from somewhere?'

Maya kept her face blank. 'Dunno.'

He looked at her again. 'Court case? Something to do with "Greasy" Saganowski, wasn't it?'

She sighed. Feet hit the wooden boards as they crossed the boundary into the Port. Like passing into another world. 'OK. My name's Maya Cassinelli, and yeah, I did a story for the *Tribune* about Lieutenant Saganowski that got me beaten in court and kicked out of my job.'

'I remember. You were right. Everyone on the force knows Saganowski's bent. But then everyone else is as well.'

'You're a cop too.'

'Suspended. Why was Blake trying to recruit you? What was he doing in there?'

She didn't answer for a while, tried to figure out what lie to tell. She'd already told him her real name, so she figured there was no harm in telling him something he'd be able to check anyway.

'I was on Green Street, wrote an article about it.'

'You know about the Curse? You're a Clock too?' The directness of the question caught her completely off guard. When she said nothing, Garrett continued, 'You gave me a fake name, and you're a journalist. You're investigating the Curse? How much do you know about Blake?'

'How do you know about the Curse?'

'I used to be on the case. I worked with the support groups for victims.'

'Used to be?'

'Let's get coffee.' He steered her on to a fishing boat which had been fitted with an outrigger and a flat deck between that and the main hull. There was a narrow counter with a pair of hot water urns set up on it, wooden baskets of tea and toasted snack food. Folding camp furniture had been crammed on to the deck, completely unoccupied in the cold night. An old man with wooden teeth was perched behind the counter. Garrett bought them both coffee in chipped enamel mugs, sat down at a table by the water's edge. There was no rail between the deck and the freezing river.

'What do you know about Blake?' he said again.

'I never met him before tonight.'

'He was at Green Street too, you know. A couple of blocks away. Did he tell you that?'

She nearly told him about their conversation, but stopped herself. Said, 'What's your interest in him?'

'He came to the groups for a while. He's supposed to be dead. Somehow he's not, and I need to know why.' Garrett paused for a moment, then said, 'If he's found a cure, or someone did something to fix him, the same thing could save the woman I love. He's got a group of Clocks in that building, and they had a bomb-maker here in the Port doing work for them. I don't know what he's planning.'

'He said he was behind the Green Street explosion.'

'I figured as much. His people killed a friend of mine. We got a call out to a building near the scene that night. You were there?'

'I was just passing through. Saw the whole thing. Nearly walked into the bomber.'

'Is that why Blake was interested in you? Because you were there at the scene and— Fuck.' Garrett slapped the table. 'Blake's people were talking about it downstairs. The case that the kid had, the one from the bomb scene. It's got to be the one Julius told me about.'

Maya felt her pulse quicken. 'A case from Green Street? Like, a briefcase?'

'I guess. I didn't stop to ask. They were looking at photos from the scene. Security cameras, probably. The bomb would've blown them out, but they'd have "before" images to work from. They've been all over the news already.'

'Jason Blake is after it.' She saw Dominic walking down Green Street. Snow hanging in the air around him. The look on his face, the expressions of the men with him. The briefcase clutched tightly in his hand. Said, quietly, 'I want to see it. I want to know what it is and why he wants it.'

Garrett stared at her, eyes narrowed. 'Something for your story?'

'Something to help me understand an old friend.' He looked blank, so Maya went on, 'If it's your cure, or something else that can help you, I'm not going to get in the way. But I want to know. I know the Port. I grew up here. I can help. You said you know where it is?'

'A guy I know here. He told me he could get his hands on it. Or at least I think it's the same thing.'

'When do we see him?'

He thought for a moment. Said, 'Now. Drink up.'

'Sorry, lad,' Julius said. He was standing in the doorway to the *Adventure*'s forecastle wearing a fur dressing gown and warm slippers. 'I'll leave a message for the boy and get him to call me in the morning, but I can't reach him now. He said he was playing it cautious.'

'Tell him it's urgent.'

Julius nodded at Maya. 'I will, my dear. I'll call Charlie as soon as I hear.'

Garrett, visibly frustrated, gave Maya a lift home. It was late, and back on dry land the city was closing its eyes for the short hours until morning. A thin inch of snow had settled on the roads, carved here and there by lone tyre tracks, other people on cold errands in the empty night. The grubby brown ridges of cleared ice and slush in the gutters were painted clean white. Newport glimmered and shone.

They said little as the car slid through the streets. Maya gave Garrett directions when needed, but that was all. They made the turn on to her road and the rows of darkened brownstones, skeletal trees pointing like exposed ribs up at the sky, parked cars huddled under the blanket of white.

'Nice,' Garrett said.

'Won't be here for much longer at this rate,' she told him. 'The Saganowski case cleaned my account and I won't be able to pay the rent much longer.'

'Shame. She deserved to go down.'

'You said.' Garrett didn't slow as they passed her building. 'Hey,' she said, 'that's it.'

He shook his head.

'What do you mean?'

'Car back there. We'll keep driving, go round the block.'

'A car? You mean, like someone watching my apartment?'

Garrett shrugged. 'You got any neighbours done anything illegal? Because if not, I'd guess it was you they were interested in. Neighbourhood like this, I doubt there's too much call for people on stakeout.'

Maya thought about Valentin's shadow, Anton, wondered if she should tell Garrett about him and decided against it. He drove them round the block, then killed the lights and the engine as they approached the intersection with her street again. Let the car coast forward until they could see along the line of parked vehicles near her apartment. Maya couldn't see what they were looking for to begin with, but then she saw that one had less snow on its windows than the others.

'That's it,' Garrett said. 'It's the heater.'

'Keeping warm.'

'They also need to melt the snow anyway; not much point watching a place if you can't see it.'

She could see the two men inside through the passenger

window, black silhouettes watching her home. The car wasn't Anton's, and in any case he'd been alone.

'Could they be cops?' Garrett said.

'I don't see why they would be.' She thought about the detectives working the groups, and wondered for a moment if they'd broken through the cover Valentin had provided for her. Pulling something like this didn't seem to fit with the weary state of the Curse investigation. They'd just call round in the daytime and give her a talking-to.

'You got enemies?'

She thought of Dominic and the men who'd come to collect him. Amanda Kent, watching him all the time. Valentin's assistant Anton on her trail. The 'others' Dominic had mentioned. Said, 'I didn't think so. But maybe I was wrong.'

TWENTY-EIGHT

Garrett started the engine, turned away from Maya's apartment, but didn't switch on the lights until he was a hundred yards from the watchers.

'Shit,' she said. 'Shit fuck ass shit.'

'You got someplace you can go?'

'Nowhere I'd trust. Fuck.'

He sighed. 'OK. You can crash on my couch tonight. Assuming my place is safe. If it's not, you and me and Emi are going to have to manage somehow.'

Garrett lived in a concrete hulk built like a proof of concept prototype for every 1980s condo block ever built, as though the architect had put together the shell to show it could take the stress, but stopped short of applying any aesthetics. There was no sign of further watchers outside. He led Maya through to the elevator, rode it up to the sixth floor.

There was a woman in the kitchen when they walked in. Emi, Maya presumed. She kissed Garrett and Maya saw a wall tumble down inside him as he hugged her, bear-like, grinning like a teenager.

'Who's this, Charlie?' Emi said. 'Oh my God! There's a hole in the back of your coat. What happened?' Tracing the edge of the ragged bullet tear with the tip of her finger.

'I went to see Jason Blake and his people. Things got lively.' A shadow across the smile. 'I didn't get the cure out of him, but I will.'

'I don't want anything happening to you, Charlie. I keep telling you. I don't want to have to keep worrying about you all the way to the end.'

'This is Maya. She needs a place to crash tonight. She was at Blake's the same time as me, been looking into the Curse.' He must've seen a question in her expression because he shrugged and added, 'There were some people watching her place. I don't know who they were but it seemed best to bring her back here.'

Maya, feeling uncomfortable, shifted on her feet. Said, 'Hi. Sorry.'

'Hi. Welcome. I'll make coffee,' Emi said.

The apartment was small and poorly lit by buried fluorescent spots that cast everything in a faintly bluish hue. The layout and the high, narrow, oddly placed windows made it seem like it had been constructed from spare space salvaged from neighbouring apartments. A broom closet from one, the corridor from another. The walls were dark, the colour of old photographs, and Garrett didn't seem to have put much effort into decorating it. There were paintings on the walls or leaning against the furniture, some big, some small, and all, Maya guessed, Emi's. On the wall by the dusty TV was a photo of a tree, and beyond it some kind of artificial metal meshwork against a cloudy sky.

They talked about very little, and took their time doing it. Emi asked her some polite questions about herself, her work, what had happened on Green Street. Garrett didn't say anything about the fishery or Blake and Maya took his lead. She asked Emi about her art, a little about her family, what life had been like in Japan with an American mother.

Afterwards, she lay awake on the couch under a comforter. Wind slapped at the window, and in between gusts the muffled voices drifting through the partition wall. Emi, seeking reassurance about something Maya could only guess at, the tone of Garrett's reply not, she thought, very convincing. Eventually, they fell away, and Maya was left alone with the bleak gale and the distant sounds of the fitfully sleeping city.

TWENTY-NINE

'**W**hat the hell was all that about last night?' Maya said as they cleared away the dishes after an uncomfortably quiet breakfast of eggs. 'The people watching my place, I mean.'

Garrett lit a cigarette, squeezed Emi's waist as she slipped past to make fresh coffee. Smiled, and Maya saw a tightness, a fear, in his eyes. Said, 'They weren't cops. No reason the NCPD would be tailing you, and if they thought you'd been up to something SOP would be to come talk to you, put you under pressure. *Then* see what you did. Clocks? Blake's people? They might have been waiting for you after what happened.'

'But they weren't here as well. Jason Blake knows who you are and didn't bother watching you.' She shook her head, reached for her phone. 'Either it's something deeper, or someone I've already told to leave well alone has a hearing problem.'

Her call was answered before it could cut to voicemail. A woman's voice, sleepy, which took her aback for a moment.

She managed her surprise, said, 'Is Harrison Valentin there? This is Maya Cassinelli.'

A pause, then Valentin said, 'Good morning, Maya. Putting in an early shift today?'

'Something like that.'

'How goes your mission? I've been meaning to call and ask; since you had your conversation with Anton I've been afraid of falling out of the loop.'

'That's exactly what I wanted to talk to you about,' she said. 'I told Anton I didn't want to work with someone breathing down my neck all the time.'

'And of course I immediately called him off.'

Didn't know whether she believed him or not. The words came easily. 'Have you got anyone else keeping tabs on me, Harrison?'

'What do you mean?'

'There were people watching my apartment last night. I want to know if they were more of yours, or if this is something I should be worried about.'

'They're nothing to do with me,' he said. Sounded genuinely concerned. 'If you like, I could ask Anton to provide you with protection, or to at least be ready to assist if—'

'No, I don't want that. I'll be careful, see if I can't figure out what's going on. I'll talk to you soon, let you know how things are going.'

A sigh. 'If you're sure, Maya. I'll look forward to your report.'

'Goodbye, Harrison. And if I find Anton or anyone else

working for you following me around after this, I'll be very unhappy.'

She hung up. Garrett said, 'Do you believe him?'

'I'm not sure.'

'How much do you know about him? You do any digging before you signed up?'

'Yes. Some. He's dangerous but I didn't have much choice,' she said. 'Not unless I can live on air and good wishes.'

'Maybe you should do some now.'

'I know Harrison Valentin,' Emi said from the other side of the kitchen.

'You're kidding.'

'Not personally,' she said. 'I have a friend who did some installation pieces for him two years ago. Valentin owns the Summer Gallery in NoMa. Gary had a month-long run there, at Valentin's personal invitation. Gary told me he was very keen. Then he was taken on for a private commission – I don't remember if this was for Valentin or someone else with a loose connection to the gallery – and he went a little strange. I haven't spoken to him for a long time.'

'Strange?'

'He cut himself off from everyone, or at least me and all our mutual friends, and shut himself away. He never said why. I don't know if he's worked since; if he has, he's doing it under a new name.'

'What was his name? His old one, I mean.'

'Gary Fisk.'

Garrett smiled and ground out the stub of his cigarette. Said, 'Do you have a phone number for him? An address?'

'What do we do if he blows us out?'

'Go knock on his door,' Garrett said. 'I doubt it'll help us; if he doesn't show up, I imagine he's running. Depends how paranoid he is.'

They sat on the jumbled rooftop of a tenement out by McGregor Hook, a frozen spit of land sticking out into the estuary where the Murdoch hit the sea. It was home to a swarm of amusement parks in the time of Barnum, long decayed by World War Two when low-rent housing mushroomed along the peninsula, before a doomed attempt at reviving it as a tourist spot to rival Atlantic City in the seventies. Now it existed in shabby limbo, a faded picture postcard of a nowhere nothing town, a tattered memory of old summers blasted by the cold wind off the ocean, watching harbour-bound ships and the rest of the world pass it by. The tenement's owner had had the idea of turning the rambling roof into a coffee house and café. Run trelliswork between the TV aerials and rusting AC units, covered over a section by the battered roof access with a green canvas bivouac, dotted wooden lawn furniture and tables around the place. Started serving customers who came up the vine-covered fire escape down the side of the building. The Hook's zoning authorities either didn't know about it or didn't care.

Maya sipped hot lemon and ginger and tried to watch the entrance. Difficult through the trellises hung with dead brown plants. Fisk had chosen the place to meet, repeatedly told them to be sure they weren't watched or followed, that he'd split if there was any sign of trouble. Hadn't wanted to leave home, hadn't wanted them to come to him, hadn't wanted to talk over the phone, so this was it. Hard, she figured, for anyone to watch who he spoke to, harder still to eavesdrop.

'Julius is taking his time finding the kid,' she said.

'He'll come through. He's a good man.'

'I hope nothing's gone wrong. A buyer already taken it, something like that.'

'He'll come through,' Garrett said again.

Sat, in the frozen Atlantic air, dead plants clattering in the breeze, and saw in every half-glimpsed movement dark figures, phantoms of Fisk's imagining. Despite the cold, there were a dozen other people up here for their morning coffee. Maya couldn't tell if any looked out of place. Movement on the stairs, and a man emerged on to the roof. Round at the middle, buried behind a bulky cold weather coat, a scarf and a hunting cap pulled down around his ears. He shambled into the shelter of the trellises, had a quiet word with one of the staff, and sat down at Maya and Garrett's table. Pulled down his scarf, said, 'Let's not hang about, huh? You must be Charlie.'

'This is Maya, Mr Fisk. Thanks for meeting us. I know it wasn't easy.'

'Not easy? Yes, you could say that. You weren't followed here, saw nothing strange?'

Maya shook her head. 'No.'

'How hard did you look? Never mind, forget I asked. Thanks,' he said to the waiter as he brought Fisk a mug of coffee. 'So what do you want? I caught the gist of your situation before you started listening to me and shut up talking about it on the phone, but I hope whatever you need is worth this. I don't like being threatened with exposure, you know.'

Garrett shrugged. 'We needed to talk. If telling you I'd spread the word you had, regardless, was enough, it was worth it. There're lives at stake.'

'Let me tell you about lives at stake.' The former artist's eyes narrowed. 'If I'm caught talking about anything I shouldn't, me and my family are dead. I've got a wife and a little girl. I only came here to get you to shut up. This getting through to you? How'd you even know to find me?'

'Emi Nakano.'

'Goddamn it. Fuck.'

'She's dying, and one of your old employers is messed up in it somehow. We want to know what you know about him. Harrison Valentin.'

'Fuck,' he said again. 'I don't need this.'

'No offence, Gary, but you sound like a classic paranoid to me. I can't believe it's all as dangerous as you claim.'

Fisk shook his head. Said, 'Pyotr Chalienski.'

'Never heard of him.'

'I have,' Maya said. It had been one of her first assignments as a rookie on the *Tribune*. She'd gone with an experienced beat reporter to the Swann Bridge and the late night suicide of a broker who'd left his convertible with its hazard lights blinking, a note saying sorry on the passenger seat, climbed the barriers and, the cops had figured, thrown himself into the Murdoch. The abandoned vehicle, tired-eyed guys in coveralls hitching it to a tow truck. The police cordon, strobes flashing. Zodiacs, sweeping the water with spotlights. No one seemed to think they had much chance of finding Chalienski, and certainly not alive. As she recalled, he'd washed up on the north shore of the harbour a couple of days later, about the same time as stories of the money he'd lost and the problems he'd had began to surface. Fifty million, a hundred million, something like that, down the drain and it had all gotten too much for him.

'You know what happened to him?'

'Jumped off a bridge.'

'He was thrown off by two guys, and he was already dead. Harrison Valentin drowned him in his bath because he was threatening to go public.'

Maya rolled her eyes.

'I was there, smartass,' Fisk said. 'Mr Valentin was running an art scam for his rich pals in what they call the Foundation. I consulted. Rich folk, see, use art like safe investments. You got ten mill burning a hole in your account, especially if it's ten mill you maybe shouldn't have, you buy yourself an old master or a fuck-off sculpture or whatever and put it in storage, and so long as the bottom doesn't drop out of the market for that kinda thing you can sell up at any point safe in the knowledge that you'll get the same value for it. Cleans your money, too. Chalienski just wanted a bigger cut; he didn't know much, and no one was gonna miss him. I was there because I was with Mr Valentin. Cleaning up the mess, right? But I saw some of the other stuff those people were into. Valentin, Ernst Kirchberg, Amanda Kent . . . all of them. I got out, and I gotta stay *out*, you understand? I've got stuff on them, so they let me breathe, but Mr Valentin made it clear if I so much as look like I'm about to give up what I know, he doesn't care that it won't stop it, he'll kill my family. I didn't even know that much, so you can figure how dangerous these people are.'

His voice trailed away and Maya saw panic on his face, the realisation that he'd probably already told them too much.

'Jesus,' she said. The wind off the Atlantic shrieked through the trellises. She saw a dozen watching figures, no more than shadows cast by the dead juddering plants, felt a hundred eyes watching her. Saw Valentin's gaze again, that night in K:Max. The smile. So hard to read.

'Rich like that,' Fisk said, 'they're a different species. A rapper or a model or a sportsman with millions in the bank, chances are they're just going to be an idiot with what they've got. Others, maybe they just want to enjoy themselves, act big, do some charity work, practise their golf game. People like Mr Valentin and those others, they're not like that. They're clever and they're predators, there's nothing they need, and all they've got left to do is entertain themselves playing with the rest of us. You doubt for a second that he'd kill me, or you, just like he did Chalienski and you're a damned idiot. That's why I don't want to be here, and that's why I want you to say what you've got to and go away.'

'You know about the Curse?' Garrett said.

'Yeah, some.'

'What would they – what did you call them? – what would they want with it?'

'The Foundation. Way I understood it, they don't like each other. If what people say about the Curse is right, the technology that makes it happen could be worth massive amounts of money. Ain't like it's really magic, is it? So there's that, and whichever one of them gets it – like your Mr Valentin – means the others *don't*. More than that, they get to control what it's used for, who gets access to it. It's all a game to them, and whichever way you cut it, that's got to be a mighty interesting prize.'

Music. 'Air on a G String'. Fisk's cell phone.

THIRTY

'**Y**ou said you weren't followed!' Fisk, in the back of Garrett's car, frantic and swearing.

'We weren't.'

'Five minutes – five goddamn motherfucking minutes – I'm talking to you people.'

'We weren't followed.'

'*Five minutes* and someone sends Helen a message that looks like it came from my phone. If she hadn't called. If she hadn't *known* to call when something like this happened . . . You *were* fucking followed, and now they're going to kill Helen and Lucy. You get it? Meet at the Ryan's Wharf ticket office? That place has been shut for years. No one to see. Right?'

They said nothing for a moment. Then Maya asked, 'What if they're tailing us now?'

'You get me to Nerio Station. There'll be too many people there. They can't do anything, even in a city like this. Probably.' He shrugged, antsy. 'Not like there's much better

I can do. It's safer than meeting at the house, and this way we can all get out of town.'

'You think they won't follow you?'

'Fuck should I know? They might ease off once I'm out of their backyard. Not like it's gonna be any worse than staying here.'

Maya thought of the call to his wife, presumably from a cloned phone. Someone must've been watching the meet, someone neither she nor Garrett had managed to spot before Fisk showed up. Acting as fast as they had, there must've been a standing order in place to swoop as soon as Fisk surfaced. Harrison Valentin smiling broadly at her over dinner, and this man in hiding with *something* worth killing for without pause. She wondered what he'd got on the Foundation. What she'd wandered into, however peripherally. Do the job, take the pay cheques and not ask stupid questions and she'd never have known.

Nerio Station was a sprawling baroque mass at the southern end of the Hook. A web of steam-age iron looping like giant Gigeresque breathing tubes over a mess of platforms fanning from the heart of the terminus. The building dated, barely changed, from the Hook's heyday as a resort in the 1800s. Numbers might have dwindled but it still served as the end of the line, and there were always plenty of people looking for a way out of the Hook, or a day on the promontory's exposed beaches and an evening ride back to civilisation. Even in the snow, thin lines of dark-clad travellers filtered through its doors like Halloween scarecrows. The heavy, peaked clock tower like a church steeple pinned through the heart of the structure was blurred by snow flurries, periodically blown to grey against the clouds.

'Where's your wife waiting for you?' Garrett said as they climbed out of the car and into the cold.

'Main concourse, under the clock.' Fisk stared past the empty bus stands to the far side of the station lot. 'I think that's our car over there. She must be here already.'

Through the mouth of the entrance, out of the snow and into the dim tunnel leading to the open, vaulted space of the station proper. Maya, glancing at every passing stranger, wondering who might work for Harrison or whoever else wanted Fisk's family dead. Footsteps and muddled conversation a hollow riot of echoes as they hit the concourse, the wide open space like a circus big top beneath a skeleton of black iron spaced by snow-covered glass tiles. A metal cube hung on baroque struts beneath its centre, clock faces on each side. There was no one waiting beneath it.

'She's not here,' Fisk said. 'Where is she?'

A coffee concession. Barista wiping tables, glancing for a moment in their direction. Three customers, talking on the phone, reading a newspaper. A snack vendor shuttering his stand after the morning rush. A couple of stores in the fabric of the perimeter, doors open, a handful of travellers. A dozen or more people standing by the departure boards, watching for their trains. The dotted specks of bright orange Transit Authority uniforms. Knots of dark-bundled figures, breath steaming, making their way from their newly arrived train and through the barriers. No lone woman with a little girl. Maya felt worry tug at her gut.

'Stay here,' Garrett said. 'I'm going to check the car. Which one did you think was yours?'

'Look, I should do it. I'll—'

'No, don't. Your wife walks through the doors, she's going to be wanting to see you, not one of us. I can see if she's waiting in the car without spooking her. I'll call if I see anyone inside and you can come join me.' He glanced at Maya and she saw something cross his eyes, a flicker of the flat, locked gaze she'd seen on the faces of emergency personnel at accident sites, reporters at murder scenes. He didn't want Fisk finding his wife and child dead in their vehicle.

'It's . . . it's a blue Taurus. Got a Newport City Zoo sticker on the rear passenger window. Lucy bought it when we went there in the summer.'

'Keep watching; don't let anything happen. I'll be back,' Garrett said. Maya watched him go, one eye on anyone who might be following him, then went back to scanning their surroundings.

'What does she look like?' she said. 'Your wife.'

'Shorter than you. Dark hair. Small.' Fisk gnawed on his lip.

There were iron footbridges crossing each pair of tracks, platform to platform, distant shadows moving along them, a couple Maya could see were motionless, waiting, or watching. A line of frosted-glass windows, an upper storey overlooking the concourse, station offices and administration. Open walkways and flights of steel stairs, closed to the public. Two men in NCTA uniform, leaning on the safety rail, talking. Movement in the roof space, tattered groups of pigeons shivering in the cold. And all around the soft raindrop patter of hurrying feet, the swirl of a dozen knots of passing strangers, and any of them could be enemies.

Then, movement beside her. Fisk, running, shouting, 'Helen!'

In the gap between a newsstand and a bank of ticket machines on the far side of the concourse, Maya saw the flash of a woman's face, pale, and the tiny hand clasped in her own, before the people with her closed ranks again and she vanished from sight.

Then Maya was running after Fisk.

THIRTY-ONE

Garrett trudged through the thickening snow skirling across the station lot. The flow of people through the station's doors dissipated and scattered, and he was wary of the few he still saw moving around as he crossed the blasted asphalt. There weren't many vehicles and he could see Fisk's car. Kept it in sight, but walked like he was aiming for something else, at an angle to it, enough to get close. Then his phone rang. Julius.

'Charlie, lad. The boy you wanted to meet is on his way. I told him you'd come to mine and we could reach an arrangement.'

'Has he got the case with him?'

'Can't say. I wouldn't count on it. He's a little antsy. You know how kids are these days. How soon can you be here? I'll put a pot of coffee on the stove ready.'

'I'm not sure, Julius.' Ahead, the Taurus. Windshield scattered with flakes, interior dark.

'Something going on, lad?'

'You could say that. Look, keep him with you. We'll be there ASAP.'

'I could rearrange it—'

'No. I want to know about the case, Julius. I want to talk to the kid. I've just been chasing a lead on something else, and it's gone screwy. I make sure this guy's family's safe and I can be right with you. Wife and child on the line, you know?' It was a cheap move, Garrett knew, but Julius prided himself on his warped sense of honour.

'All right, lad. You do what you have to and I'll keep the boy entertained. I'll add it to my cut. Broker's fee, you know?'

'Thanks, Julius.'

'Don't mention it. I'm not entirely sure what you're up to, but those fellers cleared out the fishery you asked about before. All gone last night, I hear. Someone must have stirred things, am I right?'

'I'll tell you about it some other time. I'll call you when we're on the way.' Hung up, within touching distance of the car now. He checked the lot behind him, then walked up to the rear windows. Brushed the snow away, saw the zoo sticker beneath. Looked inside.

Nothing. No one. The car was empty and undamaged. They had to be inside the station, and he knew then, at the pit of what still passed as a policeman's heart, that Fisk's wife and daughter were in real danger.

Maya, feet skidding on the Arctic surface of the concourse. Fisk somewhere ahead, scattering people as he ran, shouting.

She dodged a couple who were stepping backwards and staring after the sprinting man, made the turn and crashed straight into a gym bag lying on the floor. Felt her teeth snap together as her jaw hit the marble, the wind driven from her lungs and her knees and elbows screaming. Maya looked up, shaken, as Fisk vaulted the barrier and ran on to the platform beyond.

A mass of travellers waiting to board a newly arrived train, and Fisk weaving between them, dodging side to side, shouting louder now. 'Helen! Lucy!'

Maya heard herself yelling after him as she jumped the barriers in his wake. The train's doors hissed open and the crowd shifted, and for a moment a parting opened through their centre. She saw Fisk catch up to his wife and daughter, who were alone, plainly frightened, their escorts vanished. He skidded to a halt beside them, flung his arms around them. Maya thought she saw tears. Then three shots rolled around the station, barely a pause between them, blood splintered the air and man, woman and child dropped to the ground.

A pause for breath, and Nerio Station's travellers began to scream as one.

Garrett hit the entrance as panicking people began to stream out of it. The sound was a single, confused howl, thrown wild by the vaulted roof. He fought his way upstream, yelling 'Police!' though he doubted anyone could hear him. Burst on to the concourse, saw no sign of Maya or Fisk between lines of fleeing passengers and

NCTA staff streaming through the now-open barriers.

Flash of orange up to his left. Two guys on one of the gantries in high-vis Transit Authority uniform, one of them helping a third man, dressed in a suit and a dark coat, stuff something into a bag. Dull steel. Gun barrel. Rifle.

Garrett swore, slipped his gun into his hand and jogged towards the stairs.

Fisk and his family were dead. Maya knew it without searching for a pulse. No breathing, not so much as a flicker of an eyelid. Empty stares directed at the ceiling, across the tracks, into nothing and nowhere. Each of them shot through the chest, centre of mass, through the heart, by someone who knew what he was doing with a rifle. Maya took in the sad tableau and knew, with a stab of guilt for thinking it at such a time, that whatever else Fisk had known about Valentin, about the Clocks, everything, was gone.

When she looked up again, she saw a familiar figure walking briskly away, up the steps on to the walkway between platforms, more slowly and calmly than those who were fleeing that way to escape the shooting site. Harrison Valentin's lieutenant, Anton.

They saw Garrett as he reached the top of the stairs that dropped from the staff gantries to the passenger walkway between platforms. He'd narrowed the gap, but not enough. He could see that the guy with the gym bag, the shooter, wasn't in charge; one of the men in Day-Glo orange was giving the orders. Scarred and cruel-looking. As Garrett hit the turn, the shooter glanced behind, saw him following. Opened his mouth to shout a warning as he reached into the gym bag. Garrett jumped, hit the handrail and skidded down it, feet-first. Hit the gate at the bottom with a crash, slammed it open into the shooter's face, a *crunk* like he'd hit a pool ball with a crowbar, the bag and the man's handgun skittering across the walkway.

Garrett landed at a run, unsteady but moving fast, and while the guy in charge walked on, the third man punched Garrett in the gut, drove him back, followed up by grappling his arms before he could bring his gun to bear. The man was strong and had a grip like gnarled wood. Garrett tried to work his hands free, feeling the walkway guard rail biting into his back. A flash of orange to his right: the leader stepping through the flow of people still fleeing for the main entrance from the far platforms. Garrett moved to knee his assailant in the groin and when he moved to block he crashed his forehead into the guy's nose. Freed his hands as the man fell back, bringing up his gun, but his opponent charged him, roaring. Smashed his shoulder into Garrett's chest and bore him up, over the railing. The world flipped upside down for one sickening instant, and then he snatched hold of metal. Dangling over the tracks below, muscles already burning with the effort of keeping him there, and while his opponent prepared to make sure Garrett took the fall he seemed unable to avoid, the leader was weaving along the walkway, nearly lost in the crowd.

* * *

Anton seemed to be unaware of Maya following him. He strode briskly along with the knots of panicked civilians without a backward glance. The rumble of an approaching train, its driver presumably unaware of what had happened at the station, began to blanket the noise made by those escaping the shooting. She wondered if Anton had killed Fisk, if he'd followed her to the meeting and been the one to make the call. She shook her head, broke into a run. Shouted, 'Anton!'

He turned, but then a man coming the other way in an orange NCTA vest bumped into him from behind. A flash of steel, no more than a flicker, and Anton slumped to the floor. He didn't even move to clutch his chest.

Maya felt her heart jump, saw the killer step over Anton's body and cross the stream of people running along the walkway. Then, further back, another burst of movement and she saw Garrett fall. Rushed to the railing, saw him lying, barely moving, on the track. Saw the train on its steady approach to the platform. The killer, his mouth pulled into a leer by a scar at one corner, opening an emergency door on the far side of the walkway, an exit to some outer section of the station off-limits to travellers. Two men hurrying to join him. Garrett, still on the rails.

She swore and raced for the stairs as Anton's killer vanished. Pounded down the steps, rushed across the platform as the train squealed and clanked nearer and nearer. Garrett rolled into a kneeling position, shaking his head. She thrust out her hand, yelled, 'Charlie!'

Then she was hauling him past her, on to the platform, and the train rolled past, slowing hard, brakes howling.

'Are you OK?' she asked, panting. 'Can you walk?'

'Yeah,' he said, eventually. 'Move. Gotta move. Feels like maybe I busted my ribs landing, but I guess I'm OK. Go. Go.' Clambered to his feet, unsteady at first, and tried to drag Maya with him.

'What about the cops?' she said. 'They'll be here any minute. They're going to want to know why we were with Fisk.'

'How would they know? Ah, fuck.' Garrett clutched his side, but kept walking, steered her in the direction of a side door. 'Just bruised, I think, but Christ this hurts.'

'Security recordings. They'll watch those, see we were with him. People saw you and me acting differently from everyone else.'

'There won't be recordings.'

'But—'

The station was eerily quiet now as they entered the short corridor leading to the exit and freedom. 'There won't be recordings. Guys like that, they'll have nixed the cameras. And no witness statement made after that, so soon after Green Street, is gonna be worth shit. These people, this "Foundation", they got their guy. They were watching him, they saw he was talking to us, and they got him.'

And, Maya thought, one of them obviously decided Valentin's man would make a decent dead stooge if they needed one. She wondered if it had been planned that way, or a spur of the moment decision by the scarred man. Fisk had said the Foundation's members had little love for one another. 'What if the cops are already here, outside?'

Out, and biting cold wind on Maya's face, the glare of the snow. No police, and Garrett didn't bother looking for them as he said, 'Chopper might be here soon, but we've got a couple of minutes at least before uniforms arrive. Snow, traffic, distance to nearest precinct. Get in the car and we're gone, just like everyone else.'

She did, and they were.

THIRTY-TWO

Two months before the Green Street bombing.

Stevie Dewar whimpered as the two other men kicked him to his knees in front of Jason. Lyra, like the other Clocks, watched them back away from him with little more than a nod to their leader. Alexiy and Hume, two of Jason's innermost circle. She'd known Stevie when he was in the groups. They'd started going to them just a week or two apart. She'd left to join Jason a lot sooner, though; it had been strange to see Stevie come over to their side at all, but then people you'd never imagine could grow angry, want to act, as their time began to run out.

'This man,' Jason said, 'wanted to betray us. To betray you all.'

Maybe he just hadn't been cut out for it. The things they'd done – the things they'd *all* done or been a party to doing – could be hard to take if you thought about them too much. You had to remember that this was, effectively, war. That the rest of the world denied the

Clocks' existence or had been carefully blinded to it, and that revealing the truth, and saving those who, through no fault of their own, had been Cursed, sometimes meant sacrificing others.

That it was us, or them.

'I didn't want to do anything,' Stevie spluttered. His hands were bound behind him and blood was running freely from his nose. 'I just wanted out.'

'There is no "out", you know that. We all know that. Not everyone has the stomach for everything we need to do, and I understand that. There are plenty of you who work to support the rest of us without having to do anything you can't face. But there is no "out". As soon as there's an "out" then there's the risk of exposure and the chance that everything we've worked so hard for will be taken away. That every one of the people now looking at you, Stevie, will die from the Curse because we won't be able to force a cure.' Jason looked up, pointed into the crowd. Yelled, 'Stefan, is there an "out"?'

'No, Mr Blake.'

'You, Neil, can you leave?'

'No!'

'You.' He pointed to Lyra. 'Lyra, can any of us just walk away from this?'

She saw Stevie, kneeling there. Heard her heart beating hard and felt her stomach turning slow loops in her chest. Said, and part of her hated it, 'No, Jason. We can't.'

'You see, Stevie?' Jason said. 'Everyone else understands

this. But to make things worse, I find out you've tried to turn us in to our enemies. That you tried to contact Amanda Kent to tell her about us, and when you were dismissed as a crazy by her switchboard you tried a man called Harrison Valentin, one of Kent's cronies in the Foundation. You were going to sell every single one of us out.'

Murmurings from the crowd. Lyra heard the words and wished they weren't true, that the sense of betrayal she felt was unfounded. Stevie was crying, shaking his head. 'I didn't,' he said. 'I wasn't going to give anyone else to them. I was just—'

'You were just talking to our mutual enemies, Stevie. The very people who've put us in this position in the first place. And now you've put me in a position I don't want to be in.' Jason reached into his jacket and pulled out a gun. The metal seemed to shimmer in the stark yellow-tinged light from the bulbs overhead. He levelled it at Stevie's head.

The kneeling man began to jabber. Words poured out of him, tumbled together, a playback of a dyslexic transcript describing fear and abject desperation. Jason looked away for a moment, then pulled the trigger.

What struck Lyra first and most completely was a singular notion, something that gave her distance from what she'd just seen. *How can there be so much blood in there?* Somewhere in the recesses of her mind, a voice told her that Stevie was gone, and she didn't so much as object to it.

Jason, his face flushed, looked at the Clocks. Said, voice cold and angry, 'Does anyone else want out? Would anyone else rather betray us, our family, than face up to what we have to do?'

There was silence. No one moved. Almost no one dared meet his eyes. Lyra looked at the feet of the man in front of her. 'Good,' Jason said, somewhere in the tungsten gloom ahead of her. 'Clear him away and put him out in the harbour. We have work to do.'

THIRTY-THREE

They left Garrett's car at his apartment and took a cab back to the Port, and the briefcase. The snow had stopped again, though a thick curtain of looming grey cloud could be seen through occasional gaps in the heavy frozen fog that had blown in off the harbour. The car swam through the murk in its own disconnected bubble, beyond which were only vague transitory shadows flickering in the mist.

'Did Julius tell you anything about the kid?' Maya said.

'Not much. Just that he's edgy as hell and he wants rid of the case. He didn't say anything about the price.'

No one was on the *Adventure*'s deck when they arrived. Bosun LaBelle answered Garrett's knock and let them into the forecastle. She was dressed more modestly than she'd been the day before, but not much. Inside, the ship was utilitarian, no wasted space, no unnecessary clutter. A black and red paint job that gave it the air of a cheap fairground ride, but otherwise Maya approved. You lived on a boat in the Port, you had to maximise what you had because it wasn't like you could get any more.

Julius was sitting in the mess at a round table that looked like it might have once been the top of a cable spool. Stores and supplies hung from the ceiling, various other pieces of furniture and equipment had been folded away against the walls. Dim light through the portholes was matched by orange hurricane lamps. A stove cracked and popped at the far end and the room felt hot after the chill outside. Next to Julius was a young guy, maybe just out of his teens. He wore a grey hoodie and a woollen hat. Silver earrings, a couple of other bits of jewellery, all crucifixes of one sort or another. A jagged, fading scar on one cheek. There was a coffee cup in front of him. From the way he was twitching, Maya guessed maybe he'd had a bellyful already.

'Garrett, lad,' said Julius, waving them to the remaining couple of seats. 'This here is Chapel.'

The kid looked up. Said, ''Lo.' He was the one Maya had seen on Green Street, the one who'd snatched Dominic's briefcase.

'I'm Garrett. This is . . .'

'Maya,' she said. There didn't seem much point sticking with the cover Valentin had given her, not after what she'd learned about him. 'We understand you've got something you want to sell.'

'If you two got what it takes to buy, yeah.' Weary arrogance there, but its angles all wrong, chipped away by something else: a long, slow fear.

'We've got it,' Garrett said. 'But what exactly would we be buying? Julius was short on details.'

Chapel glanced at Julius as though he was looking for confirmation that they were on the level. Said, 'Lot of encrypted data about drug deals, some other small stuff.'

Maya and Garrett exchanged looks. 'Drugs as in blow? Why would we want that, exactly?'

'This ain't street drug deals, small timers hustling crack to nobodies. This is big time major shit. Black market commercial, maybe, or at least *serious* money business by people you'd never think. You want a piece of that action, or you wanna go to the cops, you can do it with this.'

Garrett glanced at Julius, said, 'Why the hell'd you bring this to me? What do I care about drug dealing?'

'You heard of Amanda Kent?' Chapel said.

'Maybe.'

'This is her private shit. Her *personal* stuff. You understand how big this could be now? Only way this could be a bigger deal is if God himself was involved. You crack that data and you'll have everything you need on her.'

'Tell them about the other things too, lad,' Julius said softly.

'Computer's secure, like I said, but there's a day planner and some hard copy. You got stuff on her business, some foundation she's involved with, memos about what they call "the Curse", names, dates, places. Lotta info, you want to make use of that too.'

Garrett was trying to play it cool, but Maya saw his jaw clench. 'The Curse?'

'People on the street talk, y'know? They say there're

places you go, you get unlucky and you get hexed. You gonna die, some time, and no one gonna do nothing to stop it.' Chapel shook his head. 'They say your guts dissolve to blood, your eyes burst and you scream for hours until the end.'

'Sounds like an urban myth to me,' Maya said. 'Nothing does that.'

Chapel smiled, and suddenly looked a lot older and wearier than he was. 'Yeah, I know urban myth. Grew up in the Levels, didn't I? But it doesn't matter. They only talk about it a little in the case. The rest of that stuff is worth serious money if you use it right. How much you want to pay for it?'

Silence for a moment, then Maya said, 'Why were you on Green Street, Chapel?'

His eyes widened. Maya saw his fingers trembling. 'What?'

'You were there on Green Street, or somewhere just off it, watching, where the bomb didn't touch you.'

'What're you talking about?'

'I was there, Chapel. I saw you. I saw you run up and grab the case. Why were you there? You were after the case already. Tell me, and we'll talk payment for what you've got.'

'While you're doing it,' Garrett said, 'you can explain to me how you know what's on that computer if it's all encrypted. Unless there was a Post-it on there that said "secret drug dealing".'

A long quiet. Chapel's eyes narrowed, but he eventually

answered. 'I was watching the guy with the case. Been watching him for days.'

'Who for?'

'Don't matter now. He been going into Willow Heights, talking with the gangs there. Man like that with money like that, he only gonna be there for one thing.'

'You certain of that?'

'3-Fall knew. Or that's what he told me.' Chapel stopped, realising he'd dropped a name he was maybe trying to keep secret, shook his head. 'Look, I ain't gonna lie. I want to sell this thing and be done. You guys got the cash, or not?'

Maya looked at Garrett. She had little money of her own, and wasn't keen on asking Valentin, though she could. Garrett kept his face poker-steady and said, 'A grand.'

'You gotta be fucking kidding. This is serious stuff. You crack it and it could be worth a pile.'

'If it's what you think it is,' Maya said. 'You've got no way of knowing for sure yet. It might be worth nothing.'

'It's what I say it is.'

'And if it *is* that valuable, there's going to be people looking to get it back. If that case belonged to—' she stopped herself saying Dominic's name, 'Amanda Kent and it shows she's involved in the drug trade, she'll kill to recover it. And then there're the people who set the bomb on Green Street.'

'What about them?'

'They want the case too, Chapel,' she said. 'We know that

for a fact. They're looking for it right now, and they know it's in the Port. If I were you, I'd want to shift it fast.'

She saw, then, something slip in his expression, and behind it a bone-tired fear, the look of a man harried and hunted and desperate for escape. 'Five grand,' he said. 'Five grand and it's yours.'

'Two and a half,' Garrett said. 'And that's only if we can find someone who can decrypt it. Otherwise it's worthless.'

'Two and a half?'

'We'll protect you, and the case, while we get the information cracked. Looks like you'll need it.'

'And,' Maya said, 'I want to know all about how come you ended up with it.'

'Two and a half.' Chapel shook his head, slumped a little. 'You got it here?'

'No, but I can get it easy enough. You got the case?'

'No, but I can get it easy enough.'

'Then let's all go do that and get working on this thing. Sooner we do, sooner you've got your cash and you can split.'

Chapel didn't look thrilled. 'Sure.'

'So where are we going?'

'*Number Forty-Three.*'

THIRTY-FOUR

What happened, Chapel told Maya as they walked, was that this guy 3-Fall had fucked up. He was a fixer, a middleman who'd carved out a niche somewhere in the middle of the petty smugglers, traffickers and heavies who plied Kenton and Willow Heights on the other side of the river from the Port. Somehow – Chapel was short on details – 3-Fall had found out that a suit, and a wealthy one at that, had started making regular visits to Willow Heights. 3-Fall made some tentative inquiries, careful not to disturb the delicate threads binding the local underworld together, delicately teasing out enough information to get a bead on the guy. Traced him to Amanda Kent's office, her organisation. No one talked about what he was doing, and 3-Fall didn't want to push. It was big time drugs trading, he said; had to be. No one in Willow Heights could deal weapons in big numbers; the trade in girls working the streets was well established and strictly small time. Nothing else in Willow Heights worth a damn. It had to be drugs. And that meant cash or product, either of them worth taking.

'He had me follow the guy,' Chapel said as they picked their way through the morning press. 'He was making trips every other day, similar route, easy to pick up. We couldn't get into the meetings, or figure out what exactly he was doing there. We wanted to hit them, 3-Fall figured we could take them at a meet, in the car, or at HQ. The meets were secure, bunch of guys and guns, y'know? Car was a maybe, and I was checking out that office building. Watching him when he went in, how many people he had, what they had on the doors. Like maybe we could take him on the run, be outta there before anyone heavy could come down on us. Didn't look good. But then the street blew up.' Chapel shrugged, glanced down at his feet. 'I didn't think much. I was in the alley over the road, blast didn't do more than cover me in dust, hurt my ears. I saw he was down, and I figured when the chance comes, you just gotta take it. They'd never even know the case was gone, explosion like that. Anything coulda happened to it.'

'So how come you've still got it? Are you trying to fence it for this 3-Fall guy?'

Something dark passed, then. '3-Fall's gone. I called him, he told me to sit on it for a couple of days, let the heat pass. Play things gentle. Time I moved, he was gone.'

'Gone as in dead.'

He nodded. 'Gone as in dead.'

'They knew about the case.'

Chapel looked at her with eyes that had seen too much and forgotten too little in the past few days. Said, 'Like I told you, I need the cash so I can get out of here.'

The way he found out, he told Maya, was that he had an argument with Steele, the guy whose place he'd been crashing at. Steele had come home on a mean drunk, these two girls with him, and Chapel's presence turned company into crowd. Sitting around on Steele's couch, smoking weed with the drapes closed 24/7 was, Steele explained in very clear terms, getting to be a bit fucking much. If 3-Fall wanted Chapel to keep his ass out of the public eye, 3-Fall could set him up with a hotel room. 3-Fall was probably sitting up in that apartment of his, blowing Chapel's share of whatever the score was on Filipino boys and meth. Whether Chapel joined him or found somewhere else to sling his ass, Steele said, didn't matter; Steele was fed up with him getting in the way of his shit.

Chapel carried the case hidden in a gym bag along with his other things. Took the night bus into Kenton, walked the last quarter-mile to 3-Fall's building, his mind populating the darkness with 3-Fall's imagined enemies. Remembered his advice and didn't call. Saw no one. 3-Fall's elevator was screwed, like always, so Chapel had to haul his bag six floors by hand, up a bare stairwell lit by flickering green fluorescents. The sounds of the building's other inhabitants filtered through the cheap construction, warped by the acoustics, like concrete whale song in the night. The door swung open when he knocked. 3-Fall was in his front room. He'd been duct-taped to a chair. His fingers were broken, his toes had been shattered and one of his eyes was a ruined mess. His throat had been cut. The blood was dry, but the body hadn't started to smell properly yet. Chapel wanted to puke, stomach clenching and unclenching in time to the beat of his heart. He lurched back out of the apartment and fled the building, the echoing bass of the neighbours' R&B pounding after him.

'Been in the Port since then,' he said. 'Someone else I know helped me out, 'long with their friends.'

'That's where we're going.'

'Yeah.'

'So who is he?'

'She,' Chapel said. 'And her name's Leana. That's all you need to know about her.'

They'd crossed most of the Port by now and were walking along the outer periphery of anchorages and pontoons. Ferries, little more than punts, crossed the Murdoch here, and it was at this borderline that boats working the river or come in off the harbour, too big to make their way through the maze of narrow water paths within the Port itself, would tie up to trade, load or unload cargo. No Border Patrol, no US Customs. A quarter-mile ahead, maybe more, the blocky hulks of the two former prison ships converted to refugee housing squatted grey and ugly in the water. Chapel led them past a knot of a dozen West Africans carrying unmarked cardboard boxes from a fishing boat. Cut to the left, over a walkway made from a single scaffolding plank, shadowed water sucking at the gap between boats beneath them, then across the top of a raft and up on to a small, boxy passenger ferry dating from somewhere in the 1950s, the number 43 painted in cracked yellow lettering on the side of its superstructure. Laundry was hanging outside, mismatched and plenty of it. Maya, dormant Port instinct stirring, figured maybe a dozen or more people. The deck sounded hollow underfoot. Chapel knocked three times and opened the door.

A T-shaped corridor splitting the ferry in two, a stairwell running through the core of the ship. Vinyl flooring cracked and pitted, dried into drifts of dusty flakes at the side of each hard-worn step. The walls were painted with a vivid mixture of spraybomb, new designs overlying each other as time wore on and the occupants and fashions changed. Maya could see names and faces in there, buried in the collage like they were peeping through a neon cartoon jungle. The door to the forward glass-surrounded passenger gallery was open, hinges gone, leaning inwards at a crazy angle. Through it, Maya could see rows of young hash plants growing in plastic bags, somehow surviving in the thin winter light coming through the algae-stained glass.

The body of a young guy lay in the doorway with a fat bullet wound where his nose used to be. Blood was fantailed out across the floor behind him. It was bright red, still fresh. Then, from downstairs, a woman's scream shattered the silence. High and broken by a choked gargling like she was drowning on the noise itself.

THIRTY-FIVE

'Aw, fuck, fuck,' Chapel said and froze. Garrett pulled a gun from beneath his parka and cradled it in both hands. Chapel followed suit, drawing a cheap 9mm that looked like it had passed through a trash compactor. His hand shook.

'Layout?' Garrett said.

Chapel shrugged, still twitchy. 'There're two decks below. Living space, then the engine deck. You have to go through doors from the stairwell on to both of them. It's one switchback per level. There's another set of steps like this near the back of the boat.'

'How many people live here?'

'Dunno. Never been inside much.'

'Where's the case?'

Chapel shrugged again.

Another scream, male this time. Garrett edged on to the stairs, peeped over the rail at the flight below. Started down, keeping his back pressed against the wall. The other two followed.

As they reached the turn, Maya could hear voices. A man, low and heavy, and someone else, high and hurting. Light bled through the door, which like the one upstairs had been kicked off its hinges. Sense of movement near the entryway.

'Let me ask this one more time, darling. I just want to be sure we're all clear on this. I like to be clear. Has anyone else seen the contents of this case? Have you shown it to anyone else?'

A wet, terrified sound. They crept closer.

'That's good to know.' Like a pleased father. 'And you say you can't tell me anything about this "Chapel" who gave it to you? Like, for instance, where he might be right now.'

Another wet noise. Something spattered against the deck.

'She's saying no, Mr Tyrell.' A different man. Very much a subordinate's voice.

'I see. Think hard, though. I want to be certain. This is Jonah, isn't it?' A thud, a wet snapping noise. The woman began to sob. Another thud, another, and the snapping slowly turned to mushing, like someone punching mashed potato.

'There,' Mr Tyrell continued. 'Are you sure you don't want to own up to anything, darling? I'd much prefer it if you didn't follow in Jonah's footsteps, as it were.'

'Fuck this,' Garrett said, and swung into the doorway. Fired twice, deafeningly loud in the confines of the lower deck. Maya risked a look through the opening, saw two men in winter coats lying on the floor like they'd been guarding the door. The corridor was narrow and stubby. More doors led off to either side, all open and all decorated differently. At the far end, another opened out into a wider open space, looked like a communal living area, the old crew mess, and beyond that a mirror set of stairs. There were a half-dozen more men there, in the middle of the wrecked and tossed collection of tables and bench seats. Most dressed like the two by the door, but one she guessed was Mr Tyrell in a suit and tie. He had the briefcase in one hand, a gun in the other, and was crouching next to the sprawled body of a woman with green dreadlocks and a blood-soaked sweatshirt. There was another body, a man, nearby. Maya couldn't see his head at first, just scraps of hair. Then she realised it was there, but horribly flat, all shape and form gone. The bottom of one of Mr Tyrell's trouser legs was sodden, and his shoe was covered in pasted gore. Maya felt her stomach heave, and it was all she could do to force it under control.

Mr Tyrell looked at Garrett somewhat askance, and shot the woman in the back of the skull. 'Deal with this, would you?' he said to his men. Garrett fired twice in his direction, but too fast, and both went wide as Tyrell disappeared into the stern stairwell.

Maya saw his men draw guns, and ducked back out of the way. Two more shots from Garrett, then he swung out of the doorway too as bullets slapped into the steel frame. Chapel, firing gangsta-style, unsighted. Maya felt more rounds hammer the bulkhead she was crouched against, the metal plate at her back shuddering under the impacts. Garrett leaned back into the gap and fired once, then turned, snapped the gun to the right as he switched targets and fired twice more. Silence, then, and he clapped a hand on Maya's shoulder and waved her forward. There were raised mushroom bullet welts in the wall where she'd been sheltering.

There were seven bodies in the ransacked mess. Along with Leana, Jonah and Tyrell's two guys there were three more, all residents to judge from their clothes. Two women, one man. All had been shot. One had a broken leg.

'Fuck, fuck, fuck,' Chapel yelled as they ran through after Tyrell. 'She's dead, man. She's dead.' Staring at the woman's corpse as they passed, her face hidden behind the bloodied dreads. Maya wondered if they'd been more than friends.

Through the door into the stern stairwell. Two more guys waiting for them at the first turn, guns up, but slow and looking uncertain. Chapel, firing fast and wild, caught one of them with four rounds and missed with at least as many. Garrett shot once, twice, as he vaulted the stairs. Caught the second man, crouching, in the top of the knee then in the shoulder as he fell, throwing his gun hand up and away. Garrett reached him before he finished falling and kicked him, hard, in the side of the head. Then they were past and running up the next flight. Maya saw an hourglass tattoo on the man's neck as she passed, picked out stark and clear in black and white and blood in the last flash of light from the door at the top of the stairs before it swung shut.

Up to the deck, Tyrell already vaulting over the rail of the neighbouring vessel, on to a short pontoon section.

Maya followed, lighter and faster than Garrett, better used to the surroundings than Chapel. Tyrell with the case in one hand, the other kept free, no gun. Her feet hit the wooden decking, the snow here scattered with wet sand by one of the neighbouring boats. Memories firing, the layout of the Port, the complex net of paths across the floating village blossoming and unfolding in her mind like an origami flower during a paper spring. Tyrell, storming through the morning foot traffic, took a turn up ahead on to a long line of repurposed coal barges lashed together. An engine sputtering a few yards in front of her, a narrow pirogue untying from the berth. She jumped aboard, nearly lost it, but righted herself before Garrett and Chapel thudded into the boat behind her.

'Via Riunione and the Sisters and it's yours,' she said, thrusting a twenty at the boatman, pointing with her free hand at the fleeing figure of Tyrell. 'We need to catch that guy.'

The man shrugged, muttered something in Portuguese she only half-caught, and gunned the engine, aiming for the point where the last of the barges met the next jetty, cutting the corner on Tyrell.

'What if he heads another way?' Garrett shouted over the motor. 'He'll see what we've done.'

'Can't,' she said. 'Unless it's changed, there's no way off the Sisters except the ends. They're all bulk food trade, bring stuff in by boat. Gotta keep river routes either side of the line.'

The boat scythed through the thick frigid water, Tyrell drawing closer all the while. When they reached the spot where the barges met the Via Riunione and Maya scrambled on to the snowbound jetty, he was ten yards away. He glanced back at his pursuers, expression feral, sprinted away with the three of them chasing hard. Took a turn tight left, up the gangway on to a high-sided deep sea fishing boat, and Maya followed, feet hammering on the ridged wooden board. Along the deck, across the narrow plank bridge to the neighbouring vessel, frozen plant pots dangling from the rope handholds like prayer bells. Burst through a trio of women in bright headscarves, shouts in heavily accented Spanish, then he was turning to drop down the short ladder on to the next boat. Maya saw the hoist line running down from the rusty pulley at the side of the vessel, flashed back to her childhood, racing over the Port with other kids, the cuts and scrapes and the near misses. Jumped from the side without pausing, grabbed the frozen nylon rope with her gloved hands and squeezed it just tight enough to control her descent. Prayed the pulley held, that it'd take her weight and wouldn't break free and crash down on top of her.

Down. Tyrell, startled, only feet ahead now. They were on the flat stern of an anchor handling tug, fresher markings hand-painted somewhere beneath the pockmarked covering of snow. Hopscotch. The boat held one of the Port's makeshift schools. Tyrell raced across the deck, through the door into the hollowed-out superstructure, and into a room full of staring kids, a teacher with her mouth soundlessly open in surprise. Maya was in the doorway, still running, as he cracked the teacher in the face with the briefcase and crashed through the door at the far side of the room. Screaming children, panicked by what had happened, surged away from her, from him, yelling in terror. By the time she'd fought her way through and out into the open again, Garrett and Chapel had caught up with her and Tyrell was no more than a head weaving through the knots of people making their way to and from one of the big prison ships. Maya and Garrett started to follow.

'You gotta be joking if you're thinking of going in there,' Chapel said, pulling them back. 'You don't know what it's like on the *Winter*? He's going in there, he's got friends there, you know what I mean? We follow and maybe no one sees us again.'

Maya looked up at the boxy grey hulk, pitted with rust streaks where rain had run past its dark, square windows and the lines of bars like teeth inside. Five storeys of steel-encased misery, sweat and dank air. Like most other people in Newport, she knew of the *Winter* and its sister the *Bitterness*, but they'd been towed into position and stuffed with refugees some time after she'd moved out of the Port.

'It's after my time,' she said. 'Is it really that bad in there? You said you had a police posting here, Garrett.'

'I never had a reason to go near the thing.' Garrett rubbed his jaw. 'Julius, people like him, they all warned me off checking either of them out. We need Tyrell, though.'

'He's going to come out.' She told him about the Clock tattoo. 'He has to come out. I think they were Blake's people.'

'Right now it's just him in there, and either he's gone to hide or he's got help there. But either way, if Blake wants the case, he'll need an escort for it.' He looked along the pontoon, at the straggling lines of motley-clad people shuffling in and out of the *Winter*'s narrow black maw, Tyrell now dropping to a brisk walk, one figure in the flow. A couple of them had small handcarts. 'Trade,' Garrett said. 'It can't be that bad.'

He set off again, and, left with the choice between standing on the freezing planking like an idiot or following, Maya had no option but to trail after him with Chapel in tow.

A wide steel gangway led up from the water to a watertight door leading into what had probably once been the ship's lower cargo deck. The *Winter* had been a container ship, but its superstructure had been removed and its deck covered in Lego-like stacks of welded modular units like cargo boxes, cell-like rooms joined by narrow gantries and divided here and there by wider rusted spaces open to the sky. Newport City council had run both quasi-prison barges as temporary accommodation for asylum seekers for a couple of years until they became unmanageably overcrowded and the system collapsed; they were still on long-term lease from the owner but no longer administered in any official capacity, or at least no more so than the rest of the Port.

Maya was expecting gang guards, heavies from one national group or another, to be watching the entryway. Charge a price for admission, keep out anyone they didn't like the look of. But there was no one. On the other side was a crowded hallway open to the storey above, like the main block of a jailhouse, both floors lined with tubular metal stalls draped with tattered plastic sheeting that thrummed limply in the breeze from the door and the swirl of sound. Voices echoing around the chamber like the inside of a drum, a white noise blur of different languages and dialects, hawking and haggling. The air was hot and sweaty and tasted of stale metal and old cooking spices. Fizzing orange lamps hung from the upper reaches.

'Jesus,' Maya said, feeling the crowd press against her. 'So many people.'

'There's Tyrell.' Garrett nodded towards a barred door, chained open, and a corridor that led deeper into the ship. Tyrell was weaving through it, his head barely visible above the mob.

Maya fought her way past a woman carrying three screeching chickens in a basket made from an old shopping cart, felt one hand, then another, pluck at her pockets and find nothing, heard a baritone voice bellowing, 'Water purifiers! Recyclers!' in the Port's trade pidgin. Rode the crowd's turbulence and the waves of choked stale air all the way to the door, saw Garrett elbowing his way through a few yards behind with Chapel knocked and flustered in his wake. The corridor was lined with graffiti covering the cracked and peeling stencils left from the *Winter*'s council-run days. There was a huge neon mural of a woodland scene down one wall, turned shades of muddy brown by the dim lights, and an insane mass of tags down the other. Signs near the entry pointed to the *Portal*, presumably the name for the market, and *Quarters*, *Walk*, *Boats* and *Scrubs* further inside.

The tide of people carried them inwards, sluggish and chaotic, the suck and pull of dock water trapped in the shallows. Maya instinctively drew into herself, walked defensively, wary of worse than thieves in the press now around them. Down a hallway, then, lined with people hawking wares from narrow racks of wheeled shelving – food, small jars of heating oil, strings of dead city pigeons. Past a sudden break to the left and the glare of the sky outside looking down, grey and cold and unforgiving, on a space that might have been a gap between stacks or just an opening in the core of the one above them: the Walk, a tiny frozen steel park, a glimpse of air and a reminder of the world beyond, perhaps once an exercise yard.

The hall opened out into an intersection surrounding a broad steel stairwell, switchbacks running up and down through the gloomy heart of the *Winter*. People trading junk on blankets, begging with their children or playing dice lined the junction. The air stank of mineral oil and desperation.

'Which way?' Garrett said. 'This place is a warren. Tyrell could be anywhere.'

Chapel shrugged. 'Start by trying upwards. Doubt he'd want to hide down in the dark.'

'Maya?'

'Yeah, I guess,' she said, tearing her eyes away from a twig-thin kid maybe six years old trying and failing to coax a few cents or some food out of the passing mass. 'Find some people to ask – he's not one of the locals. Someone'll know. There're only so many stacks, so many places to hide.'

Garrett and Chapel began the climb. Maya's foot was on the first step when she saw, on the wall of the flight below, a spraybomb stencil of a razor blade in deep, shadowed red. Garrett and Chapel bounded up the stairs but Maya sidestepped, felt herself drawn downwards.

'Let's split,' she said to the others, heard how abrupt she sounded, tried to explain. 'Time's ticking. You check up, I'll check down and we'll meet back here. If we don't find him either way, we can move along the ship, try the next stack.'

Garrett frowned. 'Sure?'

'Yeah. I'll be fine. Local, aren't I?'

His expression, worried and suspicious in equal measure, as she descended.

THIRTY-SIX

Emi was working on a painting when the call came. A sumi-e portrait of herself standing with Charlie, her arm round him. A parting gift for him that she'd been working on quietly when he wasn't around. Not quite right yet, something in the faces didn't feel the way it should. She stood back, picked up the phone with her free hand. Didn't recognise the number on the caller ID.

'Is that Emi Nakano?' A woman's voice, faint trace of a New York accent. 'I hope I'm not disturbing you. I'm Dr Helena Moore. I'm a biotechnician – a medical specialist – working for Amanda Kent. She met with your partner, Charlie, recently. Did he mention it?'

'Yes. What can I do for you?'

'Well, it's more what I can do for you.' Dr Moore sounded nervous, embarrassed. Not much of a phone manner. 'Miss Kent really appreciates what Charlie tried to do after the bombing, and she offered anything she could to help. We know about your, uh, situation and we think we might be able to do something about it.'

Emi felt her mouth go dry. Even knowing that it was nonsense – if she'd learned nothing else over the past year, it was that there was nothing anyone could do about the Curse – it was impossible to shake the sudden spike of hope. Doomed, stupid optimism, a lotto player's false dream. 'You're mistaken,' she said. 'It can't be changed.'

'That may not be true. We could be on the verge of a breakthrough, a new way of approaching it. Uh . . . well, it'll be a lot easier to explain this in person. Are you free at the moment? Could you come in and see what we're doing? You could decide if you want to work with us, maybe do some very simple preliminary checks?'

'Where?' she said.

'Where' was a massive house on the North Shore, a low, sprawling, ranch-style place called Shinecourt. The gates swung open as her cab approached, someone somewhere watching on camera. Up a gravel driveway lined with cedars to a dark set of double doors. Outside, under an umbrella to ward off the snow, a man in a suit, on his own. He didn't look like a scientist. Heavily scarred, like he'd had some kind of industrial accident.

'Miss Nakano?' He held out the umbrella. Gruff, eyes to match the voice. 'You talked to Dr Moore on the phone. My name's Cutter.'

'Where's Dr Moore?' A twinge of added nerves. 'This doesn't look like the sort of building where you'd do medical research.'

'You'd be surprised. I'll take you to the laboratory.'

He led her through a broad, tiled hall and down a lengthy corridor running along the spine of the building. The inside was a mix of warm reds and ochres, dotted with pot plants and carefully spaced oil paintings. Abstracts, for the most part. What Emi thought of as good corporate quality: pleasant without saying very much; decoration, rather than art.

'So you've had the Curse for a long time now,' Cutter said, no sign that it was a question at all. 'Must be difficult, having that hanging over you.'

'Yes. How do you – how does Miss Kent – know about the Curse? The police keep it a secret.'

'An acquaintance of hers had it, and, of course, she's in good standing with the cops. Main thing I'd imagine with something like this isn't so much that it's a secret from everyone, but that it's enough of a secret to keep it out of the press. Down this way.' Directing her to the right, a single walnut door whose lock audibly snicked open as he approached and held it for her. 'You got a lot of family, friends, people to support you? I suppose that'd be a big help.'

'I have enough.'

'Good, good.' The ghost of a smile on scarred lips. 'It must be a big comfort to you.'

This corridor was different, narrower and less carefully bland. There were pictures hanging from the wall every few feet, photographs, and Emi found herself concentrating on them rather than Cutter and his unnerving questions. Some of the photos were old, faded black and white, others newer. Almost all showed either formally posed gatherings or individuals, others commercial projects. At first she thought they must represent whatever business Amanda Kent involved herself in, but then she realised that some pre-dated her. Some showed public figures, both national and local to Newport City, shaking hands or standing with men and women Emi didn't know. The tiny plaque beneath one said: *Lieutenant Agnes Saganowski, services rendered on Chalienski case.*

'History,' Cutter said, beside her. 'Important to remember steps along the path, isn't it?'

The final photo before he steered her to the right, down a curving flight of stairs, showed a group of a dozen people in expensive suits and businesswear, one of whom Emi recognised as Amanda Kent. The plaque read: *Foundation annual meeting, St Nevis.*

The broad steps led down into a basement level and a bare, square space lined on one side with gleaming steel lockers, on the other by a marble table with an open metal box on top of it. Through a pair of sheet glass sliding doors, closed, she could see a wide, airy room, all soft, clean lines and touchscreen displays, dominated by what looked like an MRI machine to one side. There were two people, a man and a woman, dressed in high-collared lab whites, standing a little way inside the room, waiting for her.

'Put any electrical or electronic items in the box,' Cutter said.

'Why?'

'Interference.' He gestured at the air around them. 'The lab's basically a metal mesh cage – even got tiny wires in the glass – to keep out as much noise as possible. Can't say I really understand it all, but they don't like cell phones in there. Not that they work anyway. You pop anything like that in the box here, I'll put it in one of the lockers and you can have the key. Please.'

She looked at him for a moment, then did as he asked.

'Good,' he said. Waved a security badge over the glass doors and they hissed open. 'Let's get this started.'

THIRTY-SEVEN

The noise of the upper deck faded as Maya descended, echoed crowd hubbub from upstairs mingling with the scattered sharper sounds rising from the diesel-scented depths. She traced the outline of the razor blade tag. It overlaid several older designs but it had been there long enough to collect a thin film of grime of its own. Two people, sexless beneath layer after ragged layer, stumbled past her on their way to the Portal, speech slurred in a language she didn't understand. She saw a flash of white eyes like cave fish, pupils unnaturally pinched, and felt a momentary fear that the symbol was nothing to do with the Razor Gate but was just the mark of a gang below decks and she was walking into trouble. Carried on down the stairs anyway, round the switchback, and descended the rusting steel to the floor below.

The stairwell opened on to a relatively wide hall that ran maybe twenty yards to a plastic curtain, tied open. Beyond it, the first of them barely visible in the darkness, a dingy string of subdivisions carved out of what must once have been one of the cargo holds. There was another Gate marker halfway down the corridor, between two open watertight doors. There were three people slumped in one corner of the hall, motionless. Maya saw a rubber tourniquet on the arm of one of them. Voices came from one of the doorways, one measured, another frantic. She walked quietly, peeped through the opening.

Inside, the cramped room, which looked as if it had once been machinery space, had been converted to a kind of strange chapel. Mismatched folding chairs were lined in short rows on either side of the central aisle. Shelves on the walls held a dizzying array of items, a nonsensical mix of objects in various stages of decay, some handmade, some scavenged, others looking like antiques, little family heirlooms. Between them, hundreds of scratched words and names in a dozen different languages as well as the Port's peculiar hybrid tongue. It was lit by a mixture of dim orange fluorescents and small oil burners dotted amongst the offerings. At the back of the room was a red-painted cut steel mockup of a doorway, human-sized, in the shape of a razor blade. In front of it, a hunched, shaven-headed man in a stained brown poncho-like robe made out of an old blanket was listening to a young woman, no older than Maya, in tears as she pleaded with him in Spanish. Maya tucked herself in the shelter of the doorway, listening.

'She is so unwell,' the woman said. 'Her fever is worse and she's barely woken at all in the past day.'

'Dr Confianca, in the Third Passage?' The man, the priest

or whatever he was, answered in Port lingo. 'Have you spoken to him? He might be able to help your daughter.'

'I have, I have, but he says there's nothing more he can do. Not here.'

'I see.'

'I don't want her taken, Sevité. I don't want her to go.'

The priest nodded, and patted her on the hand. 'I cannot promise results. The Gate decides who passes through and who does not. But perhaps we can persuade it to stay closed for her.'

Maya felt a hand on her arm. Turned to see an old woman, eyes red and bared teeth long and inhuman against heavily recessed gums. Her fingers, skeletally thin, clamped round Maya's sleeve, and she hissed. Maya, shocked, jerked her arm away. Saw nothing but animal hostility in the woman's eyes and backed off. Shadows shifted in the hallway behind her, and Maya turned and hurried deeper inside the ship. Into the old cargo hold and the plywood partitions that split it into shabby, stale living quarters for individual families.

A repetitive whirr and wheeze of escaping air like a mechanical respirator or a busted iron lung. Tidelines of rising damp climbing, comb-like, from the floor up each wooden wall. Location markings, makeshift addresses like those used in the Port outside and on the signs in the upper levels of the *Winter*, but less ornate, like tally marks. As though no one and nothing down here was worth anything more elaborate. The smells of cooking and old waste intermingled and combined into a single scent like baked lentils. Voices, kept low and muffled by some common etiquette arising from the lack of privacy. The hold was lit by caged fluorescents whose plastic housings were caked in layered graffiti, a meaningless patchwork turning the light a squalid quilt of colours like a dim and hellish carnival ride.

She came to one partition whose walls had been lined with chickenwire to which had been tied dozens of rolled scraps of paper, some torn and yellowing, others neater and fresher. Dead stubs of candles sat in swirls of congealed wax by the door, and she saw several roughly made models of what were plainly gates of varying sorts. She tweaked open the end of one of the paper rolls, saw scratchy writing inside. Prayer scrolls. Wondered at the significance of this particular dwelling, whether it belonged to someone like the priest she'd seen, or if it was a shrine to a recently deceased occupant.

Crying, behind her. She turned, saw, a few yards down an adjoining corridor, a child sitting huddled against the wall with his knees drawn up under his chin. From his size, she guessed he was about six or seven, wearing goodwill hand-me-downs a couple of years too big for him.

'What's the matter?' she said. 'Are you OK?'

He sniffed. 'Doesn't matter. Don't tell him where I am.'

'Tell who?'

'Doesn't matter. Anyone. No one.'

She knelt down in front of him. Said, 'If it doesn't matter, why're you crying? You got family in here? Someone to look after you?'

A look passed across his face, and Maya figured his family might be the problem right now. 'I'm just hiding for a while,' he said. 'I'm hiding because I did wrong and I don't want to be taken away. I'll be OK.'

'Taken away? What did you do?'

'I just broke something. I didn't mean to; it was an accident.' He sniffed, wiped his nose with his sleeve. 'But my pa says if I do bad, the Ferryman will come and take me. He says that's what happens to kids who don't do what they're told. The Ferryman takes them.'

'Are you hiding from the Ferryman, or from your dad?'

He dodged the question. 'I don't want to be taken away. I've *seen* him. I've seen the Ferryman here on the ship. He'll take me away if he finds me.'

'Where will he take you?'

'Away. And then you're gone, and you don't come back.'

'Carlos!' A man's voice, behind them. Broken pidgin, heavily accented, somewhere Central American. 'You, get away from my boy. What you doing? Carlos!'

'I was just asking your son why he was upset,' she said, standing. The man was short, squat and sweating hard. He looked like a boar that had sat on a spike. 'What's all this about the Ferryman?'

'You get away from him! This not your business. You hear?' He strode up to Maya, jutted his face into hers, all jawline and scowl. Back into Spanish: 'Carlos, get over here. I've had to search all over the ship for you. You're going to have such a beating when we get home you won't be able to walk for a week. What were you doing talking to this stupid bitch, huh, idiot?'

Maya punched him in the face without thinking. Felt a stab of fear as she realised what she was doing, too late to stop it. Luckily, the father seemed even more surprised than she was. Her fist smashed into his eye and he recoiled, his mouth a shocked O, as pain lanced through her hand. She hit him again with her left, straight to the temple. Remembered something from a self-defence class years before, about not giving a sucker an even break. He dropped, moaning and dazed. By the time she turned back to check on Carlos, the boy had vanished, run somewhere deeper into the hold, gone.

If Tyrell was on this level too, he was as good as disappeared. But if they found him and the briefcase wasn't what they'd hoped, she could always bring Garrett back to take a proper look at the strange little cult down here in the dark. Movement, footsteps approaching the way she'd come, and Maya pictured the priest and the strange old woman. Cursing as she clutched her bruised hands, she walked hurriedly away, looking for another set of steps back up to the Portal and the others.

THIRTY-EIGHT

'Which gang is it Tyrell's got running security for him?' Julius asked. A couple of his people were watching the *Winter*, ready to call if Tyrell moved. 'Not that it makes much difference; as bad as each other, the whole blasted lot.'

'The people we spoke to said it was the Hierro Muerto,' Garrett said. Tyrell was, apparently, holed up at the top of the south stack with a hulker gang babysitting his people while he waited for something. Either he was folding down his operation there before returning to Blake, or he was waiting on a pickup and reinforcements. The people Garrett and Chapel had talked to didn't know either way, just that he'd taken over the top of one of the stacks.

'Don't know much about them. You wouldn't be able to buy them off at any rate, lad. Fighting through 'em on that ship will only get you killed. You're gonna need to figure this but good.' Julius stood, patted Garrett on the shoulder and excused himself.

'There's the cult below decks. We could look into that

and hope we can snatch the case on the move,' Maya said.

'I want the case.' Garrett, staring at the wall like he could see through it to where the *Winter* was moored. 'A cult can't save Emi. I want the case. Hitting them on the go's no good – too public, too much to go wrong, and if they leave by the river and the case ends up in the water it's gone. Anyone going in as well will freeze to death in no time. No, we need to get to Tyrell, before he can get off the boat or Blake's people can come help him.'

'If what's in it, those computer files, are locked, are we going to be able to crack them?'

'You're the journalist. You know anyone who can do it?'

'You're the cop,' she said. Shrugged. 'There's a guy I met at the groups, working at Bryant University, something to do with artificial intelligence research. I don't know if he'd be able to help directly, but even if he can't he must know some geek types who can.'

'Adam Nyberg?'

She nodded. 'He seemed like a decent guy. Plus he's a Clock, so he already knows about the Curse.'

'Emi knows him. Call him. Then we'll figure out how to get our hands on the case.'

Maya called Nyberg, explained the situation. Much to her surprise, he said, 'Send it to me when you have it and I'll try to break it. Tell me, Eliza—'

'Maya. My real name's Maya. It's a long story.'

'OK.' He sounded surprised, but only for a moment. 'Well, have you done anything like this before?'

'Not as such.'

'If you're lucky, it'll be like fixing a busted computer. Do you have a memory stick?'

'On my keys.'

'Download a rescue operating system on to it and boot from that. You'll be able to copy the files even if the computer's normally password-locked. Then send them to me.'

'Thanks, Adam,' she said. 'I wasn't sure you'd be able to help, or that you'd want to.'

'You said you wanted to save a friend's girlfriend before her time runs out. Emi Nakano's date's almost here so I assume it's her. There aren't so many of us it's hard to figure out, and Emi's a friend, although I've never met Charlie. And like I said, I don't want to go with any regrets. I'm happy to help. You owe me that story though.'

They'd been running through, then discarding, ideas for getting on to the *Winter* for thirty minutes when Chapel suggested the Rats.

'Leana talked about them a couple of times. Smugglers, get into anywhere, especially the prison boats, for a price. Maybe they can get us on board and up to the stacks before he leaves.'

'I'll talk to Julius,' Garrett said.

Silence for a while after he left. Then Maya said, 'So why'd you quit the Levels? Friends on the outside?'

'Some trouble.'

'Enemies on the inside then.'

'Why does it matter, girl? What's it to you why I left?'

'Just curious,' she said. 'It seems like you're short on friends now, so maybe I was just trying to get to know you a little. Making conversation. But you don't want to tell me, that's fine. I'm easy.'

Silence again for a moment, then: 'I used to hustle whatever shit I could. Pretty good at it, too. Got to be, you wanna last long in the Levels, make something of yourself. But you break the surface and things get dicey, right? You're running risks, and chances are one of them'll go bad. I was, and it did. Got in trouble with some serious people. But I knew guys on the outside, so I had a way out.'

'Guys like 3-Fall.'

'Uh-huh. Liquidated what I could, got out of there before someone took me out. Can't go back now.'

'At least you got out,' Maya said. 'The Port's hard enough to escape, but the Levels must be nearly impossible.'

The young guy looked at her for a moment, then turned back to the window. 'Guess it's easier if you don't have to do it legitimate. No one gonna give a guy living in the Levels a job. You work in cash all the time, it's not so complicated.'

'Who were these serious people? What did you do to them to have them after you?'

'Nothing.' A look in his eyes which told Maya he'd turned them over, cheated on a deal or sold them out to an enemy. Plain as daylight. Chapel might have known how obvious it was too, because he said no more.

★ ★ ★

'This is doable,' the one they called King Rat said, some time later. Outside, the early night of winter was falling fast. He had a deep, raw voice. A squat, powerful man with dozens of intricate tattoos running up each side of his muscular neck. He had a beard in two braids, piercings above one scarred eye, and must've been in his fifties. He'd arrived on the boat at Julius's invite, the man, apparently, who could get them to Tyrell.

The two other rats with him, younger and leaner, nodded. 'Lots of ways to get around the *Winter*. Some people watch, some people forget.'

'We'll have to figure out pay la—'

King Rat waved a hand. 'There's anger in Port Blackwater because of what happened on *Number Forty-Three*. You say these people did this, and they come from onshore. Port looks after its own, so this we do for the dead. Their cortège procession tonight. Rats help you as our gift for the passing.'

'Tyrell could move any time.'

The royal smile. Gold teeth glittered. 'He not going anywhere.'

One of the younger ones – Maya thought his name had been Norre – cracked a feral grin. 'Your man's holed up on upper level with two friends. El Hierro Muerto been paid to watch their asses, keep people away. And they been paid to do it until midnight. They were real specific about that.'

'Hulkers got boys on all the stairwells there,' the King

said. 'But they not too clever, or not paid enough. Rats think they only got eyes on the paths for *normals*. Rats get you in and out and they never know you were there, you quiet enough.'

'How many men?'

'A dozen, maybe more,' the second Rat said. He was taller and dressed like a ship's engineer on some Victorian steam liner. 'But if you do it right, you won't have to worry about them.'

Garrett shrugged. 'Something always goes wrong.'

Maya's phone rang. Harrison Valentin.

THIRTY-NINE

Maya, waiting on a street corner in the cold. Two blocks from the outer reaches of the Port, in a belt neighbourhood, shabbily respectable, one of those that had grown up in symbiosis with the waterborne settlement. It was as far from Julius's boat as she could get in the time between Valentin calling and him picking her up. She tried not to think about what Fisk had said: Chalienski, drowned in a bathtub for screwing with Valentin. Tried not to think too of all the time they were losing, waiting for her while Tyrell finished whatever it was he was doing on the *Winter*. And for what?

'Let's check in,' he'd said. 'I'd like to know how you're getting on and I'm sure there are ways I can help.'

'Why not talk now?'

'No phones, Maya. Let's do this in person. Besides, I have something for you. I'm heading out now. Where can I pick you up?'

Laundromats, internet cafés, general stores and light delivery services. Signs advertising bike couriers, immigration legal services, a hundred different types of international phone card. Half a dozen tuk-tuks of one sort or another, ideal for ferrying goods down into the cramped streets by the waterside. There was a bar further down the road, probably some light, inoffensive hooking, but both services were well catered for in the Port itself. The neighbourhood was flash-frozen in the day's snow, an orange-stained cinderblock update of a Dickens novel.

Then, glittering blue-white headlights, three bulbs a side, and an engine growling in the night. Valentin's Ferrari purred to a halt next to her, gleaming in the streetlamps like it was looking for a zebra to pounce on. The passenger door slid open.

'You don't believe in "low profile", do you, Mr Valentin?' she said as she buckled her seatbelt, some four-point rallying affair.

White teeth gleamed in the ice glimmer from the dash lights. 'Now, now. What's the point of having the money to buy this city twice over if you can't enjoy it? I'm happy for people to see a beautiful woman climbing into my car. So long as they don't get to overhear our conversation.'

She ignored that. 'It's not exactly suited to icy roads either.'

'Life should be risk, Maya.' He hit the gas and spun the Ferrari round, was doing sixty before they passed the next intersection.

'This is a residential area. People live here.'

'I'm a monster,' he said. Let it tick over until they turned on to one of the main feeder roads and he hit the gas on the broader streets. Evening traffic, but he swerved in and out of it like he was a cop using his lights. 'So, how are you doing in your hunt for our missing property?'

'Shouldn't you say "your search for the people who killed your friend"? Play on my emotions a little?' She felt slightly ill. Valentin seemed to have little interest in keeping the car in a straight line.

'Your priority, not mine. It's just a happy chance that they overlap.' A moment to flash her a grin, and Maya felt her pulse quicken, knowing his eyes weren't on the road. 'But you're right, I should have done.'

'It's going OK. I've got a few leads I'm following up, but nothing concrete yet.'

'Well, I'm glad I checked. Bore me with details; I'm fascinated. I know you've not visited the support groups today.'

'Even without Anton?' She caught herself, said, 'Even without him following me?' Tried not to show that she knew Anton was dead, that she'd been there with Fisk. That she knew Valentin's secrets.

'My information comes from all sorts of places, Maya. So, you've learned what you needed to from the support groups, and now you're working in Port Blackwater. Do you think our thief, or the man behind our bomber, is based there? I'd love to see what's inside that charming head of yours.'

She was quiet for a moment as the car swung on to the off ramp, centrifugal force pulling at her harness. Thought about what she was going to tell him. 'The bomber was. They had some kind of operation there, but it's gone now. He got away. I've got a couple of possible leads on the brief-case. The kid who took it was a gangbanger from Willow Heights. Dominic was doing something there, but I don't know what. The kid might have known him from that.'

'What's his name?'

'The kid? Julio,' she said, pictured a Honduran kid she'd had a crush on when she was little. 'They call him "Little Shark".'

'Interesting.'

They switched lanes, whipped past a police cruiser. No blue flashing lights behind them, no pursuit. Maya wondered if he believed her. What would happen if he didn't. 'I found a guy who knows him,' she said. 'Ex-dealer. I'm waiting to hear back from him, see if he's been able to get in touch. Then I'll see if I can cut a deal for the case. That's why I'm not at the groups.'

'You think you can do it? Any cash you need to front, just ask, of course.' He seemed almost amused.

'Sure.'

'Good, good. Now, reach under your seat and you'll find a little present.'

She pulled out a neoprene bag containing a small steel box. 'What is it?'

'Open it.' Row houses flashing past his window. They were heading back towards the Port.

Inside the box was a small chrome key. It looked like a

locker key, or maybe the sort for a small padlock. It was attached by a metal ring to a leather bracelet.

'Put it on,' Valentin said. 'You'll need it.'

'What for? What does it open?'

'I wouldn't want to ruin any surprises now. But I'm absolutely sure you'll be grateful for it when the time comes.'

The car slewed to a stop at the spot where he'd picked her up. He watched her shrug, frowning, and buckle the bracelet round her wrist, then unlocked and opened the door.

'Good luck, Maya,' he said as she climbed out. 'And don't forget to keep me in the loop. I want to know I'm getting my money's worth.'

FORTY

Cutter excused himself as the two scientists showed Emi around. 'You know what you've got to do,' he told them. 'We need primary and secondary avenues open for use. We're not going to get many cracks at this. Clear?'

Left without waiting for an answer. Forced smiles from the pair of them while they waited for the doors to hiss shut, and then they began the tour of Amanda Kent's personal investment in the Curse. The range of equipment they had was small, suited to one purpose only, which Dr Stringer, the male scientist, said was something to do with determining what chemicals the Curse generated to dissolve its microscopic toxin sacs and bring about the end. 'Crack that,' he said, showing her spinning 3D models on one of the touchscreen panels, 'and we can block the enzyme or smother the sacs to provide a second barrier layer. It wouldn't eliminate them, but it'd stop them causing, uh, well, you know.'

Death. Trying again to suppress that absurd, irrational spike of hope. 'What do you need from me?'

'We'll run some tests – chemical markers mostly, designed

to latch on to the sac walls. They should tell us something about how the sacs are made. When we know that . . .'

Dr Moore flashed Emi a nervous grin and said, 'Right, we'll do some preliminaries, shall we? Shan't take long.'

A batch of injections – trace chemicals, they said, and harmless – and a scan in the MRI-type machine. A flood of new models, charts and graphics on the screens, and Emi wondered for a moment where the old data had come from. Then they led her down another corridor at the back of the lab room, gave her a tour of the rest of the small complex. One hallway had a half-dozen rooms like hospital treatment suites, more sliding doors, all open.

'These are our guest rooms; hopefully, one day we'll be able to treat people in batches here,' said Dr Moore. 'Once we have the cure, we'll bring you back for its administration. We'll need to keep you under careful observation while we monitor its progress. Still, that's all for the future. Do you like them?'

Nervous energy from the pair of them, awkward and uncomfortable. The rooms were nice, in a sleek hotel sort of way. Pastel colours, comfortable angle-free Scandinavian furnishings, daylight-mimicking lights.

'Nice,' she said. 'If you can make a cure and I have to come back, Charlie gets to stay with me, doesn't he?'

'Of course, of course.' Dr Moore checked her watch. Said, 'I think we're done for today. No sense waiting for the test results just yet – they'll take a while to run. We'll give you a call when—'

She stopped as Cutter strode into the room, the scars by his mouth pulling his lips into a leer. 'Cancel that,' he said. 'Word from Miss Kent is that our guest should stay.'

Emi felt her gut flip. 'What? I'm not—'

'Miss Kent thinks that we should be careful that the trace compounds these two gave you don't have an adverse reaction. She thinks if there's any risk of that, you should stay here until it passes, where we can monitor you. Where, I might add, you can't have second thoughts and back out of this either. Look on the bright side, maybe they'll tell us something and you'll get your cure, huh?'

'Mr Cutter!' Dr Moore said. 'This really isn't necessary.'

Dr Stringer shook his head. 'Or helpful. This woman is cooperating with us of her own free will. Isn't she already going through enough? This is monstrous!'

'Free will, doctor?' Cutter laughed. 'Have you told her that if you can't figure out what makes the little *things* full of poison in her head, your job is to make sure that you get a sample of whatever it is that breaks them down at the moment of death?'

Dr Stringer glanced at Emi, looking miserable. Didn't deny it. 'We were hoping we wouldn't have to,' he said. 'We're confident of determining the makeup of the sac structures before then. I'm sorry, Miss Nakano. We should've said. We're under orders. But we thought – we think – we can do it.'

'And you know what'll happen – what I'll do to you – if you don't carry out those orders,' Cutter said. 'Miss Kent feels we need a backup approach on the Curse since we can't guarantee Mr Wheeler's effects will still be in a readable condition when I recover them. Without names, locations, the details of his negotiations, and with the others so close on our tail, we need a secondary way into the technology. For that we need you to do your damn jobs, and we need a Clock who's close enough to the end to mean we won't have to sit on our hands for weeks. So suck it up, or face the consequences. Miss Kent hired you because you're supposed to be the best at this sort of thing. Time to shine, doctors. No backing out now.'

'Charlie will know where I've gone,' Emi said, her heart thumping. 'I left him messages. He'll come to find me.'

Cutter held up his hand as his phone chimed. Raised it to his ear and turned away from the other three, listening. 'Excellent,' he said into the phone. 'Have your men move against the primary as soon as they're ready. I'll bring reinforcements and be at the secondary within thirty minutes. The chopper's fuelled and waiting. You're sure on both? I don't want to find out they've got another bolt-hole if they beat us to it.'

Silence, someone replying at the other end of the connection. Then he said, 'Good.' Pocketed the phone and looked at Emi. 'It doesn't look like Charlie's going to be getting your messages any time soon. Hard luck, Miss Nakano. If you'll excuse me.'

'No, Mr Cutter, this isn't right!' Dr Stringer threw himself at the other man, flailing. Cutter back-handed him across the face and sent him sprawling to the floor at the foot of the bed in an untidy heap.

'We can't do this without a Clock,' Cutter said. 'Top of your field or not, I'm not sure we can't do it without both of you. There are always more scientists. Clear? Now get out, the pair of you. We'll deal with this when I return.'

Dr Stringer picked himself up, looking close to tears. He shook out his lab uniform, smoothing out the rumples as he strode past his tormentor. Looked back at Emi over Cutter's shoulder and said, 'I'm sorry.' As she watched, his eyes flicked to the bottom of the bed, head tilted slightly.

Emi glanced down and saw the corner of Dr Stringer's security badge peeping from the shadows under the bed. Felt her heart leap, stepped forward to block it from Cutter's view. Stammered, a reason to speak hard to get out, 'Please, Mr Cutter . . . I don't . . . at least tell someone to feed my cats. I don't want them to starve.'

He left without a word, swiping his ID over the door to lock it behind him. She waited until he was long gone before dropping to one knee as if tying her shoelace, in case they had cameras watching her, and reaching under the bed for the security badge.

FORTY-ONE

Norre led them along a complex string of smaller routes, mostly steering clear of the main jetties, to an ancient lobster vessel corroding at its berth, serving as the mother berth for a string of small sampans and traders' skiffs.

'Stoker, Boss,' he said, introducing them to the man and woman who crewed one of the boats. 'Gonna get us all on to *Winter* hulk, easy.'

The two nodded, eyes disinterested. They paddled out into the current, took the boat slowly round to the water side of the prison ship. Maya wondered if they'd be spotted by anyone looking out for them, but the Rats didn't seem worried. The flank of the *Winter* that faced the open river was riddled with gaps and holes, makeshift jetties protruding into the water like misshapen coral fronds. Half a dozen small boats were tied up there, more coming and going, bringing fish, taking away garbage, routine trade best carried out on the river. The Rats brought them into one of these berths, well away from the aft stack where Tyrell was hiding out. Then into the ship itself, down a narrow flight of stairs so steep it was almost a ladder.

They took a dizzying set of turns, through narrow hallways, a couple of cramped sets of living quarters, down another flight into what seemed to be old engineering space. Past a couple of other people, Norre saying nothing, just nodding, other Rats or their friends, making connections, keeping the route clear. Up a ladder, then, and through an open maintenance hatch into what must have been either a trash clearance system or the narrow spaces left by machinery removed when they stripped out the *Winter*'s engines. Makeshift ladders made from loops of clamped steel cable broken by switchbacks through largely derelict space littered with the amputee remains of old pipework and wiring.

They emerged in a stubby dead end formed by an uneven join between units. Norre left them with some last, hissed directions at a door rusted shut and a closet marked with illegible decals, open, a padlock still hanging limp and broken from its clasp. High up in the *Winter*'s stacks, the air was colder, less stale. Garrett waited for Maya and Chapel to gather themselves, then led them down to the end of the corridor. He leaned round the corner, looked briefly along the grey metal hall to the room occupied by Tyrell. Doors all closed, no one outside. Voices and distant laughter echoed from the opposite direction; men from the Hierro Muerto, maybe, watching the stairs. He said, quietly, 'Clear. They must be inside.'

Each room had a maritime-style steel door that could be

twist-locked from the inside. Garrett saw that several of the ones they passed had clearly been forced in the past, and one was missing entirely, the opening covered in a tacked sheet of yellow plastic tarp. Tyrell's had been broken into at some point, and while the door was shut it no longer sat neatly in its frame, buckled in the centre, the hinges and bolts that once secured it twisted out of their sockets and broken. Tyrell's voice carried soft and low through the gaps, sounded like he was making a phone call, and when Garrett bent down to peep through the narrow, jagged opening he could see a dimly lit, squalid room partitioned from the rest of the cargo container-like module by a couple more grubby sheets of yellow plastic strung from the ceiling. Two guys in parkas sat in folding aluminium chairs at a small round table by this garish division. There was a pair of handguns on the table and a thermos flask. The only other furniture had been cleared out of the way, stacked against the wall.

Two, he signalled to the others. *Guns.* Mimed the partition behind them and a third man beyond it, then a T sign. *Tyrell*.

He couldn't see if there was anything holding the door closed. Probably – hopefully – just leaning in place. Another check; Chapel had drawn his gun, Maya clutched a steel baton Julius had given her, figured it was better than using her fists.

Garrett stepped up to the door, leaned back and kicked it as hard as he could, middle of the side without hinges, ready to follow into the gap, take out Tyrell's two guards or have them covered and forced to surrender before they could react. The door crashed inwards, turning as it did, but then slammed to a halt halfway through its arc, wedged like a buckled skate ramp in the opening.

'Fuck,' he yelled, feeling the advantage slipping away from him. Put one foot up on the ruined door so he could see into the room, fired a couple of times, but by then the men had grabbed their weapons and he ducked back again. Chapel leaned past, shot blind. Garrett heard the *spang* of ricochets, a wet sound and a man howling in pain. There were two answering shots over the barrier, two more metal screams as the bullets hit the hallway wall. Skittering feet, one of the guys taking cover, and his friend still wailing in wordless agony.

'Give it up, Tyrell,' Maya called out. 'You don't have to die here.'

'I could say the same. Our friends on this rusting hulk will be coming for you as we speak. I'd surrender while I could if I were you.'

Shouts from the centre of the ship. The Hierro Muerto, closing.

'Shit, man.' Chapel, agitated. He pointed his gun, arm held straight, down the corridor. Garrett could see his hand shaking. 'Shit. We're fucked.'

'Listen to your friend there. He knows how hopeless your situation is.'

'Calm down, Chapel,' Garrett said, keeping his voice low. 'Keep your eyes on what's coming. We can screw them but good.'

'You reckon?'

'Give us the case, Tyrell. I'll kill you if I have to.'

'The case? Well, if that's what you want, I might have to destroy it. We can't have it falling into just anyone's hands.'

Behind Garrett, Chapel fired his gun. Shouts, somewhere along the corridor. Garrett pictured Tyrell torching the case's contents, saw Emi's last faint hope winking out in that instant, felt a surge of panic tinged with an inevitability he wasn't yet ready to face. Another shot from Chapel, and this time an answering *crack*.

'Fuck it,' he said. 'I never was any good at this.' Tore off his coat and tossed it through the gap.

Three shots in quick succession, bullets punching through the flapping cloth. A man's voice, shouting, 'Shi—' Before the guy had finished the word, still figuring out what was going on, Garrett had thrown himself over the wrecked door. Twisted in the air, fired twice to his left. The first round smashed the guy's elbow, blew bone and sinew all over the wall, the second took him under the chin and out the back of his skull. Garrett landed, skidding, and hurled himself round to fire once more at the wounded man on the floor. Told himself the guy might've still been holding a weapon, but felt bad about it all the same.

Pause, breathe.

The sense of movement behind the yellow plastic, Tyrell shifting position, drawing a gun. Throwing a lit match? Garrett rolled sideways, squeezing the trigger again and again. Punched a line of holes diagonally across the sheeting.

He reloaded as he climbed to his feet. Breathing hard, he stepped carefully up to one end of the tarp. Flung it aside, swept the gun through the gap, ready to shoot again. Tyrell was lying on the floor by an aluminium table near the single barred window. There was a ragged hole in the side of his throat, blood running free across the steel. The case was on the table, open, its contents laid out in front. They had their prize.

FORTY-TWO

'Clear,' he said to the others. 'Get in here. Get in cover.'

A burst of firing from the corridor outside, and then Maya and Chapel clambered through the gap and into the room. Garrett ran his eyes over the case's contents. Just as Chapel had described, there was a laptop, day-planner, loose hard copy clipped into manila folders. It looked as if Tyrell had been reading from one of the files when they arrived. He said, 'We need to get this stuff out of here. Whatever happens. We got any way of sending it to Nyberg?'

'From here?' Maya left Chapel standing guard on the door.

'Your phone?'

She shrugged. 'I'll try.'

'They're coming,' Chapel called. 'I need one of you to get my fucking back.'

Maya was wiring her phone up to the laptop. Garrett watched her hands working for a second, hypnotised, seeing Emi far away. Then he snapped out of it. 'Let's get that door back up,' he said. 'Chapel, give me a hand here.'

'Means we can't see 'em coming. They'll do us like we did these guys.'

'Seeing them coming's not going to help much. And we caught those guys on the hop.' He grasped one end of the wrecked metal sheet, and with Chapel's help he managed to lever it back up and into the doorway. The fit was even worse than when they'd arrived but the extra battering it had taken allowed them to wedge it hard in place with a shriek of rubbing steel. There were narrow gaps at the sides, enough for an eyeball and a gun barrel. A thin silver of the corridor beyond, a narrow firing arc and not much help in the long run, but enough to keep the hulkers worried for a little while.

Behind him, he heard Maya talking quickly to Nyberg, starting the transfer of the encrypted files. 'Keep your eye on the corridor,' he told Chapel. 'Soon as you see anyone, you shoot.'

'Sure. How we gonna get out of here, though, is what I'm wondering.'

'No idea.' He turned, raised his voice. 'Maya, how long do we need?'

'No idea,' she said in turn.

'We need a way out.'

A pause. 'Window?'

'It's barred.'

'It's rusty.'

'It's a long way down.'

'And it's that or take the Butch and Sundance route. You

want me to get these files sent or you want me to figure out an escape? It's either or.'

'Shout if they get too close,' he told Chapel. Dashed to the back of the module and the window. He wrenched open the casement and was met by a gust of icy air sharp as razors. Powdered snow darting like river midges in the dark, glimmering in the ugly light rising from the handful of halogens marking the tops of the units below. Gunfire from the doorway, Chapel keeping the enemy at bay.

The bars were welded into a square steel insert bolted into the metal of the window frame. The bolts were rimmed with a rime frost of corrosion, salt eaten into their white-painted surface. Garrett grabbed one of the chairs, gripped it like a battering ram and slammed it into the bars. Flecks of rust spun away into the night, and the chassis of the seat buckled slightly. More gunfire. He smashed the bars again. Felt the frame judder against the bolts.

BOOM.

A third blow, and this time it was enough to shear the tops from the lower bolts. The bars hung over empty air at an angle, held there only by the bent metal pins at the top.

BOOM.

'What the fuck?' This from Maya.

'I dunno.' Chapel shook his head, bent to peer through the gap in the door. 'Sounded like a goddamn grenade going off.'

Garrett threw his weight at the bars until the stress became too much for the corroded metal and the frame came clear of the window, tumbling into the dark to clang against the roof of one of the lower stacks. 'You see anything? What's going on?'

'I could hear those hulkers trying to close up. Fired a couple of times to keep them off, but now . . . I don't know. Shit, man, it's quiet out there. Those coulda been shotguns.'

'Maya, time?' Garrett said. A couple of feet below the window, a steel cable was clasped to an eyelet in the wall of the stack. It ran out and down, looked like it ended at another wall forty yards away and two floors down. Was there a door there? Some kind of maintenance access? The dark and the snow made it hard to tell for sure. Could be it was just a solid steel wall and the bare roof of the unit below.

'Thirty seconds maybe,' Maya said.

'Chapel?'

'Noth— Fuck.' He fired twice through the gap. An answering shot, and the metal snap of a round hitting the door by his head. He backed away, gesturing at the blocked entryway. 'Guys looked like Feds, man. Suits and big winter jackets. What the fuck?'

The sound of movement in the corridor. Garrett ran over, grabbed the metal-framed furniture stacked at the side of the room and began to pile it behind the door. 'Get that thing braced,' he said. 'We need a barricade.'

A dull *tong* sound as they rammed together the ramshackle barrier. Something solid hitting the door. A sledgehammer, a police battering ram, something like that. The barricade shuddered, but held.

'Maya, damn it.'

'Done,' Maya said. She yanked the cables free, put everything back in the case and snapped it shut.

Garrett bent down and started taking the belts of the three dead guys. Tossed one each to Maya and Chapel as he got them free. Another *tong* from the door, heavier this time.

'What do we do with these?' Maya said, following him to the window. Looked out, saw the cable, and the black and deadly drop to the deck beneath it. 'You've got to be kidding.'

'We get from this stack to the next, then we get down, get away. It's this or nothing.'

She was quiet for a moment. Then, 'How?'

'Drop, catch the wire, then loop the belt over the top with one hand and slide.'

'Anyone missing that catch is dead.'

Tong. He took the case from her, gripped it with one thumb, left his fingers free, tested the weight. 'Like I said, it's this or nothing.'

'What're we worried about if they're Feds?'

'What're the chances that's what they are? On the *Winter*? Bet your life?'

Tong. A metal creak, something threatening to give way. 'You people are fucking *insane*,' Chapel said. 'Fucking insane.'

Garrett shook his head and hauled himself into the gap so

he was sitting with his feet dangling against the wall. He had the belt looped firmly around his right hand, its free end ready to toss over the wire and catch with his left, the one that held the case. The wind burned like blasted sand. He took two, three deep breaths, then dropped.

FORTY-THREE

The rush, then the bite as the cable dug into his hands. His fingers threatened to slip from the freezing steel, but he shifted his grip, his legs waving beneath him like an uncontrollable pendulum. Tried not to think about falling, his bones shattering on the deck below. Prepared to take all of his weight on his left, then let go with his right, flipped the belt over the cable. A fraction of a second, gravity burning at his arm, and then his right hand closed back over the steel again. Let go with his left, but the belt was flapping in the breeze and his fingers could do no more than brush against it. He was swaying more, now, each swing tugging more and more at the tenuous hold his right hand had on the cable. His fingers howled, wanted release. Then the wind slapped the belt into his flailing hand and he snagged it tight. Let go of the cable, hoping, as he did so, that the belt would take his weight, that it wouldn't be sawn in two by his slide. Hoped he'd survive the next few seconds as, for one brief moment, he hung, unsupported, before his mass pulled the belt tight around the wire and he began to whip

243

down the incline, picking up speed, wind and snow turning his vision to tears. The sound of the steel hawser screaming against leather, air rushing past, and Garrett helpless in the middle. Then his feet slammed into the wall and he collapsed, stunned, on to the roof of the far stack.

There *was* a door here, old and rust-streaked, but a door none the less. He rolled over, looked back, and saw Maya wedging herself in the dimly lit square of window as the sound of another metal impact rolled into the night. He watched her fall, and for a moment he thought she'd missed, couldn't make out the cable in the dark, but then she jerked to a halt and swung in place. Managed to throw her belt over the top of the wire with a little less effort than he'd needed, and began her descent. Garrett turned to the door and began to strain against the wheel locking it in place.

By the time she'd picked herself to her feet, he had it open, held in the teeth of the wind while they looked back for Chapel. He dropped, crashed into the wire with his elbows, but somehow managed to hang on and was manoeuvring his belt into place as the barricade in the doorway finally gave way with a steel crash that echoed across the frozen decks. Chapel slid, body swinging wildly from side to side, and landed as two figures appeared in the window, guns raised.

Bullets slapped into the wall as the trio ducked through the door and back into the stale warmth of the ship.

The section they burst into seemed to be home to mostly Dominican families. A lot of the doors were open, and

Garrett saw yellow, red and green cloth, people cooking *sancocho*, heard snatches of Santo Domingo Spanish as they rushed past.

Down three flights of stairs, crashing through a huddle of half a dozen guys, three of them in gang colours, trading something, and out on to a pitted four-way intersection, looking for signs pointing to the Portal. There was a steady stream of people arriving through the corridor opposite the stairs. On the wall there, an arrow next to a peeling sign depicting a man leaving the ship. Someone else had added further pictograms showing the man falling in the water, then being eaten by sharks.

'What do we do if they're watching the way out?' Maya said as they hurried down the passage. Garrett said nothing. They could see the crowds filling the Portal up ahead, a slow-moving mass of humanity wrapped and huddled against the cold air washing in through the door in the *Winter*'s side.

A few yards from the Portal, a man who'd been leaning against the corridor wall, smoking, leaned forward and clapped a hand on Garrett's shoulder. 'Rats got your back,' he hissed as Garrett jumped. 'King said to watch all the ways. Things gone bad up top, right?'

'Yeah.'

'New visitors, came in from the mainland little while ago. They left a man in the Portal, just in case. You gonna have to walk out past him.'

'There's no other way?'

'Not from here.' The Rat shook his head, lank hair swinging. 'Not with the time you got. Ship's got a thousand ways of moving around inside once you're on, but getting on and off, only a few, and most of them you want a boat, or you want it to be summer. You go out in the water now, you freeze to death.'

'So what, make a run for it?'

A lop-sided grin. 'No, *walk* for it, like everyone else. Amado distract the watcher for you. You follow, little way behind. Not have much time.'

Amado, the Rat, headed into the main hall of the Portal, lurching and swaying like a drunk. They watched him shoulder his way to the far side, close to where a guy in a suit and tie beneath a winter coat was standing, watching the crowd. Garrett thought he maybe looked like one of the people he'd seen at Nerio Station, the guy who'd thrown him off the walkway. Then Amado seemed to be struck in the shoulder, spun around by one of the passing figures. The impact carried him into the suit, sending both of them staggering back into the wall. Amado paid the guy no attention, but righted himself and lunged forward, shouting at the guy who'd struck him.

Garrett steered them through the back of the crowd as it broke to leave space around the scuffle. The guy in the suit was dusting himself off, watching, for a moment, the two men squaring up to one another. Amado and the other guy were pushing at one another, shouting, and Garrett wondered if he was a Rat too. If Amado was risking a knife in the gut over a distraction. The trio had reached the outer hatch and the first grains of dusted snow were blowing into Garrett's eyes when he heard the shout behind them, the guy in the suit spotting their exit, and they ran.

FORTY-FOUR

They sprinted along the wooden pontoon, feet slipping on the compacted snow and slush underfoot, refreezing as the long night drew on. Behind, Garrett could hear the hollow rhythm of pursuit, multiple sets of feet pounding the boards some way back. The scattered people going to and from the *Winter* moved aside, wanting no part of whatever was happening. Garrett risked a glance back, saw four guys, indistinct shadows fifty yards away, probably the ones who'd come for them in Tyrell's quarters. The mixed firelight flicker of the Port shone dully off the weapons in their hands. By the time he looked forward again, they were at a junction with one of the larger jetties. He turned, felt his feet slide out from under him, tried to arrest his skid, skittering his feet against the frozen deck before gravity overcame him and he crashed to the floor, still moving.

Splinters of ice grated against his knuckles where he held the briefcase. He clawed at the ground with his other hand, trying to slow himself. Felt his elbows bouncing over the frozen wood, knees scraping. Then there was nothing under his feet as his legs shot out over the cold, dark water of the Murdoch. He grabbed hard with his hands, felt the skin rip from his palms, and stopped before he could plunge into the river. Felt his heart crashing inside his ribs. Then Maya and Chapel were hauling him back on to the pontoon, on to his feet again. The men in suits were thirty yards away, closing.

'Via Tristezza,' Maya said.

She led them a short way along the jetty, then up a gangway and across a trio of barges lashed together. The suits had seen what happened to Garrett and slowed as they hit the turn. One briefly raised his gun, considered shooting at them, but seemed to think better of it. On the final barge, another turn, along the edge of the hull to the bow, and a jump down on to the low stern deck of what had maybe once been, decades ago, a diving support boat. The owner, shouting, and they were on to a narrow steel beam covered in textured rubber. Grab the mooring line for a high-prowed fishing boat, use the momentum to swing out and round, on to the pontoon between vessels. And then Garrett saw why Maya had brought them this way.

Ahead was one of the wider main jetties. It was walled with lights – lanterns, flashlights, some guttering candles. Scores of people lined the sides. Some were singing, and Garrett could hear drums and pipes. Down the middle, more and more obvious as they approached, was a lengthy procession. More lanterns, paper flowers, papier mâché icons, all carried by men and women wearing black with painted skull masks. Others played instruments, a blend of discordant music, at once celebratory and unsettling. And interspersed between the devotional displays, the coffins of those killed on the ferry, *Number Forty-Three*. The trio broke right when they hit the funeral route, shouldered their way to the front, and dashed across a gap in the procession. No one protested. They burrowed into the crowd on the far side and did their best to lose themselves in the mass of people.

'It's like something out of *El Dia de los Muertos*,' Garrett said. 'Where are they taking them?'

'There's an old bunkering tanker down there. They'll be cremated, probably scatter the ashes on the river. Live on the water, die on the water, you're buried on the water, you know?' A sadness on her face, then.

'You OK?' he asked.

'Just thinking about my dad. He took the same way out. It just felt like maybe, in some way, he's still out there, part of the river. One of the ghosts that holds the Port together. Everyone loses someone.'

Eventually, they left the funeral procession behind, turned on to quieter, smaller paths, and made their way back to the *Adventure* by a safely circuitous route. There was no sign of the suits.

Not until they opened the door to the boat's mess and saw the four men waiting for them.

FORTY-FIVE

Emi, running through the upper floors of Shinecourt. She'd had no trouble getting out of the lab with Dr Stringer's pass, and had grabbed her belongings from the locker before she ran upstairs. Heard people coming and made for the floor above rather than try to hide from them. She'd tried calling Charlie but all she got was a message saying he was out of coverage area and a cut to voicemail. Now she was in danger of getting lost trying to find an exit that wouldn't be watched, and knew that she might have only moments before the alarm was raised.

A door opening ahead, footsteps. She dived into an alcove and sheltered behind a potted plant. Heard a woman's voice, talking on the phone, growing louder as she neared.

'I can assure you, Harrison, I have no idea what happened to your man at Nerio Station. My people didn't see anything before they left. He might have been unlucky – it's a rough neighbourhood, after all. Perhaps the wrong person thought he was stopping them escaping and they were willing to kill to get out. Obviously there'll be no police investigation into

Fisk's death, so I don't see this reflecting badly on you. You *do* have other people, don't you?'

A pause, talk on the other end of the line. Emi stopped herself gasping at the mention of Fisk. Forced herself to hold still while Amanda Kent strode past.

'Very funny, Harrison. We both know you've got no hope of getting to it before I do. Give up, stick to something that's more your forte. And don't threaten me either. I'm perfectly happy to forget the rules and play hardball. I'm sure the others wouldn't care if it meant seeing the back of you.'

The footsteps and the argument faded into the distance. Emi slipped out of her hiding place and along the corridor. The door Amanda Kent had emerged from was still open, and beyond it was a broad, open study with floor-to-ceiling windows filling a peaked dormer between the dual spines of the roof. A glass door in the centre opened on to a narrow, curved balcony. Through it, as she approached, Emi saw a hefty pickup bearing the logo of a gardening contractor, parked by the wall. In the back was a pile of black sacks, most with twigs and leaves sticking out of their tied ends.

She headed out on to the balcony. The bed of the truck was fifteen feet or so down. She could see the gardener by the floodlights along the drive, raking what looked like the last of his shrub trimmings, heavy pruning in late winter ready for the spring revival, into two final black sacks a short way down the hill.

Breathe out, slip over the railing, and jump. The brief moment of wind rushing past and the fervent hope that the sacks were deep enough, and soft enough, to break her fall, that there wasn't anything solid or sharp to impale herself on, and then with a crunch she was sure must have been audible across the grounds she was buried in cold black plastic and the smell of cut wood. She lay there, letting her breath return, and strained to hear the sounds of pursuit.

Nothing for a long time, then feet crunching on gravel. One sack, then another, thrown on top of her. The driver's door slammed, the engine roared into life, and they were away. Her pulse beat loud in her ears as they waited at the main gate, but then the truck started up again and she knew she had escaped.

Emi gave herself five minutes in the juddering dark, then, when the engine was idling – waiting at an intersection – she slipped out of the sacks, over the tailgate and away, walking down the street as if everything were normal. Charlie's phone was still unavailable. That left her other friends, only a few of whom, Clocks themselves, knew about the Curse. She punched 'call' on the second name on her contacts list.

'Emi?' Adam Nyberg said when he picked up. 'Funny thing—'

'Adam,' she said, 'I'm on Levine Street. It sounds strange but I need you to come and pick me up right now, and I need to get to Charlie. It's an emergency.'

She was expecting him to ask why, but he just said, 'OK.

I'll be there in ten minutes.' Sounded excited. 'I know where he is.'

'Really? How?'

'I've just spoken to his friend Maya. They've found something in Port Blackwater. Something to do with the Curse.'

FORTY-SIX

'The thing is,' the chief suit, who'd introduced himself as Cutter, said, 'it's great that you've brought me the case and all, but I really need to know who else you've told about it, and what you know about the people who blew up Green Street. We clear all that up and we can take it from there. This doesn't need to be hard.'

'You work for Amanda Kent, huh?' Maya said. The men had taken the case, their phones and their weapons, and two of them were still discreetly keeping them covered. She was handcuffed to a pipe attached to the wall. The other two were cable-tied to chairs.

Cutter would've been a good-looking guy, some way shy of forty, neat blond hair and the face of a mountain climber, except for the ugly scars that etched his skin. A ragged crescent gouged in his right cheek, a slice narrowly missing his left eye, a trio of slashes that tugged the corner of his mouth up and to the side, a half-dozen small pits in the skin of his forehead like he'd been hit in the face with buckshot. Maybe he had. Maya knew him, knew the face. She'd seen him in an orange NCTA vest, stabbing Anton and leaving him to die in the station. If Fisk had been right and the Foundation existed, obviously they weren't above fighting amongst themselves if they could do it quietly.

If she'd been expecting a denial, she was disappointed. 'Not that it matters, but yeah,' he said. 'I solve problems for her. Which means there's no point saying I'll be in shit if the cops find out, or trying to bribe me, or doing anything but exactly what I say. So, tell me what I need to know and we can all get out of here.'

'Hey, fuck you, man,' Chapel said. 'You got the case, what's it matter? *Fuck* you.'

Cutter leaned forward, unhurried, and slid a scalpel blade across Chapel's jawline before he could pull away, like he was doing nothing more than brushing off lint. Chapel screamed as blood welled from the open flap of skin. Eyes wide, he slapped his hands over the wound, trying to hold it closed.

'Listen to me,' Cutter said. 'Listen. It's not going to be easy to do this with a lot of noise in the background, so you're going to have to shut up.' Chapel was still yelling as he leaned closer. 'If you don't shut up, I'll do the same thing again on the other side. Then up by your eyes, along the top of your nose, and so on, until either I run out of places to cut or you finally learn your lesson. Are we clear?'

Chapel clenched his jaw tight, and Maya saw tears glittering in the corners of his eyes. He whimpered, but Cutter seemed satisfied for the time being.

'So, back to the questions. You guys were about to say . . . ?'

'No one else knows what's in the case,' Maya said. 'We haven't had a chance to look at it. You people were chasing us. There wasn't any time to tell anyone else about it.'

'And Green Street?'

'That wasn't us.'

'You don't say, Miss Cassinelli. I know a lot about your experience there. We even had a watch on your home for a while. What I want to hear is anything you can tell me about the people who *did* bomb Green Street, and why.'

Maya glanced at Garrett. His face was taut, angry, frustrated. She said, 'I don't know why they did it. It was a group of Clocks working for a man named Blake. I don't know why he did it; he's crazy.'

'Blake? That's his surname?' Cutter leaned forward a little. 'What's his first name?'

'Jason.'

'Jason. I wonder if he was our boy Edward's brother.'

Maya's mind was a blank. 'Who?'

'It doesn't matter now. Far too late for that, and him. So Jason organised the bombing.' He grinned. It wasn't pretty. 'Great, we're getting somewhere. You know why he targeted Green Street? What he was after?'

'If you maybe know who he is, maybe he was after your boss Amanda.'

'Funny choice for a hit, but I guess it's possible. Maybe he was hoping to get his hands on the case while the smoke was clearing. Kaboom and grab it. You,' he said, looking at Chapel, who was sweating hard, the bleeding from his jaw slowing. 'You took the case. We got you on security cameras.'

Chapel said nothing, just nodded.

'What did you do with it after that?'

'Nothing.'

Cutter's expression didn't change as he reached forward and snapped Garrett in the ear with his elbow. Garrett swore, eyes watering, and hung his head, dazed.

'What you do that for?' Chapel said, looking confused.

'You are all in the same boat, no pun intended. One of you fucks around and someone's going to get it. Maybe it'll be you, maybe it'll be someone else. I don't care so long as one of you's still able to talk. You want to be the one keeps all your teeth, you better carry on cooperating unless you want to rely on these other two to do it for you. If they don't play ball, maybe it'll be you gets the worst of it. You see? It's like a game. Everyone wants to be a winner, don't they?' He carefully laid his scalpel on the table next to his chair, reached into his coat and added a toffee hammer, a pair of needle-nosed pliers and a box of nails. 'So what happened after you took the case?'

'My people didn't want it, so I hid it with friends here, tried to find a buyer for it.'

'In the Port? Really?'

'People buy all sorts.'

'Where are your friends now?'

'They're all dead.' Chapel looked away. 'Blake's man killed them. Then we killed him.'

Cutter sat back, something like a flicker of a smile passed over his face. 'And here we are. So, who else knows about it?'

'I already *told* you.' Chapel didn't look at him.

'You were trying to sell the thing, kid. How many people did you offer it to? Did anyone take a look at its contents for you, help you figure out what you had?'

'No one.'

'What's in it?' Garrett said suddenly. 'What's so goddamn important? You got a cure for the Curse, or just the Curse itself?'

'It's irrelevant now, isn't it?' Cutter stopped, checked his watch. 'What matters is that I got no more time to waste here. You all have had the chance to come clean the easy way, but I guess we've got to get right to it. While you were up on that ship, you made a call to Bryant University. Switchboard number. Who were you talking to?'

Maya felt her chest tighten, breath come harder. Garrett said, hoarse, 'What're you talking about? We didn't make any phone calls. You think we had time to sit around and chat?'

Cutter shook his head, leaned over and yanked her pinkie fingernail clean out with the pliers. She wanted to scream, but her lungs would only spasm, and by the time they were working again the impulse had passed and she was shaking and gasping with the pain. Cutter took her phone out of his pocket and held it aloft. 'You think I didn't check when we searched you? So tell me another one.'

'Fuck you,' Garrett said. 'Fuck you, Cutter. You won't get shit from me.'

This time, Cutter stood before he whipped an arrow-fast blow to the side of Garrett's head. He must've known what he was aiming for, because Garrett went limp, folded up in his chair like a sack of raw meat. 'The two of you,' Cutter said, looking at Maya and Chapel. 'Your choice now. The one who gives me a name gets to walk out of here alive. We're gonna get that name from the receptionist in time anyway, so all you're doing is cutting to the chase. I got no problem leaving you to die with your friend here, you want to play the same way as him.'

'Nyberg,' Chapel said, talking fast. 'His name was Nyberg. He was gonna crack the files. She sent them to him over the cell phone.'

'Chapel, you fucking idiot,' Maya yelled. One of Cutter's people came forward, cut Chapel's bonds.

The younger man gingerly touched the cut to his jaw. Said, 'I ain't no idiot. Fuck I want to die for? You listen to anything I told you? I just want out of this shit. Sure I hoped to sell that damn case and use the cash to get the fuck away, but I'd rather be alive and poor than dead for nothing I give two shits about. Think about it.'

'You're going to kill him anyway,' she said to Cutter after Chapel had been escorted from the mess.

'I'm hurt. Man of my reputation and all,' he said, heading for the door. 'You should never have let Harrison Valentin talk you into this, Miss Cassinelli. Members of the Foundation got no business going up against one another, and especially not against Miss Kent. Guess you get to be part of the message, huh?'

'You went up against him. I saw you kill his guy at Nerio Station.'

A ghost of a smile over his shoulder. 'That could've been anyone did that. Could've been you.' To one of the suits with him, he said, 'Get the men off, then blow this rusty piece of shit. River's a hard place, this time of year.'

FORTY-SEVEN

A short while after Cutter left the room, time spent futilely trying to free herself, Maya heard a muffled *thud* and water burbling somewhere deeper in the boat. The *Adventure* shuddered.

'Garrett! Garrett!' she yelled.

'The fuck?' He was waking, shaking his head.

'They're sinking the boat. They're sinking the goddamn boat.' She strained against the cuffs holding her to the pipe. Hoped for some kind of give in the metal or the brackets holding it fast to the wall of the room, didn't find any. 'Can you get yourself free?'

'Where's Cutter? Where's Chapel?'

'Gone. Chapel sold us out. Cutter's going after Nyberg. If they get to him, we'll never find out what was in those files or why Kent wants them back so badly.'

'Or why Blake wanted them too. If there's a cure for Emi.' Garrett tugged at the ties holding his hands and arms to the chair. Shuffled it round and began to jerk it towards Maya, using his body weight to throw himself forward a few inches at a time. 'You've got your legs free. Maybe we can both bust this thing to pieces together.'

The sound of rending metal, hollow and reverberating inside the *Adventure*. Water surged under the door and spilled into the room, an icy rising tide. Garrett's chair slipped on the suddenly greasy floor as he shuffled forward, and he crashed sideways. Whipped his mouth and nose clear of the pouring water, choking, eyes wide and shocked awake by the cold.

'Jesus, Garrett,' Maya said. 'Can you get up?'

'Not...' He spat out a mouthful of river water. 'Not gonna stay lying down.'

It took two attempts, but he managed to rock himself sideways and up on to his knees. He pulled at the ties round his legs, trying to stretch them out, down, over the foot of the chair leg. It didn't work, and he toppled forward into the water, now a good three inches deep and coming up fast. Came out, face and hair sodden, roaring with frustration. Maya could see blood in the water by his calf where the tie had bitten into his skin. Then, suddenly, he laughed.

'What is it?' she said. Her feet felt like ice, and the wet cold was spreading up her legs.

'Look at me. Stuck on the floor like a crippled tortoise with a chair strapped to my back, waiting to drown. Never thought I'd look so ridiculous when I died.' His teeth were chattering hard.

'People'll see the boat sinking.' Maya felt numb all over.

Her scalp was tight, like her hair was trying to climb away from the water. 'They'll come help.'

'They can't get down here in time. Head . . . My head'll be underwater in a couple of minutes. Don't think they'll want to get down here, risk freezing.'

'They're sinking my damned boat, are they? The devil with that, lad.' It took Maya a moment to realise that the voice was Julius's, coming from somewhere behind the mess counter.

'Julius? Julius?' There was a *crump* and the ship shuddered again. A porthole, a door, something previously watertight letting go under the pressure. The roar of the Murdoch as it claimed the inside of the vessel was constant now.

'The very same, girl.'

'Where are you?'

'Behind the counter. The bastards who put holes in the *Adventure* hit me in the head with the stock of a shotgun and left me here in handcuffs. Nothing like cold water to wake a man.'

In front of her, Garrett had his neck craned back as far as he could, trying to keep breathing. They were both shivering uncontrollably now. She shouted, 'Can you get yourself free? We don't have long.'

'I'd be free already, girl, if you didn't keep talking to me.'

She shut up then, breathing short and hard, chest tight with cold. A sweet metal jangling noise as his cuffs came free and Julius vaulted over the counter, his sodden longcoat trailing behind him like a purple peacock's tail. He had two L-shaped metal pins clenched in his teeth and a small pair of pocket wirecutters in one hand. He splashed over to Garrett and snipped through his ties. The chair fell away and Garrett lurched to his feet while Julius strode over to Maya. He tried the cutters on the chain of her cuffs, then gave up, switched to the picks and went to work on the lock.

'You always carry those?' she said.

He nodded, eyes fixed on what he was doing. 'Two sets, front and behind, sewn into the coat. No one ever finds them. You'll only need them once, but they'll save your life.'

'And the cutters?'

The cuffs sprang open. 'Counter cupboard. Even I ain't paranoid enough to have them to hand all the time. Maybe I should. You two can walk?'

'Yeah,' Garrett said. 'Swim if I have to.'

'You might, lad.'

They waded into the corridor, the water halfway up their thighs. The *Adventure* was heeling over, everything developing a distinct slant. The current in the passageway was stronger, too. Through the cold and the strain of her frozen muscles, Maya could feel it pulling against her legs and she had to clasp the rails at the sides to stop herself falling. The river was surging through a door further down, the water boiling through some hole in the hull with unstoppable force. She started in the opposite direction, but Julius pulled her back.

'This way,' he said. 'Stairs down there won't help us, just go up one deck.'

They followed him down the corridor, the going harder and harder as the water came first up to their waists, then their chests. The boat seemed to be listing more, rolling sideways under the river's onslaught. Maya was exhausted, could barely breathe. Every step threatened to drain her last remaining dregs of energy. If it hadn't been a choice between keep on and drowning, she'd have given up in a second. Then Julius lurched round a corner and on to the stairs. He gripped the railing with one hand, held the other out for her. It was trembling, but he was fighting to control it.

'Watch your step,' he said. 'Stairs go down as well as up.'

She grabbed hold, found she could barely move her fingers. Turned, did the same for Garrett. His face was bloodless, his lips blue. She wondered if she looked as deathly too.

'Go on,' he said through gritted teeth. 'Glad I didn't die in that fucking chair.'

The stairs were edged with rubber grips, and while the climb was difficult, it was possible. More water was sloshing down from somewhere higher up in a thin stream. The ship's list made the turn hard, a battle against gravity, but as they navigated it there was a deafening shriek of metal wrenching apart and the *Adventure* lurched back to the horizontal. They hung tight to the railings, rode out the bucking motion. Heard the water's roar rise in a triumphant crescendo and suddenly the river was thundering up the stairs, climbing as fast as they could run.

'It's the hull,' Julius shouted. 'The hull's gone completely.'

Up another flight, Maya fighting collapse from fatigue, each step slower than the last. The water was up with them now, boiling around their knees and showing no sign of slowing. They reached the door on to the main deck, saw more water streaming around its edges; the boat was a foot or more below the surface. Julius glanced at it, carried on up. Maya saw Garrett struggling behind them, gave him her hand, hauled him with her, body and mind separated, like she was controlling her limbs from afar, clumsily, with strings. Even the sound of the water was muffled, turned to white noise in the deep background. Garrett said something to her, but she couldn't hear what it was, just saw his mouth move.

Then they were outside, in the scything bitter wind and the snow blowing down from the night like stones. They were on top of the *Adventure*'s forecastle, the jetty a few yards away and a few feet above. People from the Port, cloth-wrapped shapes shouting in the dark, were clustered nearby. Two of them had thrown a rope to Julius, others were casting around for more. The water behind them where the rest of the boat had been was a churning mass, air rushing from the last remaining pockets in the ruined hull. Julius tried to loop the rope over Maya's shoulders, but she shook her head and pushed Garrett forward. Once secured, he leaped, dazed, into the river to be hauled up on to the jetty by those waiting there. The rope was thrown back, a second with it. Julius grabbed one and was about to loop the other under her arms when the boat lurched again, crashing sideways.

The line tore from her grip, and Julius, held fast by his own, was left behind as she followed the forecastle over, into the river. For a second, she saw Garrett's face, ghost-like, staring down from the jetty's edge, and then the river's current grabbed her and everything went cold and dark.

FORTY-EIGHT

Someone flung a blanket that smelled of darkness and the memory of sweat over Garrett. He was dimly aware of hands stripping his waterlogged clothes, others replacing them with dry ones, too big, too small, hanging all wrong. Mostly all he felt was the scratching of the wool, saw Maya's face over and over, caught in the moment between the *Adventure* capsizing in its death throes and the river swallowing her, the current sweeping her away, under the jetty, into nothing. How alone she'd seemed, and how lost. Except sometimes it wasn't Maya but Emi, and she was crying out to him.

The warmth returned quickly though, and it wasn't long before someone helped him to his feet, still swaddled in the stranger's blanket. Port faces clustered around him, people guiding him wordlessly to the flat deck of a neighbouring boat and a chair by the brazier there. A large, chipped mug full of lukewarm tea was pressed into his hands and someone said, 'Drink, drink. Finish this, I'll give you more. Mustn't have it too hot, but it'll get you warm again.'

A community, closing ranks in the face of a tragedy. Like when they'd cremated the dead from the ferry. Like when they'd helped Garrett and Maya on to the *Winter* to recover the case, before it was snatched away again.

Julius trudged into the circle of light by the brazier and lowered himself into one of the other chairs. He was wrapped in a blanket and clothes that weren't his. In a beige sweater and brown cords, shorn of his usual trappings, he looked disturbingly normal. He accepted a cup of tea and leaned closer to the coals, warming his face. Garrett saw the ugly, bloodied lump on the back of his head where Cutter's people had knocked him out. The locals had stepped back, some leaving altogether. A private circle around the two of them; everyone had seen Maya thrown to her death and they seemed to want to give the two men some space to come to terms with it.

'How'd you feel, lad?'

'Not great.'

'I'm colder than a witch's tits in winter. Head hurts like a son of a bitch too.' Julius sipped his tea. 'There's nothing left of the *Adventure* above the water now. I had a look. Anchorage is too deep. She was a good boat. A good home. Bastards must have screwed her but good to send her down like that.'

'Do you think there's any chance Maya made it?' Garrett said after a moment's silence.

'The girl?'

'Yeah.'

'People have spread the word, watching for her, but . . . It was one of the outer berths, away from the shore. With the tide as well, the current can be strong – strong enough, anyway. If she'd caught herself on a line on the other side of the jetty, grabbed one of the boats there, straight away, they'd have pulled her out. But she was down and gone. Could be anywhere. Even if she broke surface some way further along, no one can survive water that cold for more than a few minutes, and we'd all already spent long enough in it inside the boat.'

Garrett shook his head, drank some tea. It was murderously sweet. 'Sounds pretty final then, huh?'

'I don't like to sugar-coat anything, lad,' Julius said, patting Garrett on the shoulder. 'I ain't saying it's not *possible*, just that it ain't *likely*. People've gone in the Murdoch in weather like this and come out OK before. They get swept past a little skiff or a sampan on their way out into the middle of the river, and someone plucks them out of the water and manages to keep them warm until they get to shore. Or they get tangled on an anchor line and some sharp-eared fellow hears them crying for help and gets them back up top. Word doesn't get out that's what's happened for a couple of hours.'

'It does happen.'

'It does. But you've got to be real lucky. Best you face the most likely outcome and deal with it, then anything else that happens is a nice bonus, right?'

'Fuck.' Silence for a while, then Garrett said, 'I don't feel very lucky today. We lost Maya and they'll have got to Nyberg by now because that Chapel kid sold us out, and I got no idea where to find Blake. Which means we're pretty much fucked, me and my girl. Might as well give it up. You ever had a girl, Julius? Not like your "bosun", whatever her name was— God! Was she on the boat?'

'No, just me. Keep things private-like when there's business going down.' He shrugged. 'I should give her a call. Except my phone's full of water.'

'You ever had someone you were properly in love with?'

'Proper serious *in love* in love? Something that happens to other people, lad. That kind of attachment's difficult for a man like me.'

A hint of something there but Garrett was too caught up in himself to want to explore it. 'I love Emi,' he said. 'But she's going to be dead in a few days. Right now, and right up to the moment it happens, she's fine. I look at her and she's just like she's always been. And then, suddenly, she'll be gone. We don't even know the time, just the day. Just that, at some point, in the middle of something, with no goodbye, it'll be over. And I could've saved her. This guy, Blake, is alive when he should be dead. He's got a cure. Maybe the cure was in the case and that's why he wanted it, to make sure he was the only one who got it. But now I don't know where Blake is, Cutter's got to the guy who could tell us what was in that case and we'll never find out. And I've spent Emi's last few days chasing after nothing when I could've been with her.'

'You could go after Cutter, stop him getting to your man with the codes.'

Garrett gestured at his blanket-clad form. 'You think I'm in any shape to do that? Everything hurts. My weapon's at the bottom of the river. I don't think shouting at Cutter's going to do any good even if I could catch up to him, which I can't. How much of a head start did he get? Shit.'

'Well, lad, I guess life really has fucked you but good. At least you've still got a home, though.' Julius caught Garrett's eyes and smiled wryly. 'Seriously, you got my sympathy. Hard thing to deal with.'

'What'll you do about the *Adventure*?'

'Nothing I can do. She's gone and I doubt the city'll pay to have her raised and mended. Water's probably deep enough to reuse the berth. There'll be another boat. Even if I have to start with a dinghy and work up.'

'Not going to take up a life on land?'

Julius's smile broadened. 'I'm Gentleman Julius Poll, lad. I couldn't go leaving the Port now, could I? Disappoint my public?'

The crowd slowly faded away. An old woman wrapped in a half-dozen carefully interleaved layers of different coloured fabric came and quietly told them their clothes had been taken to Indio's Laundry to dry and they could pick them up in the morning.

'Via Pulito,' Julius said. 'Next jetty landwards.'

Then there were gloved hands on Garrett's shoulders. Emi, come through the night so quietly he was certain he was imagining it. And behind her, a man he recognised from the groups. Nyberg, alive and well.

'Charlie, what's going on?' she said. 'People working for Amanda Kent tried to keep me at a house of hers so they could work on the Curse. There was a man called Cutter who I think was coming after you. Someone helped me escape and then I called Adam to bring me here. What happened to you? You look . . .' She stroked the side of his face. It hurt.

'They tried to take you?' Garrett swore, felt fear and guilt mix with anger in his gut. That they'd failed was one thing, that they'd tried, that Kent had tried, abandoning all pretence at wanting to help, was another. And Cutter . . . 'I'm sorry, Emi. I'm so sorry. I should've been there. It's just that I was this close to saving you.'

'I worry about you, Charlie. I didn't know it was going to be like this, what you're trying to do.'

'I don't want to lose you,' he said. 'That's all that matters. I'm going to get the cure.'

'And I don't want to die alone.'

'You won't.' He turned to Nyberg. Said, 'You must have left just before Cutter reached you. He was heading for the university after you.'

Nyberg shook his head. 'I left when Maya sent me those files. The way she described what's been happening, I figured that wasn't the place to be looking into them. I cracked them at home. Then Emi called.'

'What was in the files?'

Nyberg pulled his chair closer. 'I haven't been able to break the encryption on them all, but I don't think it's too difficult to figure out the type of thing they contain. The case belonged to a man called Dominic Wheeler, and he worked for Amanda Kent as a kind of spokesman or assistant. The bulk of what you have falls into two categories. The encrypted material seems to concern negotiations between Kent's people and some sort of gang whose turf borders Willow Heights who they think have a connection to the Curse.'

'She wants to know how the Curse works.'

'That would be my guess. The money she could make from the technology involved in it . . . well, it'd be astrono-mical. The person who created it has cracked some of the key engineering problems associated with developing func-tional nanotechnology. He just happens to have been . . .'

'Mad?' Garrett said.

'It seems so.'

'So she's trying to get to the creator? How close have they got?'

Nyberg shrugged. 'Hard to say without the rest of the encrypted data. Close, certainly. And from the rest of what's there, unencrypted, I'd suggest they're either very close indeed or expected they would be by now. Maybe enough to find where it's made without negotiating access. Amanda Kent will be conducting a TV interview with Shellie Lyon at her penthouse tonight. Dominic was supposed to provide her people with security protocols for the building, instructions and a schedule. Reading between the lines of some of Kent's instructions to Dominic, she's going to be revealing the existence of the Curse. If the interview is still on, there'll be extra interest in it if she reveals that the Green Street bombing was the work of Clocks.'

'If she tells people that, there'll be an outcry. The public'll want every Clock watched or rounded up in case they go crazy too. The people who kept the case quiet will be sacked and everyone will be sued into oblivion.'

'To say the least.'

'And she'll come out shining white. No one'll begrudge it to her when she reveals she has the cure, or patents the tech, or whatever it is she does.'

'*If* she goes public.'

Garrett thought back to the *Winter* and what he'd heard before crashing into Tyrell's room. 'The interview. That's what Tyrell was telling Blake.'

'Blake? Jason Blake?'

'When we snatched the case, Tyrell was dictating things to Blake over the phone,' Garrett said. 'That was it. I couldn't hear more than a few snatches, but there was something about door codes and security passes.'

'Then that was it. There's nothing like that in the rest of the stuff here.'

'He's going to be at the interview. Blake wants Amanda Kent, maybe something to do with his brother – Cutter seemed to know him, so there's got to be a connection there. He's going to crash the interview and fuck her up or pull some kind of shit like that and get the whole thing on tape for the TV. Where does Amanda Kent live?'

'The codes were for her penthouse in Arel Spire, right at the top.'

'I've been there. Either she's got the cure, or Blake has. I get in there and I can still save Emi.'

Nyberg looked at Garrett sadly. Said, 'Charlie . . .'

'Just tell me what you've got. I'm going in.'

FORTY-NINE

Maya drifted, pressed in on all sides by cold, solid force. A chill personal gravity that seemed to be making her smaller and smaller, existence shrinking to a flickering singularity. She remembered running from something, but the details were gone, stripped away like dreams. Probably, she figured lazily, not important.

Shapes. Shapes in the dark. A brief surge of panic, the realisation of water all around, unable to breathe, steel and wood and fibreglass and mooring lines. Movement, upwards, sudden, a cold so fierce on her face that it cut through the total numbness that encased her. Air. Hands, shaking her, turning her over. The shapes of people, vague shadows against the scattered black beyond. Voices, garbled and wordless. Something closed in over her and she blacked out again. Retreated into the singularity and safety.

Occasionally there were interruptions, moments when Maya found herself dragged away. More movement, someone with a gruff, old voice saying, 'She's breathing again. Huh. What d'you know?'

Another voice. A woman. 'Is she going to die?'

A different voice, her own, asking almost the same question years before, about her father. The memory brought with it the bitter bergamot smell of the tea 'Brass' Veloso liked to drink as he tended to her dad. The quiet of the funeral procession and the light flat and cold on the top of the cardboard coffin.

Warmth, then, and the scent of half-burned petro-chemicals. Maya managed to force open her heavy eyes to see a corrosion-streaked narrow steel room. It might have been a cell or a shipping container. Torn posters in a language she didn't recognise were plastered on the walls. An old man swathed in layers of wool overcoats was hunched by an oil burner at the far side, stirring something in a pot. Maya was lying on a stained mattress beneath a couple of blankets that smelled like charcoal. A girl maybe eighteen years old, dressed like the old man, grubby and thin, had Maya's right foot in her hands and was massaging her toes, rubbing them hard to warm them, keep the circulation going.

The girl saw Maya's eyes open. 'She's awake,' she said. 'Hello?'

'Don't stop,' the old man said. 'Don't want frostbite.'

Maya couldn't move; her muscles wouldn't respond. Couldn't speak either. Something wrong with her throat. Her eyes lolled and she felt herself nodding again. The last thing she saw as the shades came down again was the razor blade design of the girl's earrings.

The old man again, this time with two others near the oil burner. No sign of the girl. The newcomers were better dressed than the two who'd been caring for her. Heavy longcoats that seemed to have been stitched together from other, smaller garments in blocks, then bleached white. Dark sweaters underneath. A man and a woman, both with the sides of their heads shaved. They looked lean and hungry, hollow eyes shadowed and shining.

'In the river,' the old man said. 'We were on our way home when Miriam's oar struck her.'

Something inaudible from the newcomers, voices too soft for Maya to hear.

'I don't know. Thought she was dead to start with, surprised me we got her back. She ain't woken much, in and out, but I guess she's not going to die.'

Maya wanted to move, to shout out, but she couldn't do more than blink. She could feel her fingers and toes though, tingling slightly, like permanent pins and needles. Warmth at the foot of the bed, something hard wrapped in wool. A swaddled plastic bottle full of hot water, keeping her feet warm. Her throat was raw and ragged and she wondered if it was from swallowing river water or hacking it all back up again when they rescued her.

'Dunno,' the old man was saying. 'Miriam did what she could. Frostbite doesn't look too bad. Seen worse. Ha! I've had worse. Hard to say how deep it goes, but maybe we got it in time.'

Another soft line of questioning from the newcomers. Maya strained to hear, feeling the weight of sleep coming down on her again as she forced herself to concentrate. She saw the old man nod, heard him say, 'That's right. The Gate.'

The next time Maya woke she was no longer on the mattress, but lying on what felt like a thick sheet on the floor of the metal room. The girl, Miriam, was kneeling by her head, hands working to tie something like she was doing up a shoelace. Maya saw a wooden pole there, running from under the sheet on which she lay. She was on a stretcher. They were moving her.

She tried to talk, but broke into a cough instead. Miriam started at the noise, said, 'You're awake again. Can you hear me?'

Maya, still coughing, nodded.

'What's your name?'

She fought her lungs back under control. Forced her arm to move. It took all her strength to lift her hand a few inches and bring it out from under the blanket, clasp Miriam's hand. Maya felt tears pricking her eyes at the effort it had taken. Her fingers were blotchy red and white, yellowing near the tips, swollen at the knuckles, but not as bad as she'd feared. She croaked, 'Where are we?'

'The *Winter*. We're on the *Winter*. Can you sit up, do you think?'

Maya tried, but didn't have the strength or the energy. Miriam managed to prop her up into a reclining position with a couple of bags behind her back and head like hospital pillows. Then she picked up a mug and pressed it to Maya's lips.

'What is it?'

'It'll help you get your strength back. Help your throat too.'

'Your friend . . . is he the Ferryman?'

Miriam smiled. 'What? That's just a bogeyman for children.'

The drink was warm, lemon-tinged and sweet as syrup. Maya gulped it down, felt its heat spread through her chest. She settled back on the makeshift cushions and was asleep again before Miriam had taken the cup away.

FIFTY

Chapel felt like a million bucks and looked like a dollar fifty and change when he walked into a shabby dive bar on Carnivale Street. His jaw was freshly bandaged, one hand clutching the bus ticket in his pocket, and Chapel himself still riding the high of being alive. Cutter had been as good as his word, and although Chapel had expected to wind up with a bullet in the skull and a cold, wet grave, Cutter's men had instead taken him topside and turned him loose.

'Get out of Newport. Right now,' one of them had said. 'Don't come back.'

'Don't talk to nobody, I guess,' Chapel said, surprise at his good luck overcoming his common sense.

'People like you don't talk. And you're small time; you don't know anything about what you got yourself into, do you? Don't waste the boss's generosity.'

'Not me. Small time, you got that right.'

It was good being small time, he figured. OK, so he'd sold

out the girl and that cop to save himself, but you had to look after Number One. And they hadn't paid him or anything. He didn't owe them, and it wasn't like anyone in Florida was going to know who he was or how he'd got there. Clean slate.

'Three shots of tequila,' he said to the barman, grinning. 'You want something?'

'Nah. On duty. You won the lottery or something?'

Chapel shook his head. Knocked back two of his shots, looked around the bar. 'You know,' he said, 'I really, really hate this town. I mean, I fucking *hate* it. I hate the people, I hate this bar, I hate you. It's gonna be so good to leave.'

The barman looked at him like the feeling was mutual. Also like maybe he didn't disagree. Said, 'Where you going?'

'Miami. Gonna be a world away from all this snow.'

'Got friends down there?'

'Not yet.' Chapel downed the last of the tequila, flung the empty glass to shatter in the far corner of the room and tossed a twenty on the counter. Left with a cheery, 'Fuck you, man.'

Cold wind like needles of ice, and the sidewalk was slippery. He hunkered into his coat, watched his footing as he walked the couple of blocks to the bus station. People trudging in the opposite direction, vague neon ghosts in brightly coloured parkas. The neighbourhood was a bleak commercial jumble, the bare concrete props and beams that held up the film set facade of downtown Newport City.

On the ramp down to the bus station's sprawling parking

lot were a mixture of homeless people and scroungers. Guys hunched behind tattered signs reading *Need fare to Philly* and *Ten bucks short, got to get to Boston.* Toothless, weathered faces peering from beneath multiple hats and hoods next to the tiny ramshackle huts made from layers of cardboard lashed together with duct tape, they lived in 'Newport igloos'. The last time, he figured, he'd ever have to see them. Didn't imagine they had them down in Florida.

A rattling noise, and a can rolled out from the gap between two of the frost-streaked structures, bounced over the ice and came to a stop against his foot. He glanced down at it, had enough time to see it had no label, just a funny symbol, a red pictogram of some kind, and, from the corner of his eye, the hunched shape of the homeless guy who'd dropped it. Then something stung the side of his neck, hard. Two heartbeats and the world spun, his stomach heaved. Movement, people around him, and everything dropped into night.

FIFTY-ONE

Garrett, his eyes on the glittering colours of downtown Newport turned to soft neon fog by the snow, a glimmering halo around the crown of every tower. He was surrounded by shining concrete ghosts, six blocks from the bomb site on Green Street. Arel Spire was the tallest of them, a spike of steel and glass that looked like it had been hacked out of a glacier, ringed in gold. Two other, smaller towers framed the landscaped plaza at their centre. A further glimmer in the dark gap between one of these and Arel Spire – the lights of a battered advertising blimp, tethered at half the height of the artificial downtown canyon beyond. He'd seen it from the cab, straining in the wind against the four steel cables pinned to the street floor, the sides bowing in the gale, no longer perfectly inflated. When Kent's people had brought him here before, they'd come a different way, round to the rear entrance. Now he remembered the place well. On the opposite side of the street, the Borges, which housed an ultra-exclusive restaurant, two nightclubs in its upper floors and a small mini-mall full of designer stores selling designer goods to designer clients. Garrett had taken Emi there once. They'd bought ridiculously overpriced coffee and browsed some of the stores, pretending to be rich, until Garrett had chased her through the fountain in the middle and they'd run, laughing, into the evening before Security caught them. Life as far from the Port and the Curse and everything else Garrett had known for the past year as it was possible to get.

He crossed the plaza, walking beneath dead trees diamond-frozen in blown snow. Had a gun he'd bought in the Port to replace the one lost on the *Adventure*. 'Three hundred,' the woman who'd sold it to him had said, 'but I buy it back from you for one, you return it to me soon.'

'I'll only need it for a night,' he'd told her. On the mainland, he'd backed it up with a taser and an extendable baton. Bought a cheap pre-pay phone and given Emi the number.

The front of the building was a sweep of near-seamless curved glass rimmed with faint amber light. Behind the glass, a broad lobby clustered with potted plants and, at the centre, a single knotted birch with sheer white bark and a scattering of leaves gleaming like gold. Steel and brass elevators at the back, reception desk made from the same materials off to the right. Two men in security uniform that made them look like Tokyo *sararimen* stood behind it, unmoving. The doors were almost indistinguishable from the rest of the glass, shown only by the faintest of seams at the edges and a change in the lights around them. A message appeared in burnt copper text on the surface as Garrett approached, politely telling him that Arel Spire was closed to non-residents and that he should either enter his personal passcode or call for the porter. A touchscreen alphanumeric keypad and call button shimmered into being next to it.

Garrett typed in the code provided by the material in the briefcase and hoped it was still current. The pad disappeared and the message on the door changed to: *Thank you, guest. Welcome.* The doors unlocked with a muffled click of electro-magnets and swung inwards. Garrett stepped through, into the warmth, and heard them snick shut behind him as he walked towards the elevators, head down, like he had good reason to be here.

'Excuse me, sir,' one of the guards said, voice clear and precise in the echoing marble quiet. 'You need to sign in before you head upstairs. Fire regulations.'

The elevators were twenty yards away. Garrett stopped, breathed hard, and turned to the desk. Managed what he hoped was a look of innocent bafflement. Said, 'Oh, sorry. First time I've been here.'

The two guards watched him, implacable. They were older than him and had the flat look of ex-mercenaries. The desk was high and narrow, topped by a glass sheet over matt grey steel. One of the men tapped something behind the counter and a brief text form and keypad appeared in orange light on the glass.

'All very impressive, this,' Garrett said as he filled in an invented name and reason for being there. 'Never seen so much touchscreen stuff outside an Apple store.'

'Uh-huh.'

'My apartment block, you're lucky if the doorphone works.'

The first man glanced at his entry in the visitor list. Said, 'You're going up to 2501?'

'Yeah.'

'Purpose of your visit?'

'I'm an outside PR consultant for Perry-Whittle Media. They're doing an interview with Miss Kent.'

The guard's expression didn't change. He said, 'We'll need to see some ID as well. It's a requirement for visitors to the penthouses.'

'Sure.' This hadn't been in the entry plan in the briefcase. Garrett pulled out his wallet, flipped through it until he found his driver's licence and slid it across. Looked bored, heart thumping, and slipped his hands back into his pockets. As the guard frowned at the name on the licence, Garrett tasered him in the neck.

The other man took a second to react, mouth dropping open, reaching into his jacket for a weapon. Garrett clubbed him in the face with the baton as it extended, swung himself over the desk as the guard staggered back, yelling. The guy had enough presence of mind to backhand Garrett across the chin with the grip of his pistol. The impact rattled Garrett's teeth and sent pain shooting across his face, but didn't slow him down. He hit the guard a second time with the baton, then kicked his legs out from under him and left him on the floor, stunned and moaning. He turned, did the same to the man he'd tasered. Took their weapons, covered their mouths and eyes and bound their limbs with duct tape.

There was a door, flush with the wall behind the desk. No obvious way of opening it until Garrett took one of the men's badges and waved it round the edge and it slid away without a sound. Behind it was a spacious security and administration suite. Screens showing feeds from surveillance cameras covering all the building's public areas, filing and computer equipment, and in a second, smaller room a number of steel lockers and a toilet cubicle. There were no other staff. Garrett dragged the two men into the locker room, double-checked to make sure there was nothing there they could use to free themselves, then slipped out. As he did, the screens changed, a central window outlined in red opening as the software managing the feeds detected and concentrated on a camera that had picked up movement. Three men, entering an elevator.

He left the office, quickly made sure there were no alarms winking on the reception desk, and headed for the elevators before the men could arrive in the lobby.

FIFTY-TWO

Swaying motion, and cold in her lungs. A bird shrieking high above Maya, call warped to a hollow keening by the Doppler effect as it banked and wheeled away. She opened her eyes, saw whorls of wind-twisted night cloud like spectral armies reflecting Newport's ugly light. Snow blew down in flurries, dancing like crazy glitches in her vision. She was buried under layers of blankets in a narrow boat rocking on the river waves. She felt better than before, less exhausted. Slowly, awkwardly, she pushed herself into a sitting position, out from under her covers. The man and woman who'd been talking to the old guy were at either end of the boat, each of them with a paddle in hand. Maya looked down and saw that she was dressed as they were. The stitched-together coats they wore were heavy, but kept the wind and the cold out. By the feel of it, most of her things were gone, though she still had Valentin's key round her wrist. The Port's lights were a long way behind them and they were slowly cutting their way along the deserted commercial reaches of the sluggish Murdoch, the snow like clumped mist around them.

The man, sitting in the stern, said, 'She's awake, Teri.'

The woman turned, laid her paddle down. She pulled her scarf down from her mouth and clambered to the seat in front of Maya. Said, 'How are you feeling?'

'Better, some.' Her throat was still sore and her voice was raw and scratchy, but she could talk. 'Who are you? Where are we going?'

'Food,' the woman said. She pulled a tiny charcoal stove made from a steel lockbox out from beneath the seat, clamped it to the wood, and lit it. Clipped a kettle to the top and flipped open the spout. 'We've still got a way to go. You should eat. I'm Teri and this is Stian. We're on our way to the Gate.'

'The Gate? We're going there? Why? How?'

'Old man Huayna said you'd been trying to say it in your sleep but you couldn't do more than whisper it. He thought you said you were trying to get back there so he called us to bring you home.'

Maya shivered, hoped it didn't show on her face that they had her wrong, that she wasn't one of them, but Teri was checking on the kettle and its contents. The first wisps of steam were rising from the open spout and a rich vegetable scent hit Maya's nostrils. Her stomach growled. She wondered how long it had been since she'd eaten and couldn't remember.

'How did you end up in the river?' Teri said. 'Not a good time of year to take a swim.'

'The boat I was on sank. Someone sank it.' Her memories of what had happened on the *Adventure* were jumbled. She remembered Garrett's face, looking down at her, guessed he'd survived. What had happened to Julius? Had he made it? She didn't know.

'Why?'

'They wanted something I couldn't give them. Who are Huayna and Miriam? They found me in the water.'

'Just Port people. They live on the *Winter* and have a boat berthed at the riverside hatches they use for scavenging and fishing, which is how they found you. They know about us, of course, but they're regular folk.'

'Turn's coming up, Teri,' Stian said from the stern.

'Watch the soup,' she told Maya. 'Make sure it doesn't boil over.'

Teri returned to the prow and helped Stian steer their craft towards an opening on the far side of the river, fighting the current, until they passed through its mouth. Darkened industrial wharfs guarded the entrance to what seemed to be one of the dozens of narrower, half-channelled tributaries of the Murdoch. Maya had no idea which one it might be, only that it was still within the commercial wasteland fanning out from the harbour districts.

Once they were safely free of the Murdoch's current, Teri laid her paddle down again and took the kettle off the stove, emptied the hot coals into the water. She poured the soup into three mugs and passed them round. Maya clasped hers, enjoying the warmth through her gloves, inhaling the thick vegetable smell as they slowly passed by deserted factories gently blanketed by the drifting snow. A ghost landscape, dead and empty, forgotten by the outside world.

The soup was long gone and they'd taken another couple of turns into a narrow network of canal docks by the time Teri picked up her paddle and helped Stian swing the boat into another, shadowed entryway. A couple of dozen yards inside was a steel guillotine lock. The two of them brought the boat to rest in front of it, next to where a rusted intercom unit was mounted to the channel wall. When Teri pushed the call button, a pair of red lights flicked into life over the boat, casting everything into a harsh crimson. Maya saw, then, the pattern of holes and gaps cut in the surface of the barrier. Like a huge, bloody razor blade, half sunk in the red-stained water.

FIFTY-THREE

The numbers over the door, displayed like roman numerals on an old-style clock face, scrolled past, smooth and steady, every three breaths. Garrett checked his reflection in the mirror at the back. Saw the faint text of a scrolling news ticker across the bottom of the glass and the logo of Daedalus Venture laser-etched in the corner. There was an ugly welt across his jawline, broken by a red slash of slow blood. He wondered if Blake was already here, and if so, how he'd got in without trouble from the guards. A second point of entry through the parking garage below, maybe. The way they'd brought him on his first visit here. Or perhaps he wasn't coming at all, and if Kent didn't know the cure herself then this was going to be for nothing.

'Please let it go, Charlie,' Emi had said before he left.

'Don't you want to live? We've got a chance to save you. Why don't you want to take it? I don't understand you.'

'It's not going to work.' She'd touched his face, and he'd pulled away, angry. 'Tell me how it helps if you get yourself killed or arrested. I haven't got much time left and I want you to be here. I don't want to die alone. And I don't want to die knowing that you haven't come to terms with it yet.'

'It doesn't have to happen.'

'Even if you find out how Jason Blake survived, what are the chances of the cure being something you can acquire for yourself right then and there, get back to me, and administer it before my time runs out? You're not thinking straight, Charlie.'

'I'll be back.'

He felt the elevator slow and stop as the floor counter ticked round to 25. Ran through the rest of the entry instructions in his head, one more time. Figured they probably wouldn't be worth that much by now, but the closer they got him to Kent the easier it'd be and the sooner he'd be out.

The door slid open to reveal four corridors running from the elevator core in an X, one to each penthouse. They were lined with plate windows and floored with thick ruby carpet, and resting squarely on top Garrett could see the underside of what he guessed was a helipad. The metal strutwork was arched and styled like the ornate framework of a European king's airship from a hundred years before.

It was the whiff of cigarette smoke that warned Garrett the Clocks were there before he saw the two men waiting. A little and large pairing, dressed down. They looked like most of the guys he'd seen in Copeman Fisheries, and he saw the hourglass tattoos on the backs of their hands. Both of them were carrying shotguns.

He fired his taser at the first, the guy jerking spastically as the current rippled through him. His finger yanked the trigger of his weapon, the gun's blast high and off-target, closer to his friend than it was to Garrett, and it probably saved Garrett's life. The second guy ducked, lost his aim and fired wide. Garrett felt a couple of stray pellets whip through his side like hot wire. He threw himself forward and swung the baton at the man's neck, but he blocked with the barrel of the shotgun, smashed the stock into Garrett's chest. Shooting spike of pain as a rib snapped, and he nearly froze in shock. Saw the man's eyes and the fat empty barrel of the shotgun as it came back down. He grabbed it with his free hand, ignoring the pain, and crashed the baton into the side of the guy's neck. Kept hold of the gun as the man fell, and hit him again. Felt something snap and the guy went limp.

Swearing, behind him. Garrett spun and saw the man he'd tasered forcing his ragged muscles to act, to reach for his weapon again. Their gazes met for a fraction of a second, then Garrett pulled the trigger and the man's face vanished, turned to red, pink and white. His body collapsed, began to bleed thickly out. Garrett didn't want to look too closely at it.

The shots would have alerted the others. Time was almost up. He jogged, wincing and bloody, towards the door to Kent's penthouse.

FIFTY-FOUR

'It's Teri. *Patefacio quod universa.*'

No answer from the intercom, but Teri sat back and as the light flickered out the gate began to shudder upwards, screeching and grinding, metal shearing against metal. They paddled through it, Maya half expecting it to come crashing down like a blade as they tried to cross the boundary, into a short, dead-end stretch of dock surrounded by a single U-shaped decaying warehouse unit. There were a dozen more boats moored here, none of them, Maya noticed, fitted with a motor.

They tied up by a rusting ladder and Stian steadied Maya as she pulled herself up the first few rungs and left the boat behind. Her arms were aching, legs unsteady, by the time she reached the top of the wharf. The warehousing was heavily modified. The huge loading doors were gone, the openings yawning wide with a newer, cinderblock wall inset a couple of yards behind them. It ran all the way round the perimeter of the building, turning the front of the warehouse into a sort of monastic cloister. Dim light spilled through some of the windows on the upper floors, enough for Maya to see, high up on the wall facing the gate, a painted red razor symbol identical to those she'd seen on the *Winter*.

Teri patted her on the shoulder. 'Are you OK?'

'Yeah,' Maya said. 'Yeah. I'm just a bit dizzy. Standing and walking's going to take a little while to get used to.'

'I'll help you inside.'

'Thanks.' She turned her gaze away from the razor emblem, wondering if there was, even now, someone inside the warehouse being given the Curse, having their life irrevocably changed while they lay helpless and drugged. Whether Teri and Stian were Clocks too, or some kind of perverse servitors of whoever was behind the Curse.

She let Teri steer her into the colonnade, out of the snow. Along its strange industrial–religious length for a way, then through a door on to the old warehouse floor. A long, lofty chamber whose high windows were long boarded up, heated by two rectangular firepits sunk in the concrete floor and carefully ringed with steel fences and spark guards. Four long tables, interlocked pasting benches, ran almost the length of the room, lined with seats. A third, much smaller fire at the back of the room was capped with a metal grill holding a couple of large cooking pots. There were at least forty people in here, eating and talking. Some were dressed like Maya and Teri, others had red or black tabards over the tops of their makeshift longcoats. The wall at the far end bore another razor emblem, huge and ornate, and a motto underneath: *To soar higher and carry us all*. The air reeked of smoke and cooked food. It was a refectory, and she'd clearly arrived during the evening meal.

'You want to eat?' Teri said. 'You'll feel better.'

Maya did, but couldn't face all those eyes, waiting for someone to mark her as an impostor, or simply cracking under the deep, deep strangeness of it all. Since Harrison Valentin first told her of the Curse, she'd imagined plenty of places she'd find its creator, many ways it might be sustained. This was nothing like any of them.

'No. I do,' she said, 'but I feel like I'd just throw up. I must have swallowed half the river . . . before. I'll leave that until tomorrow.'

Teri smiled, and Maya wondered why she was here, keeping the Curse alive. 'Sure. Let's get you to your cell.'

She led Maya through another doorway at the end of the refectory under the enormous razor emblem, into another part of the warehouse. There was obviously a mezzanine floor here; Maya could see the underside of some of its connecting gantries, but the gaps between them had been blocked with thick, red plastic sheeting to split the area into two distinct storeys. More of the sheeting had been strung from this new ceiling to make walls subdividing the space beneath into scores of individual rooms and connecting corridors. The doors to each of what she realised Teri had meant by 'cell' were simply flaps of this plastic that could be tied open or lashed in place. Light was provided by bulbs in safety cages suspended from the gantries above or bolted into the floor, the plastic painting everything in shades of crimson.

She stopped, said to Teri, 'Look, I'll make it to my cell from here. You must be starving. Go get something to eat. There's no sense letting me hold you up, not after you brought me all the way home.'

'Are you sure? I don't mind.'

'You've done so much, Teri. I'll be fine, really. What can go wrong from here, right?'

'Well, if you say so.' Teri's gaze shifted over Maya's shoulder. 'Shepherd Arcus,' she said, bowing her head. 'Good evening.'

Maya turned. The man behind her was wearing the same coat as the others, but his black tabard had a painted white book at its centre. He was tall, with a shaven head, a pair of eyebrow piercings, and a jawline like an iron girder.

'Good evening, Teri,' he said. 'Everything well in the Port?'

'Yes, all as it should be. We also found one of our own who'd nearly drowned in the river. Some hulkers picked her out of the water and asked for our help. She's a bit shaky, but she's going to be OK.'

'I'm glad to hear it.' Shepherd Arcus smiled.

'Be sure to check in with me in the morning,' Teri said to Maya. 'I want to be sure you're better for a rest. Take care, now.'

'Thanks. I will,' Maya said, thinking: please don't leave me alone with him. But Teri turned and headed for the refectory and food.

'Walk with me a while,' Shepherd Arcus said. 'If you're

able. This won't take long. There's something we should attend to.'

She wanted to object, but she couldn't find an excuse that wouldn't lead to further complications. He gently guided her in the direction of one of the plastic-lined corridors then walked beside her at a measured, easy pace with his hands clasped together in front of him.

'Teri and Stian did well today,' he said, softly, as they walked. 'But you're not one of us, are you?'

FIFTY-FIVE

Before tonight, the penthouse had been immaculate. When Garrett opened the door he was presented with a high, ornate hall that wouldn't have looked out of place in Versailles. A huge oil painting on the far wall showed a night-time view of the city skyline broken, he saw, by a series of twelve towers. One of them was clearly a heavily stylised version of Arel Spire, the others he didn't recognise. Beneath the painting was the slumped body of a woman, ivory white, covered in blood. It looked as if she'd been shot in the gut. From one of the rooms to the left, down a short corridor lit by amber sconces that led to the private elevator Garrett had entered by before, he could hear shouting. Two men, arguing.

He was almost there when the door thudded open and an angry guy in a longcoat strode out, looking like a stockbroker about to go non-linear after a market crash. He had a gun in his hand, some kind of street SMG, a Tec-9 knock-off, wildly incongruent with the rest of his appearance. He saw Garrett lurching towards him, said, 'Fuck!' and Garrett shot him in the chest. Didn't think about it, just acted on instinct. The recoil jarred his busted rib and a fresh wave of pain washed through him. The guy folded against the wall, moaning frothily, his gun gone and forgotten. Garrett figured he wouldn't last long. A burst of talk from the room he'd come from, then a cold silence.

Garrett limped up to the doorway, hissing every breath through clenched teeth. He wondered how many of the rest of them had weapons, how many 'the rest' were. Probably not a lot; to sneak anyone up here, unnoticed, must have been difficult.

'If this is some kind of dumb-ass rescue attempt, you'd be advised to stay clear until we're done here,' Jason Blake said, somewhere on the far side of the doorway. 'I'll happily kill Miss Kent here the moment we have any trouble. I'd like to talk to her for a while longer, but not so much that I'd let her be taken back. It's your choice.'

The voice, so long imagined. Garrett saw McDermott dying in the snow, Emi, crying and alone, Maya's face as the river swallowed her. Fought the pain and bitterness he felt and managed to say, 'I don't care what you do to her. This isn't a rescue. You're the one I want to talk to, Blake.'

'Charlie Garrett again? Well, well. This *is* interesting. What brings you here?'

'I want to know how you did it. How come you're still alive. How you beat the Curse.'

Laughter. 'Our hostess is the one you should be talking to if that's what you want. Once we've finished our business here you're welcome to ask her anything you like.'

'I'd be happy to do it the other way round.'

'I'm sorry, Charlie. We need to get this done. None of us are coming out until we're finished, so either you take your chances and walk on in, or you've got nothing to do but wait and hope we get done before the cops show up. Before the *other* cops show up, I mean.'

Garrett pictured a handful of men, armed, watching the door while Blake held a gun at Amanda Kent's head. Said, 'Did you manage to decode any of the stuff in that case, Blake? Do you know what she's been up to?'

He waited a second, let Blake begin his answer, draw his men's attention for a moment, and then twisted into the doorway, ignoring the agony in his chest, shotgun up and ready. There was more than a handful of Clocks here. Seven of them plus Blake in a sprawling suite carved and painted like a Revolutionary-era ballroom. Blake was sitting opposite Amanda Kent, keeping her between himself and the door, with a pistol wedged against her forehead. One of the others was covering a group of civvies. Some of them were obviously part of the TV crew, and terrified. Amongst them, though, were some of Kent's security people. A TV camera was fixed to a tripod, pointing at Kent's face. Lights blared on stands behind it.

'Anyone so much as twitches and I'll turn you and your "hostess" to red paste,' Garrett said.

'You'll die before you can pull the trigger.'

'Bet your life?'

Blake smiled, seemed mildly amused. 'What is it you want, Charlie? I don't think I did much to you. Don't tell me this is revenge.'

'Emi,' Garrett said. The name sounded strange, hollow, as he said it here. 'Her time's almost up. You're alive and I want to know why. Miss Kent's been talking to the guy who made the Curse in the first place. I want to know how to save her, and at least one of you's got the answer.'

A long hard silence. Then Blake sighed, softened his posture. 'Emi. How is she?'

'How d'you think?'

'Do you love her? Stupid question. You wouldn't be here otherwise.' He looked at Kent. 'I can't help you, Charlie, but maybe she can. What do you know about what she's been doing? I'm genuinely interested. I think, in our own ways, you and I are here for the same reason.'

'How did you survive, Blake?'

'Charlie . . .'

Garrett blinked, adjusted his grip on the shotgun. 'How?'

'You're the only one in this room who doesn't know. I tell all my people once they're a part of the family,' Blake said. He sounded sad, pitying. 'I never had the Curse, Charlie. I lied to the cops to get into the groups, but I was never Cursed. That's why I can't help you.'

FIFTY-SIX

Emi was waiting with Adam Nyberg in one of the Port's little deck-top bars when Harrison Valentin and four men strode aboard. She could see the bulges of guns under their jackets. Slipped her hand into her bag and hit the call button on her phone a couple of times, knowing the redial would put her through to Charlie's new, temporary, number.

'What do you want?' she said.

'You, Miss Nakano. Please,' Valentin said to Nyberg, 'sit down. I have no great desire to have to do anything to you, but I will if you make it necessary.'

'I'm not going anywhere. This is a public place,' Emi said.

'Which makes no difference. Not to me, and not tonight. I've had eyes on this area since I knew my little helper was working down here. I know who you are, and I know who your boyfriend is, and I know your circumstances. Things are moving, Miss Nakano, and I have to race one of my rivals, who I'm sure you know, to a very tempting prize indeed. Time is ticking and it'd be a shame if you missed out.'

'Sir,' one of the guys with him said, 'Mr Cutter—'

'Yes, I know. Time to go, people. Miss Nakano, if you would.'

FIFTY-SEVEN

'I don't believe you,' Garrett said. Felt everything threatening to come loose. He'd expected that Blake wouldn't help him, thought that he or Kent might not be here, might be dead, imagined all kinds of different scenarios, but not this.

'That's your choice, but it's true, Charlie.'

'So why are you here?'

'Tell him, Amanda,' Blake said. 'Tell him why I'm here.'

Garrett glanced at the woman in the chair. Amanda Kent, one of the richest women in the city, if not the country. So calm and slick the first time they'd met, now cold and taut and furious. And looking, he thought, nothing like a hostage. She didn't return his gaze but kept her eyes on Blake. Said, with withering contempt, 'This is ridiculous. I've told you already, and now Mr Garrett, coming in here like this, should know too, that this is going to end badly for you all. Regardless of what happens to me.'

'You were going to go on air about the Curse,' Garrett said. 'That was the plan. Reveal its existence, get everyone freaked, and quietly take the technology for yourself. You took Emi to try to figure out how to break it. Have you done it already? Have you got a cure?'

'Cutter should have done his job a little better. I'll have to reprimand him when he returns.'

Garrett said, quietly, feeling his voice tighten and choke, 'I want the cure. I don't have much time. I have to get back to Emi. I don't care which one of you has it or nearly has it. Please.'

'You're not the only one who wants it, Charlie,' Blake said. He nodded at those with him. 'Look at these people. You think they don't want to live? We all want the same things. Except Amanda here.'

'You don't. You just said you never had the Curse. You've got no idea what you're talking about.'

Blake's eyes narrowed. 'Do you remember Edward Blake, Charlie? He only went to the group meetings a couple of times. I don't know if you were on duty when he did. He was my brother and he got the Curse. I was in Iraq. I couldn't help him. I shouldn't have needed to. See, Edward worked for Daedalus Venture. Even more than that, Edward was Ms Kent's man. She has a thing, it seems, for taking a fancy to her underlings, rather as I imagine a Roman empress would with some of her slaves.'

'She let him die?'

'Better.' A grim smile. 'Before Edward was affected, Amanda had no idea the Curse existed. And when he told her about it, she wanted it. Didn't want my brother, though.

She had her pet doctors at her mansion give him all the tests they could, told him to keep it quiet so they could "work on a cure" in peace, and froze him out. Stupid son of a bitch had been idiot enough to think he loved her, and she dropped him as soon as he was no use to her. Cops told him to keep it a secret too, and I was gone, so he had nowhere to go. He wrote me a letter before he died. Explaining. You understand now?'

'You blew up Green Street. You killed nearly fifty people.'

'I needed revenge. We needed leverage. Amanda's not the only one trying to get her hands on the technology behind the Curse. There's a group of wealthy like-minded individuals she belongs to, like a private members' club. They're not supposed to act against each other, though I guess you've seen they do when the greed's strong enough, but they're free to screw with the rest of us for fun and profit. Any one of them could get the cure. I figured if we take one of them out, threaten to do the rest, it'd give them a real incentive to help end the Curse.'

Blake shook his head. 'Except we missed her. Our information was that Amanda would be in that car, and we were wrong. A second chance might've been hard to come by. But when our spotters saw that kid snatch the case, I did some digging and realised there might be some very useful information indeed in there. So here we are. I want Miss Kent here to admit everything she's done, on camera. To wreck her life in the way she wrecked Edward's. And to give up what she knows of the Curse and a possible cure. I promised my people as much.'

'So what do you know?' Garrett swung the barrel of the shotgun to point at the back of Kent's head. Didn't care what the Clocks did now he was no longer threatening their leader. 'What's the cure?'

She turned then, looked at him for the first time. She had the face of a fine sculpture: beautiful, but unyielding and soulless. No pity in her eyes, only contempt, as she said, 'There isn't one. Not yet.'

'I don't believe you. You must've been looking at this for ages. You know something that could help.'

She shook her head, slowly, like she was talking to a child. 'Not yet. We're close. We'll have it very soon. Between the information Dominic was carrying and our own efforts on the ground, we've found it. Not that there's any guarantee of a speedy result. If your girlfriend hadn't run from us, we'd have had something in a couple of weeks. Even when we know how the Curse is made, working out how to stop it killing will take time. You fools should have come here in a month or so.'

'You're lying!'

'Charlie—' Blake, his voice heavy and calm.

'You're fucking lying!'

'Charlie, she doesn't have it. No one does. We can use her to put pressure on the others for a cure, but it'll take time. It's the best we can do. She can't help you right now. Do you understand?'

A long, sad pause. Then Blake said, 'Go home, Charlie. I don't know if there'll be cops or security or anyone downstairs by now, but none of my people will stop you. Go, be with Emi. Someone should.'

Garrett backed away. He wanted to kill Kent, or Blake, do *something* to persuade himself he hadn't wasted all the time he'd left Emi alone, gone against her wishes. No one paid him much attention, as if he'd ceased to exist. He'd so desperately wanted to rescue her, to come through at the last minute on a white horse, cure in hand, and give her back her life. He'd been fooling himself.

His phone rang. So strange, in these surroundings. And only Emi had the number. When he picked up, there was no talk, just muffled sounds, and then Emi's voice, talking to someone else. For a moment he wondered if she'd dialled by mistake, but then he heard the other side of the conversation and broke into a run.

Into the hallway, and right there were two clusters of men in SWAT gear, no police insignia. They were carrying fat shotguns and wearing gas masks. The lead man froze, shocked, as he saw Garrett. Garrett flinched, jerked back into the doorway. There was a crack, and a slug slammed into the wall where his chest had been.

FIFTY-EIGHT

'Frankie, Sharpe,' Blake said, 'keep these people covered. The rest of you, on the door. Miss Kent stays with me. If it looks like we're screwed here, no one makes it away, clear? Sorry, Charlie. Guess none of us get to go home just yet.'

'Or at all,' Kent said. 'Regardless of what happens in here, none of you will be leaving.'

'Not an especially smart thing to tell me, in the circumstances.'

'I hate to see people chase fool's dreams. You can still decide how quickly this all ends.'

A voice out in the hallway, shouting, 'You have five seconds to throw down your weapons and surrender, then this is all going to turn ugly.'

No negotiation, no pretence of wanting to talk. Garrett remembered the gas masks. He found a cloth, dunked it in a vase of flowers and tied it, sodden, over his mouth and nose. As he did so, he saw a phone lying on the floor, looking like it had been kicked or knocked there during whatever struggle had happened before he'd arrived. Expensive, elegant. And on the screen, updating as he watched, a map and a GPS marker moving across the city. It was tagged 'CUTTER'. Not far from Willow Heights. Amanda Kent's phone, Cutter en route. He thought back to what he'd heard of the conversation between the men who were taking Emi, surely Harrison Valentin or someone like that. They were moving too, about to seize the prize. They were trying to race Cutter, and therefore wherever Cutter went, that's where he'd find Emi. He pocketed the phone. If only he could get out of the penthouse.

The Clocks were taking up watching positions. The two covering the hostages had forced them to lie on the floor and were hunkered down nearby. Blake pulled Kent away to the side of the room and shouted, 'We only came here to talk. If you want to make it ugly, make it ugly.'

The metallic *spang* as a bulky grenade hit the wall just inside the doorway, bounced and rolled into the room. One of the Clocks fired, futilely, into the hall as it went off, spewing gouts of white vapour into the air.

Choking and coughing, those nearest the door catching it the worst. People shouting. Garrett felt his eyes prick as the tear gas spread. Then, gunfire. Three shotgun roars from behind the cloud in the doorway, answering wild fire from the Clocks, unsighted and reeling from the gas. Garrett heard screaming, saw a woman rolling around on the floor, clutching her thigh. Realised that Kent's people were shooting baton rounds. Probably why they felt they could be so gung-ho. He pulled away to the back of the room, blew out one of the floor-to-ceilings, glass and ricocheting buckshot spattering his clothes and skin. Icy air blasted inwards, took some of the pain of the gas away. More gunfire, and he saw a black-clad figure in a gas mask drop just inside the doorway, the faceplate punctured and red sheeting all over the inside of the plastic.

'Down, down, down!' Garrett couldn't even tell which side the man shouting was on. Two impacts snapped the air by his side, rubber slugs hammering the wall, and he dropped, flipped the table in front of him on to its side and ducked into the cover it provided. Dark figures skittering, predatory and alien, through the gas and tears and smoke. Shotgun blasts and the baton rounds pounding like a bass line, return fire like a driving drumbeat, and over it all the shouting and screaming of people unable to see or breathe, people in pain, people terrified and panicking.

Then something smashed the lights and the room filled with sparks and darkness. Gunfire now lit the shadows in strobes, turned the streaming gas to glowing fog, the people within it to ghastly frozen spectres. Garrett saw two of the Clocks, crouched, coughing, and firing almost blind, take slugs almost simultaneously. One was struck in the head, blood held for an eyeblink in a rooster tail, a flap of skin torn loose from his brow, waving free as he twisted under the impact, already unconscious or dead. His comrade was hit in the shoulder, spun, screaming, his weapon arcing away from him into the stuttering black. Garrett popped over the top of the table, fired twice at what he thought were guys in gas masks, but couldn't be sure. Looked across and saw Blake huddled by one of the cracked windows, Kent still clutched in front of him. Red-eyed, watching what was happening in front of him and, from his expression, not happy with it. As Garrett watched, he pushed Kent away, said something to her, just a couple of words, and then shot her in the back of the head. His face was a blank, taut and drawn. The tear gas made it look as if they were both crying. Her body slid to the floor and, in the next gunshot strobe, Blake was gone.

The gas was beginning to dissipate, turned to tatters by the wind whipping through the missing window.

Another boom, a flash in the dark, and pain tore through his chest. It felt like he'd been hit by a car. The faint impression of a masked figure, framed in the dark, and there was no floor beneath Garrett's feet. Then the ceiling fell away from him, gravity closing around his body like a fist, and he was through the window and skidding head first down the crystal pyramid slope of Arel Spire's upper floors on his back, winded and stunned, helpless.

The whine of the glass beneath Garrett filled his ears and shook his teeth as he slid down the snow-dusted surface like it was a ski jump, faster and faster. His chest was agony, and he could do no more than flail his arms ineffectively, nothing to even slow his descent. Then, suddenly, the glass was gone and the wind tore at his hair as he shot out into the howling night, twenty floors of nothing beneath him.

FIFTY-NINE

Thunder roaring in his ears, air resistance like a wall beneath his limbs. Time running slow, but Garrett couldn't feel afraid. Felt nothing at all, as if all the regret and anger and guilt had been left behind in the penthouse when he went sailing through the window. Just empty and sad that he'd not had the chance to say goodbye to Emi, that he'd be leaving her in the hands of their enemies. The snow whipping away from him, like lines of white rain falling past him, into the void.

Then he crashed into something, as if he had hit a vast vinyl bag full of water. Saw a huge shape away to his right like the tail of a gigantic fish, flapping and bowed by the wind. The advertising blimp. He'd landed on top of the blimp.

And was sliding again.

Garrett forced his body to twist, threw himself on to his front. Fingers scrabbling against the surface of the blimp as he slid down from its crest, searching for a seam, a handhold, something to anchor him as it bucked and swayed in the gale. Found nothing. His legs slid out over the void and he was falling again, but then a webwork of cords was skipping past his hands and he hooked his fingers round one and clung tight. He was dangling from the net of polymer lines at the base of the blimp that distributed the load evenly between its four mooring cables. A hundred and fifty feet beneath him, Garrett could see traffic, lights high and wide in the driving snow. The nearest cable was six yards away and might have been a mile. His fingers burned and his shoulders were raw, and his ribs were racked with pain, but, he told himself, it was hang on or die. He had a second chance, and daren't squander it.

Release, lunge, grab. Pause for breath. Concentrate. Release, lunge, grab. Pause for breath. Concentrate. A foot at a time, Garrett slowly swung to the steel mooring cable, which was thrumming in the wind. One hand closed on it. Then he swung out his feet, wrapped them around it. Then, heart pounding and hardly able to breathe, his other hand. Pictured his grip slipping from the metal, or sliding uncontrollably, skin flaying from his palms, slamming into the street. But neither happened. He gripped the cable grimly, and slowly, very slowly, edged his way downwards, one breath at a time.

By the time his feet touched solid ground, he could barely see, couldn't feel anything at all. He collapsed into the snow that caked the sidewalk and lay there for a time, trembling.

'Hey, you OK?' A woman, wrapped up in a thick red scarf and matching hat. 'You need a hand getting up?'

Garrett stared at her for a moment. Wondered how he must look, bruised and bloody. Said, 'I'm OK, yeah.'

He rolled over and forced his shattered muscles to push him to his feet. Wrapped his coat tightly around him, hoping she hadn't seen anything that gave away what had happened to him.

'You sure you're all right?' she said. 'You look pretty dazed. I can call the paramedics, if you want to get checked out.'

'No, no. I'm mostly just cold. I'll be fine once I get home. Thanks, though.'

'Well, if you say so. Be careful, huh? I guess it must've been some fall.'

'Yeah,' he told her. 'Yeah, you could say that.'

Checked his pockets for Amanda Kent's phone and its GPS tracker and found it safe. Staggered into the street as he saw headlights approach and held up a hand, not even a badge or a gun, nothing to force the driver to stop short of sheer willpower.

The vehicle skidded to a halt in front of him. Of all things, it was a cab. The driver stuck his head out of the window and yelled in a thick Russian accent, 'You only had to wave.'

'Sorry. I'm a cop.'

'You are a mess.'

'You got to drive, real fast.'

Moments later, the cab was screaming through the streets of Newport. Garrett held the GPS tracker on the dash so the driver, who said his name was Anatoly, could work out his route. The marker had passed Willow Heights, circled over the harbour and was now heading upriver into what Garrett vaguely remembered as a mouldering commercial district.

'I know that area,' Anatoly shouted over the engine and the wind rushing through his open window.

'You do? What's there?'

'I don't know what is there before, but now is place for filming documentary, I hear. Word just go out on radio that no traffic through area, roads closed. Not that anyone goes through there anyway; five years I drive this cab, I not go within half a mile of the place. But still, they say.'

'A documentary?' Garrett shook his head. Cover story, he guessed. Good one, too; unlike a movie, no one would ever go in the cold to see a glimpse of filming when there were no stars, no Hollywood. 'How soon can we get there?'

'Ten, fifteen minutes. I drive well.'

Garrett used the radio to file a garbled report, giving McDermott's badge number, something about commandeering a cab to respond to an emergency. Then he sat back and let Anatoly drive. As good as his word, the Russian had them across the river and scything past deserted industrial lots with barely a pause. By now the GPS marker was stationary, locked over a block a short way ahead. Garrett tapped Anatoly on the shoulder, yelled, 'Stop the cab. Stop.'

'Why?' But he did.

'You've got to get out. Where I'm going is very dangerous.

I don't want you getting killed, clear?'

Anatoly frowned. Shook his head as he got out and said, 'Better be good fare for this. And story after.'

Garrett shrugged. Fumbled in his pocket for a wad of notes. Said, as he climbed into the driver's seat, 'If I make it back I'll tell you whatever you want.'

Belted up and hit the gas. He was doing fifty by the end of the next block, across a narrow canal, and accelerating now he was on a clear straightaway to his destination. Didn't have a plan for what to do when he got there, but hadn't that been the case the whole evening?

Then he saw the road run out up ahead, too late to do anything much about it. Someone had demolished the bridge over the next strip of water, left nothing but a halfway skeleton of girders in its place. No chance to stop in the snow, given the speed he was doing. Garrett aimed for a metal beam that looked like it'd best serve as a ramp, and kept his foot on the gas.

SIXTY

The day of the Green Street bombing.

Mikkel Thoresen looked at his watch yet again: must have been a hundred instinctive, nervy flicks of the wrist by now. Found a little irony in a Clock needing to know the time. The bomb vest he wore was heavy but not uncomfortable. The others had made it well and it hung evenly from his shoulders. All plastique, no metal packing, no shrapnel; Jason had been very clear on that. He'd been assured there was no chance he wouldn't die instantly and painlessly. He rubbed the hourglass tattooed on his hand. The Curse would take him in less than a week anyway. He'd carried the knowledge of his death with him for so long that knowing it was almost upon him – under his control – was, now he faced it, a relief. His fear was that it wouldn't work, that the bomb wouldn't explode, or that he'd be hit by a car or stopped by the cops before it happened.

In his pocket, a photo of himself with Anya. She'd left

when he told her he had less than a year to live, said she couldn't face it, deal with the certainty of losing him. Maybe he'd shouted at her, maybe his mood had changed; he knew he hadn't dealt well with finding out he had the Curse. Memory was a blurred half-picture now, a torn piece of paper. He'd nearly ended it all then. She'd been the best part of his life. But Jason had helped him see that he still might have a purpose, that he could still *do* something. It wouldn't help him, but it might help the others. Might make Anya appreciate what he'd been going through, how many of them there were, and how little aid they'd had from an uncaring city. Yes, he knew people would die with him, but that was the way it had to be; the message had to be impossible to ignore.

He sighed, pulled his hood up, hauled his heavy coat on over the top of his sweater, itself over the bomb vest. Checked that the radio detonator was secure round his wrist, ready to slip into his hand at the vital moment. Stepped out of the back of the van, into the snow-filled alleyway where Jason and three other Clocks were waiting for him to finish composing himself. Wordlessly, the trio shook his hand in turn. In their eyes he saw what his sacrifice meant to their cause. Felt proud, and afraid. Then Jason hugged him, patted him hard on the back, didn't seem to worry about the explosives he wore.

'Are you ready, Mikkel? You look like it, but let me hear it.'

'I'm ready, Jason.' Smiled, ruefully. 'If I don't do this

now, I'll only have another few days anyway.'

'But you're willing to do it. It's important to me and to all of us that this is your choice.'

'Yeah. Yeah, I am.'

'Tell me again what it is you have to do.'

In his mind, Mikkel saw the face in the photographs Jason gave him to study. A face etched hard into his memory, every line and crease. Others – the building, the street at this time of day. So that he had a picture of exactly what he'd confront. No surprises, nothing he hadn't imagined doing a hundred times already.

'I wait for the call to say that the target's vehicle is on its way,' he said. 'I head on to the street and wait for her party to leave. I should be careful, but in the weather and the dark, I shouldn't worry too much about drawing suspicion. When I see them leave the building, I walk to the road, between twenty and thirty yards from the vehicle. Closer makes me look more suspicious. I give them time to get between five and ten yards from the vehicle, then I detonate the explosives.'

Jason looked at him and smiled. Confident and sad at the same time. 'Good man, Mikkel. You're a good man. It's been an honour to know you.'

'Thank you.' Nerves now, but he knew what he had to do. He shook Jason's hand and walked down the alley. Three blocks away, the evening rush hour was beginning on Green Street.

SIXTY-ONE

Her adrenaline was surging, but Maya knew she didn't have the strength to fight or run. Certainly not with so many people one cry of alarm away.

Shepherd Arcus smiled wryly at her. 'Relax,' he said. 'You're in no danger here. Indeed, you're welcome to our home.'

'You'll have to excuse me, but I have a hard time believing that.'

'You're certainly not the first visitor to reach us. You don't think we were all here already, do you?' Through a door, a proper, solid one, and away from the red plastic maze. Up a flight of stairs. 'I'm taking you to meet the Curator, so you can best understand our purpose.'

'You give people the Curse.'

'We do. But you need to understand *why*. Through here.'

A corridor, doors open along its right hand side. Through them, Maya saw a large, cleared space with mats and prayer cushions arranged around the edges. Then a workshop, two men in red tabards carefully and silently fiddling with something tiny and delicate under lamplight. 'What exactly is this place?' she said. 'The uniforms, the cells, your title . . . it's like a monastery.'

'A fortress – monastery, to be precise. The neighbouring blocks are ours too. We took down all surface access across the waterways a long time ago. It's like a moat around the Keep.' He must have seen Maya's expression because he added, 'The canal network's irregular. You wouldn't know we'd sealed this section off unless you looked for it, and since the area's ours, no one has a reason to come here. Most of this district's derelict anyway.'

'You bring all your victims in by boat, then?'

'Our guests, everyone. People who, for one reason or another, seek us out or want to know what's going on here. People like you. Most are unconscious or blindfolded, but not all. As I said, we all came here from somewhere. No one starts out as a member of the Flock.'

Maya said, 'And you all believe you're helping people? You're willing to kill innocents for . . . what? The notion that it's good for them?'

'People are willing to do all sorts,' Arcus said. 'How many people, every day, are willing to destroy themselves simply to murder others because of their nationality, religion or skin colour? We as a species have a deep need to believe that there is a purpose to our lives, something greater than ourselves. Here, we have a purpose. We might argue the morality of it, but we all believe that out of this some good may arise. In fact, we know that real, tangible good has already arisen. This is the Gallery.'

He showed her through into a dimly lit hallway. Its walls were lined for some distance with photographs, each with a piece of paper bearing a name and a small, in some cases very small, block of text beneath. There must have been scores of them.

Maya looked at one at random. The picture was of a man in his thirties with mousy brown hair hanging down beneath a striped knit cap. He had a short goatee and the ruddy face of a guy who spent a lot of time in the outdoors. He looked, as they all did, as if he was sleeping, already dead. The epitaph read: *John Austin: Reconciled with father. Travelled with family to Australia for first time.*

'Every single person we've taken is up here,' Arcus said. 'This is the record of their last year, a catalogue of what they've done, or not done, with the time they've had. We don't judge; it's not our place. We all make our choices.'

'How do you know what they do?'

'Some we cull from news reports, information online and other public sources. Some, people supply us with. We have quite a network, sources few would suspect or even notice. It's my job to oversee the collection and organisation of all the data. We want to know that our work isn't devoid of results.' He pointed to one of the pictures. 'Formed a community group to improve his neighbourhood after he was gone.' Another. 'Turned her house into a shelter for the homeless.' Another. 'Aid volunteer in the Sudan. I don't like that people have to die for this, but I still think we're doing right.'

Maya looked down the line of photographs until she saw a face she recognised, that she wouldn't forget. 'Mikkel,' she said. 'Killed forty-eight people on Green Street and injured many more because he couldn't handle what you'd done to him, and because a man called Jason Blake was able to turn his despair to violence.'

Arcus nodded, said nothing.

'So what happens to me? Once we see your "Curator"? Give me the Curse and turn me loose, lock me away, what?'

'It's late now, and a long trip to anywhere much, especially in this weather. You can stay with us tonight, get your strength back, and then one of our boats will take you back to the Port. Or anywhere else along the water, if you'd prefer.'

'That's it? No threats to secure my silence, no demand for secrecy?'

'No. That's not the way we do things, not if we can help it. Mind your head.' She ducked through a low doorway, newer, framed by steel beams. 'What happens afterwards is up to you.'

'And no one ever talks?'

'We have a lot of people here, and more outside. The Keep needs food, clothing, material and so on, so our members have to be out in the community and stories do spread, even if there aren't that many. The kind of people who seek us out are the kind most likely to stay. They want something to belong to. And if they don't find it here, they're still unlikely to talk. They're alienated from regular society already.'

The door opened into a long, uncluttered space running through the central core of the Keep; there were no windows in here. The walls, floor and ceiling had been coated with some kind of spray resin to form a seamless white plastic shield. There were six work stations, three on either side, before a glass partition cut off part of the far end. The closest four stations each held variously sized pairs of stainless steel vats connected to clusters of monitoring equipment, fixed tubes and glass remote manipulation fish tanks of the sort used to handle nuclear material. The final two were home to single items of boxy, almost analytical-looking apparatus connected to computers. Everything was, to Maya's eye, of laboratory grade. This was no back alley scrounger job; it was maybe little wonder the authorities hadn't found a cure for the Curse yet. Nine men and women in booted blue coveralls and face masks were working the equipment, and none paid Maya any special attention as she followed Shepherd Arcus.

'Don't we need protective gear as well?' she asked.

'These technicians work here all the time. The machines are sealed, but to reduce the risk of accidental contamination . . . Visitors like us are a minimal risk.'

'You're not a technician, then?'

He shook his head. 'I run the archive.'

'Where did all this stuff come from?'

'All will become clear. Shh, we're here.'

They had reached the glass partition. On the other side of the barrier, two Flock members in red were checking over an unconscious patient strapped to a plastic-draped operating table under the gaze of a man clad in charcoal grey. He was fully dressed and seemed unharmed, wired up to an EEG and a cardiograph. Maya couldn't see his face, just the dark lines of gangland tattoos up the side of his neck. She realised to her horror that this stranger had just become the Curse's next victim. She wondered if he had a family waiting for him, loved ones he'd leave behind a year from now when his time ran out. She rested a hand on the glass, willed the guy to wake up, somehow break free, but knew he wouldn't.

'You're killing him,' she said.

Shepherd Arcus rapped softly on the glass. The man in grey turned, nodded. 'Yes, we are,' Arcus said. 'This is the Curator.'

SIXTY-TWO

It started, the Curator told Maya, with a single man. He called himself Professor Rayner, though no one knew if that was his real name. He had been a research scientist in the field of nanotechnology and bioscience, working on a string of corporate-funded projects trying to resolve the problem of manufacturing nanoscale materials. However, wary, he said, of his sponsors, he began to hold back potential breakthroughs and to work on them himself, in private, using his own considerable resources. When he eventually perfected a biological molecular self-assembly process, not only successful but, like most biological systems, relatively robust, he decided to keep it hidden. The Curator said he didn't want it to fall into the hands of private interests; Maya thought, if the story were true, he'd probably just gone insane, become the classic mad scientist, obsessed with his work. Either way, he acquired this building and others through a series of fronts and blinds and moved his working materials here in secret, to create the lab in which they stood.

The professor's process allowed the to-order creation of liposomes – bubbles of fatty membrane that carried all sorts of payloads within individual cells in the body – as well as other biologically derived molecules, specifically the neuro-toxin used in the Curse. Surface compounds or structures on a biological 'baseplate' allowed the liposomes to bond or interact with specific cells or matching chemicals in the body. Most important of all, the same biomanufacturing breakthrough enabled him to crack one of the great stumbling blocks in nanotechnology: a functional, reliable clock mechanism, also biological, powered by chemicals in the human bloodstream, with a preset cut-off switch.

'So why did he use it to create the Curse?' Maya said. 'He could have cured all sorts of diseases, fixed so many problems . . . I just don't understand. He did all this – and I've got to believe he did, because the Curse is real – but of all the ways he could have put it to use . . . Did he really want you to kill that woman in there? Or any of the others who've died? This is insane.'

The Curator looked at her sadly. 'People have to be allowed to die. You're right, the professor's discoveries might extend our lives by another ten, twenty years, maybe more. But is that fair on everyone? Can the world afford to have its richest citizens consuming its resources for longer?'

'So don't use what he learned. Let them die. But why the killing?'

'The professor could see that as soon as his process became public, it would serve both good and bad purposes.

It might spare people suffering, but it could equally be turned to nefarious purposes by governments, intelligence agencies and the like. And, for a time at least, it would only continue to expand the divide between rich and poor, benefiting the few instead of the many, like most technological and medical breakthroughs.'

The Curator watched as his assistants covered their latest victim with a sheet and wheeled him away. 'And what is life, anyway? We, the rich few, have become comfortable and lazy. We drift through our day-to-day existence, with little reason to pursue anything greater. We could be so much more, but it takes effort. We have become a society of lost potential. The professor saw a way to change that, at a considerable cost. We are – usually – at our best in adversity, when there is no choice but to stand and be counted. The greatest advances in science and social change, the occasions when we show the most altruism and selflessness, are in times of war or disaster. When we are united in a common goal, freed from the comforting expectation that life as it is will continue for ever, unchanged. The professor could not give us a war, but he could give us that freedom.'

Maya shook her head. The Curator shrugged. 'Believe me, I can understand your feelings. We give people a time limit, a deadline by which they must achieve everything they wish. We free them from fear of long-term consequences, or dreams of long-term rewards, and allow them to act entirely according to their wishes. We allow their true selves to shine forth. We give people life in its most concentrated form, but only by taking it away again.'

'You're insane. What right do you have to do that to these people? Why should you be the one to choose?'

'Almost all of us harm others,' he said. 'We all make that choice, without having the right to do so.'

'Bullshit.'

'What about your clothes? Your shoes? The material possessions that make your life so comfortable? Made by those less fortunate than you, who live in conditions you can't imagine, exploited by companies who grow fat on your dollars. This happens because you want it to. What right do you have to force grinding poverty and slavery on others? Ultimately, which of us is doing greater harm?'

'Dozens of people died on Green Street because of you. I was there.'

The Curator shook his head. 'Not because of us. Mikkel was responsible for his own choices.'

'You don't know the pressure these people are under. What it's like to have your own death hanging over you like that. I've been to the support groups. I've seen it.'

'You're wrong,' he told her gently. 'The professor's no longer with us because the first person he used his discovery on was himself. He gave himself a year to establish this place, to begin his work. From the first of us who were drawn here, he asked for a volunteer to take over when he was gone. The condition the professor set was that his successor must make the same choice. Anyone seeking to be Curator must be given what you call the Curse themselves. I have already begun training the woman who will succeed me. My time will run out in less than three months. I don't regret my decision. The ethics of what we do are difficult, and the points you've just raised are constantly debated here at great length. But I still believe in it. We don't do what we do out of hatred or anger, we aren't bad or violent people. We do what we do, genuinely, out of hope.'

Silence for a while. Maya thought of those in the groups, how little joy this man's 'hope' had brought to most of them. 'So you know everything he knew? You could fix it if you wanted?'

The Curator looked at Maya with something like sympathy. He gestured at the machinery around them and shook his head. 'No, we can't undo what's been done or alter what we do. We know enough to operate the process, the feed materials for the biological vats, the use and maintenance of the atomic force microscopes used in the lithography process which constructs the finished article. We don't know how the self-manufacturing system in the vats works, how to change it or how to undo it. That knowledge died with the professor. We can maintain what he built, but not alter it.'

'A lot of people think you can. Amanda Kent wants your technology for herself.'

'The Flock was contacted by her people, but we've been careful to keep her at a distance. She doesn't know – I hope – where we're based, though I'm sure she's looking for us with every means she has. The meetings were always carried out a long way away in the territory of third parties. We have no interest whatsoever in dealing with her, and absolutely no intention of allowing our equipment to fall into her hands. It was unfortunate that one of our chosen was a lover of hers.'

'Why did you pick him if you didn't want to get her involved?'

'We don't choose beforehand, but we do observe afterwards. We want to know what results our work here has.'

'I don't believe there's no decision beforehand,' she said. 'You must watch people and see something of their routine.'

An uncomfortable glance between the Curator and the Shepherd. 'There's some . . . *preparation*,' Arcus said. 'More systematic, perhaps, the longer our work has continued. There's been some worry that this is leading to more deliberate selection.'

'The professor's instructions were that the choice should be entirely unbiased.' The Curator shook his head. 'I'm not sure we've ever been completely true to that. But then, we are only human.'

A sound, thrumming, rapidly growing somewhere in the night beyond the monastery walls. They all stared at the ceiling, then Arcus tugged on Maya's arm. 'Come with me, quickly,' he said.

'What is it?'

He led her out of the lab, the Curator left standing sadly behind them. 'I don't know. Not yet.'

Down a corridor, breaking right towards a maintenance exit. Outside at a run, and up a steel staircase to the pitched roof of the building. Maya arrived at the top out of breath, her legs aching. By now the noise was deafening and the source of it was right in front of her.

'You might have tried to keep Amanda Kent, or others like her, at a distance,' she said as a bell began to toll, too late, 'but it doesn't matter. They've found you. They've come for the Curse.'

A helicopter was hovering over the watery heart of the Keep. Four ropes, uncoiled, hung from its open doors, and men in military gear were deploying on the docks, assault rifles up, more rappelling down behind them. Maya saw the face of the last to swing down from the chopper. It was Cutter.

SIXTY-THREE

Shouting, the sound of running feet. Cutter's men, firing staccato bursts at targets Maya couldn't see. Flock members, panicking, trying to flee to safety. She suddenly felt the fear she'd consciously expressed, but never experienced, of the Foundation gaining access to the Curse's technology. The fear, too, of what they'd do to get it, how many people would die here, including her.

'We need to go,' Shepherd Arcus said. His face was grim, worried. 'You need to leave.'

Back, down the flight of stairs, at as much of a run as the snow would allow. Maya, behind him, said, 'What are you going to do?'

'Fight. We're not without protection.' More shooting, the dull crump of an explosion. Doors slammed downstairs. 'But I must also,' Arcus said as they dropped down another level, 'remove our secrets from their grasp.'

'What do you mean?'

Yelling, shouted orders. Maya could hear people whimpering with pain. More gunfire and the *thunk, thunk, thunk* of bullets slapping into – through – the walls of the building. Flock members passed them at a run. There was a thin drift of smoke wafting through the air and the smell of cordite.

Shepherd Arcus grabbed one of the passing cultists, a man dressed in the red of what Maya guessed was their medical contingent. Said, 'I'm setting protocol. Pass the word.' The man nodded, ran off.

'What does that mean?' she asked. 'What are you going to do?'

'Protocol. If there is a grave danger of our work falling into the hands of others, the Keep is to be destroyed. I hope the Curator has managed to get our last guest to safety. I think there was time. It wouldn't be right for him to die too. But we can't let what we do be taken.'

Into the warren of the living quarters, but cutting across them, not heading the way Maya had come when she arrived. They were bound for the cloister surrounding the inner dock. 'You're going to kill everyone?'

'We all know this,' he said. 'The protocol was set a long time ago. There's a corridor running towards the outer walls. That's where I'll leave you. You should be able to escape. I'm sorry I can't do more.'

'Hold on a minute,' Maya said. 'You take down the building, they're still going to pick through the wreckage. You can't stop that. At least give me some information, something we can use to make a cure for those who want it. It's not like it's going to be a secret after tonight. The cops, the news . . .'

'On a night like this, in a district like this, in a city like this, no one will know what happened until someone finds the bodies. Which may be never.'

They came to a closed steel door. Shepherd Arcus flung it open and moved to steer her through it. Maya stood her ground in the doorway. He shook his head. Said, 'I have to do this. You know what will happen if someone like Amanda Kent has control of the process? The untold evil she could wreak? You do, I'm sure.'

Three gouts of red burst from his chest, sprayed Maya with hot mist she could taste. She felt three bullets rip through the air next to her and embed themselves in the wall. Arcus dropped like dead weight, didn't so much as put out a hand to break his fall as he slapped into the floor. Behind him, through the fluttering plastic fronds that had divided up the Flock's living space, she saw the faintly insectile armoured figure of one of the Foundation soldiers, still with his rifle raised and pointing at her. She snapped herself out of the doorway, into the corridor. Saw the empty, straight, protectionless hall stretch before her and pictured for a moment how easy it would be, if he chose to pursue her, for him to gun her down as she fled. Instead, she flattened herself against the wall by the door and ducked down, below his sight level. Hoped it'd be enough to catch him off guard as he came through, make a fight of it.

Nothing, for a long time, long enough for her breathing to slow. The gunman had obviously decided to stick to his position or moved on, knew she was no threat to him. Beside her, Shepherd Arcus managed to turn his head towards her. Each quick exhalation saw gobs of pinkish fluid dribble down his chin and on to the floor. Bleeding hard, and dying. He tried to talk, licked his lips, tried again. 'Do it for me,' he whispered at last. 'If none of the others can. There's a small office. Left, to the south, twenty yards. Overlooking the dock. Behind the desk, you'll see it. Combination is 1420. Once you use . . . the switch . . . you have two . . . minutes. Please.'

Fear in his eyes. Not of death, she knew, but of Amanda Kent holding the Curse for herself. 'I wasn't going to run anyway,' she said. 'Who were you before you came here?'

A smile, and blood now flowed freely over his teeth and on to the concrete floor. The words came more easily as well. 'It's not important compared to who I am now,' he said. 'Thank you.'

She glanced through the doorway, saw no sign of Cutter's men. The living area was a mess of drifting plastic where bullets had severed the lines that had held the makeshift walls and ripped whole sheets to rags. She ran low, through the mess, towards the cloister. Gunfire and the sound of rounds tearing through the brickwork beat a jungle rhythm all around her. Through gaps in the red plastic she saw a few Flock members, running to take up positions, finding cover, hoping to protect their insane dream. One guy younger than her, not much more than a kid, hunched and crying in the refectory doorway at the far end of the room. She wondered, for a fraction of a moment, about what he must be feeling, whether he regretted the choices that had led him here. Then he screamed, 'You're not taking my home, you fuckers!' and leaned into the gap, firing a pistol at whatever lay beyond. She didn't wait to see what happened to him.

The door to the cloister was wide open. She quickly scoped both ways along the narrow covered walk along the inner rim of the Keep, saw no sign of Cutter's men. All inside, she guessed, aiming for the Curator's lab. Ducked out and ran, but as she broke across one of the open gaps to the dock she saw an armoured figure waiting there in the helicopter-blown snow and smoke. Maybe the one who'd killed Shepherd Arcus, gun raised, the single eye she could see cold and implacable as it sighted along the barrel at her. Behind him, distant movement across the dock, some of the Foundation soldiers heading into the Keep, or, like him, forming a rearguard perimeter by the water. Their chopper, still waiting overhead. The ropes used for rappelling still dangled beneath it but now, she saw, one ended in what looked like a cargo harness and the others in hooks and clasps. They were prepared to airlift the Curse back to Kent.

Maya's legs bunched as she tried to throw herself at the gunman, a last, vain attempt to reach him before he could fire and cut her down. Then the gate to the dock exploded in a hail of flame and shattered steel behind him. She saw a piece of shrapnel shear through his arm and bury itself in his side, and then the shockwave knocked her back against the wall. The Razor Gate was destroyed.

SIXTY-FOUR

Emi flinched as the noise of the explosion rolled along the canal. Valentin, at the controls of the hovercraft, didn't move, let it reverberate around him while tiny chunks of brickwork and flakes of metal rattled on the craft's hull. His people, working in the shallow, silted water beneath the entryway, had quickly wired the gate with what he'd said were shaped charges, and were now moving in. Valentin revved the hover's engine and grinned at her like a Disney tiger.

He'd driven her straight to the river after snatching her from the bar. Him in a sports car, his men in a rather more practical blacked-out SUV. The sort that drug dealers and presidents used. He had some kind of open phone connection with the SUV and others, on conference. Occasionally, graphics which looked like sat-nav maps or Google satellite shots of Newport flashed on the car's windshield, sometimes with markers, sometimes without. Commercial zones, riddled with waterways. Like a heads-up display in a fighter jet. She'd asked him one more time why he needed her, what possible use she could be when Charlie had no interest in him or whatever it was he was up to tonight.

'I'm just covering all eventualities,' he'd said. 'Tonight will see the end of the old order and the beginning of the new. When one's bringing about a fresh era, Emi, it's best to be prepared. I'm sure you could yet be valuable collateral or a useful tool. Besides, I find I always perform best when there's a beautiful woman looking on.'

They'd driven into a large boat shed, a covered repair dock, to find the hovercraft waiting. It looked like a military model, bulky and armoured, about the size of a van, but much lower to the ground save for where the two fan housings rose from the rear. It was matt black and sat on a thick, heavy skirt. Valentin's men had changed fast and snatched up equipment waiting for them on folding tables while he led her up and into the cramped, awkward hull. Two of his people came with them, watching her, the rest, now in wetsuits and some kind of body armour, grabbed the secure handholds that dotted the hull and found stable perches as Valentin engaged the engines and inflated the skirt beneath them.

The fans roared, the vibration rattling Emi's spine, and then the craft had thundered out on to the water and into the night. The journey down the Murdoch and into the web of small industrial canals that fed into it had taken little time. They'd run without lights, using night vision equipment instead. The constant pitch of the fans, and the bone-jarring force with which every turn and burst of speed threw Emi against her seat. The men, barely visible, seated on the hull outside. Like the two behind her, they seemed to be more than simple thugs or ex-military types, carrying a swagger and a grin as if they'd been infected by Valentin's apparent belief in his own immortality. Emi had clamped her teeth together and thought of Charlie, where he might be, whether she'd see him again.

Now, the craft cruised into the smoke-filled space in the deep centre of some kind of former factory or warehouse. Valentin's men were swarming up the canal sides like predatory sea life. He dropped the fans to a low, idling hum and picked up a microphone from the dash. Emi could see the broad smile on his face, his eyes shining, in the dim reflection on the windshield as loudspeakers somewhere on the outside of the hull blared into life as he spoke.

'This is Harrison Valentin,' he said. 'I'm sorry to say that your employer, Miss Kent, is dead. My sources say that one of her various enemies stormed Arel Spire and removed her from play just a short while ago.' A metal spattering sound from outside the hover. Emi realised with a sudden flush of adrenaline that someone was shooting at them. 'She is no longer in a position to take the prize on offer, and nor is she – or your Mr Cutter – in a position to pay you for your night's work. The Foundation is changing, as of tonight. The new order is here, gentlemen. You can either embrace it and be welcomed, or stand against it and be ground into the dust of history.'

Another couple of insignificant metal noises. Valentin's

men opened the hatch and swung out, one covering the surrounding roofs while the other swarmed up the ladder on the wharf beside them. In the open night air, rattling gunfire, and shouting. Valentin popped open her harness and reached out a hand to help Emi up.

'Come, my dear Emi,' he said. 'Let's see where you were, if you like, made.' She must have twitched as another couple of shots sounded, close this time, because he grinned at her. 'People like me don't die. The universe needs us.'

Out, into the bloodied dark, and deepening chaos.

SIXTY-FIVE

As the explosion at the Gate faded, Maya felt a sudden urge to have a weapon, something to protect her in the madness of the Keep. She darted forward to search the soldier, not sure if he was dead or dying. He was gurgling, but looked unconscious. A quick check revealed no sidearm, nothing she knew how to use or cared to carry. As Harrison Valentin's voice – no time to figure out what he was doing here – rolled across the dock, audible over the roar of the helicopter and a second, similar engine sound, she slipped back into the deeper shadows of the cloister and edged her way along, trying to follow Shepherd Arcus's directions. There was a door, still closed, some way down, past a couple of open entryways into the Keep's cavernous innards, and two dead Flock members in the further of them. A sudden burst of fire from the direction of the water and one of Cutter's men sagged out on top of them. She flinched, ducked into the cover of the nearest entryway. The movement saved her life.

The sharp *crack* of a gun behind her, hot gas wash over

the back of her neck. She was dimly aware of brick dust exploding from the wall ahead as the bullet sailed over her head, missing by inches. Maya spun, found she was in the Flock's supply stores, sacks and boxes stacked in neat piles between skeletal remains of the old warehouse structure. Just a yard behind her, just inside the entryway, was another man in a helmet and body armour, carrying a handgun. Scarred face sneering behind the iron sights. Cutter. A moment of recognition as she finished her turn and punched him, hard, under the chin. The strap of his helmet took some of the impact and she felt it cut into her knuckles, but his head still slapped back and she heard him grunt. Operating on adrenaline now, she tried to knock his weapon hand away but his strength was too great for her and it barely budged. As the scarred mouth began to leer back at her, she settled instead for kicking him hard in the knee and running for cover. Threw herself over a pallet-load of rice sacks and heard more shots, bullets thumping into the heavy bags beneath her, as she flew.

Landed, rolled, looking for a length of wood, a lump of metal, anything she could use against him, and seeing nothing. Ran again as she saw him advancing on her, slid behind a stack of boxes marked TINNED GOODS, rolled across the bottom shelf of a steel stack running to the ceiling and pressed herself back against some rolls of sheet aluminium. Up to her right, high windows in the side of the Keep, snow drifting in, whipped to flurries by the rotors of the chopper above.

'Didn't you hear, Cutter?' she said. 'Valentin says your boss is dead. Maybe Blake got her after all.'

'There's always succession.' The reply drifted back. She wondered how close he was now. Saw the blank, unconcerned look on his face as he slashed Chapel across the face. The icy waters of the Murdoch rising to drown her, along with Garrett and Julius. 'And if there's a successor, there'll be me. I'm not a money man, but money men always need people like me.'

Closer, definitely. She crept further down the row, into the shadows of a tarp-covered pile of crates. Saw him through a gap in the canvas, rounding the corner of the shelves, gun sweeping towards where she'd been. She turned, looked the other way for an exit and found only another set of shelving and a blank brick wall behind it. She was trapped.

Back through the gap, she saw he'd reached the coiled metal. Moving slow and careful, not letting his guard slip. Limping slightly, she noted with a touch of pride.

'Time's almost up, Miss Cassinelli,' he said. 'Miss Kent had me run a make on you, you know? You're a Port rat, aren't you? You should probably have just let the river have you when I gave you the chance before.'

She clenched her fists, breathed hard, ready for a last stand. Then the outer wall of the Keep burst inwards in a shower of crumbling brickwork and masonry.

SIXTY-SIX

The cab seemed to be in the air for a long, long time, and Garrett wondered for a second if it was falling too far, plunging through the broken bridge and into the canal, but then the nose tilted down, road ahead, and his view filled with asphalt. It hit with a colossal *bang* like it had torn in two, but somehow the back landed as well with the vehicle still in one very battered piece and the engine still running. The tyres shrieked over the cracked asphalt. Ahead, dim lights ringing an industrial unit picked out plumes of smoke, and, he saw through the splintered windshield, a helicopter circling above with cargo lines trailing from its belly. No need, now, to follow Cutter's GPS marker.

The road was pitted and strewn with wreckage and trash. The steering was heavy; each turn of the wheel needed more and more of his strength and the back began to fishtail. The car slewed as it closed on the building, thundered up a kerb and over a sidewalk. He cranked the steering again but this time the wheel held for a second then spun free. Tried pumping the brake but nothing happened. The wall of the warehouse loomed large in front of him as Garrett shielded his eyes.

Boom as he hit, an impact which snapped him against his safety belt, flung his head into the rapidly mushrooming airbag. Felt pieces of glass or masonry whip against his skin, immediately smelled oil smoke and the thick scent of spilled fuel. The driver's door was gone, torn off in the impact. He clawed at the belt release and fell, winded, past the deflating bag and out into a jumble of broken brickwork. Saw, as he forced himself upright, that he was in what looked like a store room, and up ahead was a man in something like SWAT gear raising a gun in his direction. Familiarity in the way he looked and moved, but Garrett couldn't place it.

Then a woman in white swept out behind the guy with a brick held in her hands and drove it into the back of his neck, below his helmet. Garrett saw his face then, and knew him. Yelled, 'Cutter!' and broke into a run.

Cutter, downed, fired once, up at the woman, but missed. She smashed him in the face with the brick as Garrett reached them. He kicked Cutter's gun away, stamped on his other arm, and knelt on top of him. Cutter's face was a bloody mess, his nose broken and a couple of teeth gone. He roared wordlessly at Garrett, clawed for his throat, but then down came the brick again. He snapped back against the floor and lay still, fluid first rattling then gurgling in his throat, as though maybe he was drowning. The man had tried to take Emi, been happy to torture Garrett, Maya and

Chapel, and left them with Julius to die in the *Adventure*. Garrett did nothing to help him. He looked up at the woman in white and thought for a second he'd hit his head when he came through the wall.

'Maya?' he said. 'Maya? I thought you drowned.'

She was bloodied and wild-eyed. Dropped the brick, let it clatter to the floor. Said, 'So did I. Why are you here?'

'Emi.' He felt himself recover, snap out of whatever daze he'd been in. Flames roared around the car behind him, painting them both in vivid yellow firelight. 'Harrison Valentin took Emi. I think he was coming to the same place as Cutter.'

'He's here. He came through the gate on the water. He was talking over a loudspeaker. He'll be heading for the lab.'

'Has he got Emi?'

'I don't know. I didn't see him. I was trying to get to the controls to demolish the building. They— It doesn't matter. There's a way to stop the Foundation and anyone else getting access to the Curse.'

Garrett thought for a moment. Picked up Cutter's gun. Said, 'How long will it take?'

'They told me it's a two-minute timer once the switch is tripped. It's not far from here.'

'How far's this lab?'

She gave him what she could remember of the route she'd taken as they hurried to the room's main entryway. Said, 'It won't take you long.'

The dockside was quieter now. Any remaining fighting

was taking place inside. There was a man in something like a wetsuit, gun in hand, just about visible across the far side of the space near what was probably a doorway. Maya nodded, said, 'Must be one of Valentin's men. Watching the way out.'

Garrett saw one of Cutter's dead soldiers on top of a pair of corpses dressed like Maya a few yards down the corridor. He scurried over and took the man's rifle and spare clips. Tossed Maya Cutter's pistol and said, 'Give me a bit of a head start, then trip the switch. My guess is if we're not on our way out in a couple of minutes, we won't be coming out at all.'

Then he ran past Maya, heading for the lab.

SIXTY-SEVEN

Emi trailed in Valentin's wake, one wrist clamped in his free hand, as he made his way through the Keep accompanied by two of his men. The others had left to deal with resistance elsewhere. The sight of so many people dying and dead made Emi nauseous and bitterly, bitterly sad.

'Why are you all doing this?' she said. 'What can be worth this misery?'

'This is, Emi. This – what you have and what these people create – is the thing I've been waiting for. The thing that changes the game.' Something in the earpiece he wore, because he steered them hard left at a turn. 'The others don't understand because they're so very, very locked into the old school of thought. For them, this is something that will make them obscenely wealthy.' Another turn. 'They already have, we all already have, more wealth and influence than we can use up in a lifetime. More is meaningless. Sure, there's getting one over on the competition – did you know they have a little rule that Foundation members shouldn't actively fight against one another? Just business. Of course, it doesn't stop them doing little things if they can, like having one of my men killed at Nerio Station in a vain bid to tie me to the killing of someone who really should've kept our secrets to himself. I don't deny I *love* the fact that I've beaten that bitch Kent to this, even if she's no longer alive to see it, and I'm sure there's plenty of money in it for me too. But the thing . . . You know, the others look down on me when we meet? My father made our fortune when the Soviet Union collapsed. They consider it bad form, little more than theft. What he knew then, and what I learned as a child, is that when the chance to change the rules comes along, if you're decisive enough and fast enough, if you don't let anything dissuade you, it's you who makes the new world. And the old one, well, that becomes irrelevant.'

'If you're ruthless enough.'

His grin again. 'You might say that. Ah, here we are.'

They strode into a room Emi felt she should recognise, but didn't. The singular stands of apparatus. The broad, empty space. And at the far end, a bright, glass-walled chamber with an operating couch and medical equipment.

Standing in front of it, alone, was an older man in a grey uniform of some kind. Valentin gestured at their escort and the two men fell back into step a couple of yards behind them, let him take the lead. 'So this is where it happens,' he said. 'This is where you make magic.'

'There's nothing for you here,' the man said calmly. 'The inventor of all this died a long time ago. No one, not even me, knows how he made it work. I've disabled the machines.'

'You must be the, uh, leader of all this?' Valentin waved his gun hand at the walls around them.

'I'm the Curator, yes.'

'And you think I can't repair whatever you've done?' Valentin didn't sound angry, only amused. 'You wouldn't believe the things I'm capable of.'

'I would. But for what, money? How pathetic.'

'Ah, but as I've just been explaining to Miss Nakano here – who I believe you've met, briefly – I'm not here for the money. Nothing so mundane as claiming the process as my own invention and licensing it to others. No, I have no interest whatsoever in marketing the technology behind your Curse. I want the Curse itself. I want what Jason Blake has had with his private little band of Clocks. People who'll do anything for a cure, or for revenge, who will volunteer to die. It's a marvellous tool for control, the Curse, used correctly. The things I could do with such control . . . And more, taking the technology further. You, Curator, have shown me that it's possible, however indirectly. I suppose I should thank you.'

With that, he shot the old man between the eyes. Inclined his head towards the two men with him and said, 'Have the others finish their sweeps and prepare to load the cargo.'

SIXTY-EIGHT

Maya scurried down the remaining stretch of cloister, afraid that at any moment one of Valentin's men would see her moving and open fire. No bullets, no alarm. Still the rumble of the helicopter, circling the warehouse, apparently unsure of the situation on the ground, then a *whoompf* as, she guessed, Garrett's car went up. Orange lit the smoke and haze over the compound.

Then she was through, into a small, dusty office. A row of old filing cabinets. On one wall, an intercom and a single fat lever switch on a circuit box; the one that opened the Gate, she presumed. Following Shepherd Arcus's instructions she found the steel box by the wall behind the desk. Dialled the combination and opened it to reveal a mundane-looking switching unit. No lights, no extra switches, and no countdown readout. Just one single master toggle looking somewhat ridiculous on its own. She waited, counting in her head until she thought she'd given Garrett enough of a start, then flicked the switch.

Gunfire. She glanced through the windows, saw Valentin's distant sentry turn, head into the building. Maya swore and ran back towards the lab.

SIXTY-NINE

Garrett stepped into the doorway as one of Valentin's bodyguards turned, talking into his radio. The man saw Garrett just as Garrett squeezed the trigger on the assault rifle and sent three rounds punching through him. Quick turn, three more into the second guy before he could react, and then Garrett was sighting up on Valentin and advancing into the room.

Valentin hugged Emi closer, pressed his gun to the back of her head, and grinned, ferally. 'You must be Charlie. Charmed to meet you. You see, my dear? I knew you'd be useful.'

'Let her go or you're a dead man.'

'No, no, I don't think I'll be doing that. I've got all the time in the world.'

Garrett glanced at Emi. Walked, slowly, towards them, and round, circling. 'You're Valentin, aren't you? That guy Maya was working for.'

'Was, and still is,' Valentin said, smiling. 'Without her, I would never have found this place. Exactly what I employed her for, in fact. If you see her again, do tell her I consider it a job well done and that her payment for services rendered is in her account.'

'What do you mean "without her"?'

'Not directly. I gave her a little something. Something that, since she'd been so prone to vanishing from the reservation, gave me a way to check on her whereabouts. I didn't expect it to produce dividends so soon.' Garrett saw the little key on Maya's wristband that she'd had since going to meet Valentin the night they found the briefcase. Swore to himself. 'A simple radio transmitter,' Valentin said. 'Very small, of course. Like a Lo-Jack. And here we all are. You could surrender before more of my people show up.'

'Let Emi go. I don't give a shit what you do with the Curse. Take it, enjoy.' Hoped that Maya had reached the destruct already. Wondered, if she had, how much time he had left.

A pause, then Valentin said, 'Deal. Take her.' With that, he pushed Emi towards Garrett and stepped back quickly.

Emi's gaze flickered from Garrett to something behind him and he turned to see one of Valentin's guys step into the doorway, gun raised. Before he could fire, though, there was a single shot and blood spouted from his throat. Then Maya was running past his falling corpse and Emi was in Garrett's arms. He looked for Valentin, saw him diving behind one of the final, blocky pieces of equipment on the Curse's assembly line, pistol up as he flung himself into safety. Garrett shot, raking the area with bullets, seeing sparks fly and the glass of the Curse operating room shatter and sparkle like diamonds. Valentin fired twice, blind, dust cascading down from the roof as the moulded plastic interior of the lab was breached. Another burst from Garrett as he pushed Emi back, towards the cover of the vats.

'It's time to go,' Maya was shouting. 'Garrett, it's time to go!'

With a screech of metal, the frame of the operating room, shorn of the base of its supports by Garrett's fire, tore free of the ceiling and a cascade of heavy plastic and steel rained around where Valentin was sheltering. Garrett heard him trying to move and swearing. Another shot from his pistol, but wild, obviously blind. He stepped forward, intent on finishing everything for good, but Maya and Emi pulled him back.

'Thirty seconds,' Maya said. 'At most. Then the building explodes. Go!'

They ran. Through pain and fear and relief at his reunion with Emi, to the maintenance exit through which Arcus had led Maya to the roof, then out, over the side and a fifteen-foot drop into the snow banked high against the side of the warehouse. Precious seconds picking themselves out of the white blanket, then they were running again.

Gunshots behind them, splintering glass. They turned and saw Valentin, free of the wreckage that had pinned him, jump from one of the upper windows and catch one of the ropes trailing beneath Cutter's helicopter.

Then, a single loud crack followed by a string of thuds

like meteor impacts. The blast wave battered at Garrett's face, left him staggering. Tossed Valentin on his string like bait in the breeze. Roiling clouds of dust erupted into the air, turned yellow-grey in the night. They could hear fragments of masonry rattling from buildings, spattering off rooftops and falling like volcanic pumice all around. Behind the wall of smoke, the Keep was gone, and with it the Curse.

Valentin recovered himself as the chopper shied away from the explosion. They watched him shimmy up the rope and over the side. Saw light glint from a gun in his hand as he pointed it into the cockpit. Whatever he said to the pilot must have worked because the helicopter abandoned its station near the Keep and swooped past them. As it did, Valentin stood in the doorway, one hand holding himself in place, the other waving at them, and once again that dark and feral smile.

Then he was gone, and they were left with the trudge towards the nearest canal and, if they were lucky, a boat, and freedom.

SEVENTY

A strange kind of dark when Chapel woke up, and cold. Thin grey light washed uneasily through taped-over splits and folds in what he saw were sheets of cardboard made to form walls, a ceiling. The place reeked of ancient body odour and piss. His muscles were stiff, and memory was a loose, splintered thing he couldn't yet grasp and assemble into a whole again. Shouldn't he be on the bus to Miami by now? He'd blacked out before, drunk or high, but never without any memory of what had led him there in the first place. The snow . . . something that looked like a guillotine, picked out in red . . . At least he still had his wallet and watch. He hadn't been mugged.

Suddenly a hole opened in the wall and a hideous, jagged-toothed man's face appeared in the gap, snow whipping around it. His eyes widened at the sight of Chapel, and he snarled, words slurred together into meaningless noise. He gestured at the world outside.

'Sorry, man,' Chapel mumbled, rolling on to his front

and crawling through the doorway. 'I dunno how I got there. I didn't mean to sleep in your spot.'

More growling.

'I said sorry. Shit, it's cold.' He stood up, looked around. The bus station was there, a couple of hundred yards away from the cardboard igloo in the little homeless camp by the entry ramp. It was snowing hard, no sign of the sun, no clue as to the time. How long had he been out?

Chapel patted his pockets, checking to make sure he still had his ticket. Didn't know if it'd still be valid, but maybe he could get a replacement for the next bus. Felt something rustle inside his coat and found a folded sheet of paper stapled to the breast lining. Opened it as he walked down the ramp.

I'm sorry, it began. *You have only a year, from the day you read this, to live. This is not a trick, a joke or a scam. Nothing anyone can do will stop this from happening. What you have been given is incurable by anyone, even me. It will be sudden and painless. What you choose to do with this information is entirely your choice. You have a year.*

The snow fell on, spattering across the letters, blanking them out.

SEVENTY-ONE

When her time came, Emi said she wanted to go back to the Garden of Song. They sat on a bench amongst the snow-covered birches, watching fat white flakes drifting down like ash. The air was still, the winds of the storm outside caught, dissipated and deflected by the lattice of baffles and cables that made up the park's roof. Snow, whipped and blown into chaotic flurries, hit the boundary and was instantly calmed, left to settle slowly and peacefully in the magically still air. The roof whistled and hummed, pitch and volume rising and falling, a melancholy symphony like a blend of pipes and whalesong. Dressed entirely in white, her dark hair hanging loose to her shoulders, she looked like a ghost, already passed into the monochrome fields of distant memory.

For a while, they sat in silence. Garrett looked up at the dim, moonlit sky above the garden's spiderweb roof. Saw, for the first time, how like a gilded clock face without hands the pattern looked. Then Emi said, quietly, 'I'm glad we came, Charlie.'

'Me too.' Speaking hurt, even though the injuries he'd suffered in the mad days leading up to the destruction of the Keep were well on their way to healing. He put his arm around her and she rested her head on his shoulder, nestled into it as if she was burrowing for warmth. 'I'm still sorry, you know,' he said. 'I should've listened to you all along. I should have just been here for all that time instead of trying to fix everything.'

'Yes, you should have.' She lifted her head, kissed him on the cheek, settled back again. 'But I forgive you. Don't feel bad about it. I know you tried for us. It just wasn't meant to be. You made it back, we both did, and that's the most important thing. We've been together. We're here together now. That's what matters to me.'

Silence again for a while. Garrett found it deeply strange, knowing this would be the last conversation they'd ever have, that it could end any time. No obvious sign it was coming, nothing to help them prepare. No beeping hospital machines or grieving relatives, no blue flashing lights, nothing to make the elephant real.

Emi must've felt it too, because she said, 'I want to know you'll be OK after I die, Charlie. Now we're here. Don't fall apart.'

'I won't. I'll be OK, eventually.'

'Like you mean it, Charlie.'

A smile. He couldn't help himself. 'I promise.'

'I'll hold you to it.' She fell quiet again, listening to the sing-song of the wind. 'I love it here. I want to stay all night.'

'Sure.'

'When I was a little girl, my mom took me to Kanayama Lake to go ice fishing for wakasagi. Everyone wrapped up in their winter clothes, completely blue sky and a completely white lake, and dotted all over it were all sorts of different tents and shelters, dozens of colours and shapes. Some of the men were so still and so concentrated on their lines, trying to catch these tiny fish. Others talked, had their children with them, laughing and playing on the ice. It would be silent, like being in a church, and then suddenly voices would echo across the lake. You couldn't hear what they were saying, but they were so full of happiness.'

She shuffled along the bench, lay down with her head in Garrett's lap. He stroked her hair, let her carry on talking, enjoying the sound of her voice. 'It had been quiet for a while and I was busy with my fishing line when I heard my mother singing "*Fuyu no Uta*". She had a voice like crystal, singing this silly children's song about winter. And then another voice joined in, and another. Soon the whole lake was singing. When we reached the end, everyone cheered and applauded. Then we all went back to our own worlds. I don't think I ever saw any of those people again. I always thought that was life, in microcosm. To enjoy the few moments we have singing the same song as others before we pass on. I still think that. The song's almost over for me, Charlie, but I'm so happy I got to sing it with you.'

Garrett, sitting in the snow with tears running down his cheeks, through the long quiet until dawn, and Emi cold and still against him.

SIX MONTHS AFTER THE GREEN STREET BOMBING

Maya Cassinelli walks through the doors of the *Newport Post* building and swipes her security pass across the reception gates. Says hello to a couple of faintly familiar faces – after five months working here, she knows a few people outside her immediate circle of co-workers well enough to say hi, but the place still feels a little alien at times. It probably always will, given the circumstances. The board of directors, she knows, are watching her. They told her as much before she started. Standing in front of them in the top floor office, the prospective contract on the table in front of her.

'Ordinarily we wouldn't have taken you on,' one of the interchangeable suits with faces had said, 'given your past record. But a request has been made by one of this newspaper's most valued benefactors to take you on staff. To give you a second chance. You understand there won't be another.'

She'd shrugged, unconcerned. She'd passed through the Gate, with all that had entailed, and wasn't about to be cowed by some jackass in an old school tie.

'Out of respect, we've agreed to make you this offer, and we think you'll find it acceptable. But there is a caveat: everything you do here, everything you write for us, how you act and what you say, will be monitored closely. Should you so much as imply anything without the strictest basis in proof, or otherwise conduct yourself in a manner that reflects poorly on this newspaper, its sponsors or the city, your employment will be terminated, at once and without benefits. And I promise you, you will never work in respectable journalism in this country again. Is that understood?'

She'd considered flipping them the bird and walking out, but it was a job and it paid the bills. Harrison Valentin had indeed paid her, presumably out of his twisted sense of humour, but the money wouldn't last for ever. Let the Foundation think they had her tamed, under control and safely out of the way. It'd give her the time and the respectability she needed to make a concrete case against them. Go public too soon, with the Curse a faded memory, the few remaining Clocks winding down their last days in private, and nothing irrefutable to back up what she'd seen and what she knew, and she'd be just another crank. Another Bilderberg conspiracy nut or an anti-capitalist whack job with too much time on her hands. After all, she had a record for unreliability, didn't she?

Maya smiles as the elevator doors swish closed in front of her. She has work to do.